It was a place of beginnings...

Noah led Anne down the winding stairs into the library, then stretched her out on the thick carpet, with only the light of the fire illuminating her pale body. "This is where we started," he murmured.

In the fitful glow of the firelight Noah looked almost demonic, his body taut and golden, the muscles etched in shadow.

"Shall I give you one more chance? A five-minute head start? Do you want to leave me, Annie, love? Do you want to sleep alone tonight? In that narrow bed with its clean white sheets?"

"If I said I did would you let me?"

"If you meant it I would." And then he added, "But you'd be lying. Wouldn't you?" His voice was barely audible as his head dipped toward hers. "Wouldn't you?"

"Yes," Anne said, the sibilant sound long and drawn out. "Yes, yes, yes."

ABOUT THE AUTHOR

Anne Stuart had her very first work published by *Jack and Jill* magazine at the age of seven and has been writing professionally ever since. She is the author of five Gothic romances and two Regencies, as well as four American Romances and two Intrigues. Anne currently resides in an old farmhouse in Vermont with her husband, one dog and five cats.

Books by Anne Stuart

HARLEQUIN AMERICAN ROMANCE

30—CHAIN OF LOVE
39—HEART'S EASE
52—MUSEUM PIECE
93—HOUSEBOUND

HARLEQUIN INTRIGUE

6—TANGLED LIES
9—CATSPAW

These books may be available at your local bookseller.

Don't miss any of our special offers. Write to us at the following address for information on our newest releases.

Harlequin Reader Service
P.O. Box 52040, Phoenix, AZ 85072-2040
Canadian address: P.O. Box 2800, Postal Station A,
5170 Yonge St., Willowdale, Ont. M2N 6J3

Housebound

ANNE STUART

Harlequin Books

TORONTO • NEW YORK • LONDON
AMSTERDAM • PARIS • SYDNEY • HAMBURG
STOCKHOLM • ATHENS • TOKYO • MILAN

Published March 1985

First printing January 1985

ISBN 0-373-16093-3

Prologue

It was a very old house, sitting at the end of the long, rutted driveway, surrounded by a shawl of ancient oaks that protected it from the extremes of the climate. The gray stones were weathered from a thousand storms; the wavy glass windows had looked out over more than two hundred years of seasons, harsh and gentle. Within its strong thick walls families had lived out their lives, children had been born, old people had died, marriages had been consummated and destroyed, and still the house lived on, eternal in its graceful mass.

But age was beginning to take its toll, to tear away at the sturdy fabric that had held the house together since before the birth of the country. The slate roof was patched and leaking, the foundation crumbling; the sills were rotting and the plumbing and electricity rebelling against their anachronistic location. The house was dying from the inside out, and there was nothing that could be done.

For more than two hundred years the huge old house had been filled with families—grandmothers and grandfathers, babies and pregnant women and maiden aunts and bachelor uncles. But now it was empty and lonely, most of its rooms unused, with no laughter or life flowing through the gracefully paneled interior. There were no children to stare with wonder at the bullet holes and ominous brown patches that were sworn to have come from the Revolution. There were no young lovers to run laughing through the weed-choked gardens that were now brown and midwinter dead. The beautiful old house was dying, and one lone woman couldn't stop its demise, no matter how hard she tried.

She could throw her heart and soul into it, she could single-handedly patch and pray, she could spend every waking and dreaming hour working for the house, for the money to keep it going, for the energy to struggle after the interminable repairs. And she could steadfastly ignore the fact that bit by bit it was slipping away from her like a distracted lover who'd found someone new. The only way she could save her house was to let it go, and that was the one thing Anne Kirkland could never agree to do. So she watched it die, day by day, as she fought against the encroaching darkness.

And the house waited.

Chapter One

Anne Kirkland absently rubbed the back of her neck as she replaced the plastic cover of her Selectric. She was fond of the creature—indeed, countless times Edmund Jolles had begged her to accept the wonders and glories of word processing, but Anne had been uncharacteristically obstinate.

"If I were a secretary I don't suppose I'd have much say in the matter," she'd replied just that afternoon with the easygoing charm that had so often aided her in getting her own way. "But I've got the exalted title of assistant editor, and the amount of typing I do is minimal. For heaven's sake, Edmund, I only work part-time. How can you justify the expense?"

"It's thanks to you that our tiny publishing house can afford such luxuries. I want to reward you suitably." He ran an exasperated hand across his shiny pink skull. Years of running his hand through his thinning hair had created a habit even baldness couldn't stop, and Anne smiled at him fondly.

"You can always reward me with more money," she suggested lightly.

"But I couldn't write that off on my taxes. Besides, you'd just pour every penny into that damned house and still end up needing more."

"So I would," she agreed, unabashed. "So no raise. But no word processor, either. I love my Selectric." She gave the brick-red machine an affectionate pat. "And she serves me very well indeed. If you're feeling guilty, give me an extra couple of days this week— Holly and Ashley are coming down with a group of friends."

"I shouldn't do it. Why should you want to take days off just to cook for a horde of starving artists?"

"They're very successful artists, and I like to cook. Don't worry about me, Edmund. I can take care of myself quite well, you know."

"Maybe," he replied, unconvinced. "You can have as many days off as you want—you know perfectly well I'm damned lucky to have you. But take the Chinese manuscript home with you and see if you can put in a few hours on it. The thing's Greek to me, and Harvey Etling needs some feedback by midweek."

"God protect me from insecure authors," she said. "I'll do my best."

"And try to have some fun."

"I expect to. Wilson will be there at least part of the time, to make sure I don't work too hard."

Edmund made a rude noise. "Wilson Engalls is about as much fun as a Victorian novel. How a bright, beautiful woman like you could possibly get engaged to such a stuffed shirt is beyond my comprehension."

"Love is blind," she replied blithely, having heard all this before.

"It must be. You and a lawyer!" He snorted, drifting back toward his office, mumbling indiscernible imprecations.

It was pitch-black by the time she left the rambling Victorian house that held the offices of Jolles Publications, a small publishing house that specialized in textbooks, arcane dissertations and insolvency. Of course, Bucks County wasn't the best possible place for publishing, but the Jolles family had lived there since the Revolution, and the very thought of moving the business to New York or even Philadelphia turned Edmund pale with horror. Publishing's loss was Anne Kirkland's gain. Working three days a week, a scant seven miles from the tumbling-down estate on the New Jersey side of the river that still housed her professor-father and her artistic siblings at odd occasions was a job made to order. Tossing the five-hundred page manuscript onto the frayed front seat of her aging Volvo, she slid behind the wheel and offered up a silent prayer to the god of automobiles. On this occasion he was disposed to be merciful, and after only one complaining sputter the engine chugged into life. Pulling out into the rush-hour traffic on an early February evening, she mentally reviewed the dinner for that night. There would most likely be at least seven. Her father, the original absentminded professor, had no classes that night, and Ashley could be counted on bringing at least two of his hangers-on. As his success as an abstract artist increased, his coterie did likewise, efficiently devouring all of the quite fabulous sums Ashley could now command for his massive, somewhat dour paintings. Sleeping arrangements might be tricky, depending on who accompanied him and which way he was swinging, but Anne decided not to worry about it. It had never proven to be an insurmountable problem before.

But Holly was a different matter. As cellist in the renowned Mellon String Quartet, she spent a great deal of time on tour, and her visits to the old house were far too infrequent. And this time she was bringing someone special. Not that all her men weren't special, to

Holly. But this one was even more magnificent, or so she had informed Anne the previous night on the telephone.

"I've heard that before, Holly." Anne had been skeptical. "How long have you been seeing him?"

"Well, that's the problem." Her younger sister's breathless, bubbly voice carried over the line from New York. "I've only just met him, and I'm not quite sure what he thinks of me. He's absolutely the sexiest man alive, but I sometimes wonder whether he's taking me seriously."

Anne had stifled her instinctive retort that Holly had yet to take any man seriously. "What is he, besides the sexiest man alive?"

"Right now he's a lawyer."

"Yuk."

"Now don't be prejudiced, Annie. You're engaged to one. And I've known some incredibly charming lawyers in my time."

"You've known some incredibly charming everything in your time, little sister." Anne's voice was caustic. "What did you mean by 'right now'?"

"Mmmmh?"

"You said, 'Right now he's a lawyer.' What did he used to be? Knowing your recent taste I bet he was a punk rocker."

Holly giggled, a lilting sound that had enchanted more than one man. "Certainly not. That was last fall. Noah's a lawyer, all right. I just don't know how long he'll be one. He seems more than a little disenchanted with the legal system."

"That's a point in his favor. And he'll be good company for Wilson."

"That's not exactly what I had in mind," Holly drawled. "I was counting on him being good company for me. Besides, I wouldn't really think Noah would be Wilson's type at all."

"What type is he?"

"Absolutely charming, and absolutely beautiful." She sighed soulfully. "With a divine touch of cynicism and a touch-me-not heart that is completely irresistible. He was widowed several years ago, and I gather he hasn't been seriously involved since. It's all so marvelously romantic, though he's not at all a tragic figure. You'll adore him."

"He doesn't sound like my type either," Anne responded. "So you want this Noah put in your bedroom?"

"Nooo!" Holly shrieked. "I told you, we only just met. I'm planning to use this weekend to seduce him. And I need your help, darling."

"Holly, I draw the line at pimping for my siblings."

"Must you be so crude, Anne? You've been reading too many thrillers. I'm not expecting you to push him into bed with me, I just wondered..."

"Yes?" Anne waited patiently.

"Could you possibly put him in your room?" It came out all in a rush.

"I don't know what Wilson would say to that," Anne replied.

"Not with you there, idiot!" Holly shrieked. "Besides, I thought we agreed he's not your type."

"The sexiest man alive isn't my type? Thanks a lot."

"You said it first. And you know what I mean. You like them a bit more sedate. Like Wilson." On the other end Anne winced, but Holly continued blithely on. "Besides, Noah's too young for you. He's only thirty-two."

"And I'm thirty-four. Such an insurmountable age difference!" she scoffed. "It would serve you right if I

did share my room with him. You're not very flattering
to my ego, dear one."

"I've put my foot in my mouth again, haven't I?"
Holly's voice sounded mournful.

"You have, darling. But you do it so charmingly. So
you'd like me to vacate my room for the youthful Noah
so that you can manage to have your wicked way with
him. So be it. There's a perfectly comfortable bed in
my studio. Never let it be said that I stood in the way of
true love."

"Oh, bless you, Anne! You don't think Proffy will
mind, do you?"

"About me vacating the bedroom or your sharing
it?"

"The latter, of course! He doesn't care what you
do," Holly said artlessly, and Anne, inured, ignored it.

"Of course not. As far as our father's concerned you
can do no wrong. He makes it a practice to ignore what
goes on upstairs, which, considering Ashley's habits, is
a very fortunate thing."

"Is Ashley coming? I haven't seen him in ages."

"He's coming, with several of his cronies, I don't
doubt. Will you be riding down with your precious
Noah?"

"Don't I wish! No, he has to work, of all things. I'll
be down early afternoon, and I expect he'll arrive
around dinnertime. Are you sure you don't mind, Annie darling? I hate to evict you."

"Anything for romance, Holly. I'd like some nieces
and nephews."

There was an audible gasp. "Well, he may be the
sexiest man alive, but I don't know if I like him that
much! Babies are so… so permanent. Besides, Noah
definitely isn't the sort to settle down. I don't see him
as the home-and-hearth type, which is part of his

charm. I think you'll have to make your own babies, darling. Talk Wilson into it, why don't you?''

"I'll do my best," Anne said dryly. "By the way, do you suppose you could help out a bit on the expenses? Feeding seven people on a long weekend get's a little pricy. Father's only on half salary now, and my money doesn't go very far."

"Of course, dear, though I must admit I'm a trifle short myself. I guess it's my artistic temperament. Thank God we have someone practical like you in the family."

"Thank God," Anne echoed wryly.

"And I've brought back the most marvelous silks from Italy. Do you suppose we might have time to work up a few things for me? I'm afraid I'm desperately in need of something new to wear onstage. The others say they're tired to death of my current wardrobe."

"I'll do my best."

"Of course you will, darling. You always do. Ta."

As Anne crossed the bridge into Lambertville her fingers clenched the steering wheel for a moment, then relaxed. No life was without its little frustrations, and Holly's artless selfishness was more than compensated for by her charm and affection. Doubtless when Anne arrived home at the rambling stone farmhouse Holly would greet her with hugs and kisses, and with strange and wonderful and completely useless presents from the exotic places she'd traveled to. With the proper amount of coaxing Anne could even persuade her to lend a hand in the kitchen; that is, if her father didn't demand her presence by the fireside for a leisurely brandy while Anne cooked dinner.

Now where did that sudden, irritated thought come from, Anne wondered, once more loosening her grip on the steering wheel. She must be more tired than she thought.

Turning past the crumbling stone fence that marked the boundaries of their property, she drove down the long, rutted driveway that eventually led to the rambling old house that Anne loved with a passion. As the gray stone walls loomed up out of the darkness a feeling of peace and contentment washed over her. As long as the mass of stone and wood was safe and secure, so was she. The light spilled in welcoming pools from the deep-set windows, almost every one sending a warm yellow glow into the dark winter night. All very beautiful, Anne thought, until you considered the electric bills. She drove around back to the kitchen entrance, parking the old yellow Volvo under the portico, and with an unusual weariness climbed out, the weighty manuscript in one arm, a few last-minute provisions in the other. Holly had said her sought-after Noah liked fine brandy. There could be little more conducive to romance than a shared midnight brandy by a flickering fire. It would be up to Holly to procure either the living room or the library for the private tête-à-tête—when Ashley was around, his entourage tended to spill over into every available space. Besides, Holly and Noah were just an excuse—Anne had craved this particular cognac for ages and denied herself that luxury. It was nice to have an excuse. She could only hope the two lovers would be more interested in each other than in her precious cognac.

There was no one in the long, low kitchen when she let herself in the door, dropping the manuscript on the scrubbed oak table and setting the brandy down with the care such a work of art deserved. It was extremely fortunate that the majority of the dinner had been prepared at six that morning and was waiting in the fridge for its final cooking. It was more than obvious that help was not on its way.

"Anyone home?" she called out, wandering up the short flight of stairs to the main floor of the house, stripping off her hat and gloves as she went, shaking free her curtain of midnight-black hair around her slender shoulders. No one answered. The living room was deserted, the empty glasses with half-melted ice cubes attesting to its recent occupants. With a sigh Anne eyed them. Three of them, one bearing Holly's particularly vivid shade of lipstick. Obviously her father had made it home early. But whose was the other glass? Noah What's-his-name wasn't due till later, Holly had said, and Ashley would be bringing at least two if he ran true to form. And for that matter, where were they all? The house, for all its blazing electricity, was completely empty.

With a sigh Anne went through the first floor, turning off half the lights, stoking up the impractical but romantic fireplaces, gathering up glasses and ashtrays and heading back down toward the kitchen. A hastily scribbled note by the sink provided her with a partial answer.

"Gone skating at Yarboroughs'. Sorry to miss you— can you hold dinner? We'll be back around nine. Proffy's with us—I might even get him on skates. Be nice to Noah when he arrives and send him along. Holly."

"The sink's a pretty fitting place for a note, Holly, dear," Anne said out loud, her voice caustic. "I am not in the mood to play Cinderella." The stone walls echoed her voice eerily, and she shrugged as she crumpled the paper, tossing it into the trash as she headed toward the narrow, deep-set door at the far end of the kitchen. It was barely two feet wide and six feet high, and the foot-thick plaster walls were flaking a bit on the tile floor. But beyond the narrow, whitewashed door was Anne's private domain. It had once been a combination pantry and wine cellar, built into the hillside, dark and cold. Anne had played in it as a child. It had been an Indian tepee, a princess's castle, a Gypsy encampment and anything else a quiet child could imagine it to be. As soon as she was old enough she had staked it as her own, spending her first year's salary in having the heavy outer doors knocked out and replaced with glass facing south over the rolling woodlands. The walls and ceilings had survived three coats of white paint with only minimal peeling, and the wood floor, once scraped clean of bird droppings, old paint and myriad other strange, gummy things, had turned out to be oak. It had taken Anne two years of on-and-off work to get it to its current lustrous state, and then all her willpower to keep her siblings from taking over. Ashley, with self-righteous indignation, had announced it was the perfect studio for a real artist, and didn't she have a generous bone in her body when he so clearly needed it?

Holly had begged and pleaded and even managed a tear or two. After all, it was far away from the rest of the house—no one would have to listen to the obligatory four hours of practice she had to put in every day. Even Proffy had done his best to sway her, but Anne, when her mind was made up, could be adamant, and she had never regretted it, even when faced with Ashley's long-suffering sighs and Holly's wistful expressions.

One of Ashley's less-morose paintings adorned one wall, a gift when he grudgingly accepted his fate. Anne's drafting board and dressmaking supplies were in one large corner, her mother's spinet in another.

The narrow mahogany daybed served as a couch, and the stereo was far better than the one currently ensconced in the living room. Anne surveyed it all with a pleased smile, noting the stack of historical romances by the couch. They would have to wait until the Chinese manuscript was whipped into shape, but God willing, that wouldn't take long. However, the god of editors couldn't always be counted on—Etling was a professor of Chinese studies at Rutgers, and academics were notoriously poor writers.

Stripping off her subdued work clothes, she yanked on a well-worn pair of Levi's and oversized chamois shirt, and tied her hair back with a ribbon, hoping belatedly that she'd brought enough clothes down to last her the weekend. She didn't relish traipsing into the bedroom of the sexiest man in the world for more clothes.

Anne had a very good idea of what she looked like, and thanked a merciful providence that no one important would see her like that. She knew perfectly well that her narrow face was pale and tired after a long week, that the dark, black-fringed eyes were shadowed. What she didn't realize was that even as tired as she was, the dark eyes glowed with intelligence and humor, that her lustrous black hair, pulled roughly back from her face, was thickly beautiful, and that her tall, slim, gently rounded figure was enhanced rather than hidden by the faded jeans and loose shirt.

She was in the midst of making a huge tossed salad, a snifter of the magnificent cognac by her side, when she heard the distant tones of the doorbell.

"The legendary Noah," she murmured to herself, wiping her damp hands on the hips of her jeans, which were already well covered with flour from the rolls she had made. Anne hated aprons but couldn't bring herself to wipe her hands anywhere but on her person. She allowed herself one last glance at the coq au vin heating slowly in the oven before scampering barefoot up the stairs to the front hallway. The stone beneath her feet was chilly, and she wished she'd remembered to grab her moccasins. Well, she didn't need to stand on ceremony with the sexiest man alive, especially when he was a babe in arms, she reminded herself cheerfully, opening the door into the cold February night.

"Hi, I'm—"

"I know exactly who you are," she greeted him with a smile, swallowing her disappointment. "We've been expecting you." If this was the sexiest man the world had to offer, then she'd gladly make do with steady, unexciting Wilson. Granted, this Noah Whatever was handsome enough. Wavy blond hair, styled just so, white, perfect teeth blazing out at her, an impossibly cute nose, and blue eyes as bright and opaque as china. But there was something just a little...contrived about him. Besides, he looked quite a bit older than thirty-two, and was trying to hide it. Well, there was no accounting for tastes—she'd never been much taken with Holly's crushes in the past, either.

"The others have gone skating at our neighbors'," she continued affably. "Would you like to join them, or can I offer you a drink while we wait for them?"

"I brought my skates," he said with a grin that didn't quite reach those bright blue eyes. "Would the neighbors be hard to find?"

With mingled relief and irritation she gave him the instructions, then watched him drive off in a shiny new BMW that set her to gnashing her teeth in envy before she trudged back to the kitchen. "So much for sex gods," she informed the mushrooms. "If that's the best thing Holly's ever seen, she must have lived a more cloistered life than I realized." Shaking her head, she addressed herself to the salad once more, glancing at the clock every now and then. At five of nine irritation began to grow, and she opened the red wine with a little too much force to let it breathe. By nine-fifteen she turned off the oven, watching in despair as the chicken shrank from the bones. At nine-thirty she dumped the meal on the sideboard warming trays in the dining room, served herself a plate and headed toward the kitchen, her temper well beyond the boiling point.

The doorbell rang just as she was heading down the stairs. For a moment she contemplated ignoring it. Finally her customary even temper reasserted itself, and she headed for the door, still holding her plate.

Chapter Two

A man was standing there in the doorway, a lean figure just under six feet tall, with a kind of wiry strength and casual grace that radiated from both his jeans-clad body and the slow smile that lit his face. He was very tanned for February in the Northeast, with thick, wildly curly black hair that fell across his forehead, high cheekbones, a slow, sensual smile, and blue eyes that would put Holly's Noah to shame. The heavy wool sweater clinging to his narrow body couldn't disguise the strength in his shoulders as he lounged against the door, and Anne swallowed once, twice, in sheer awe.

"Hi." His voice was even worse—impossibly low and beguiling. A voice to charm the senses out of anyone, she thought dimly. "My name's Grant. I believe I'm expected." Those blue eyes caught the plate she was holding in one numbed hand, and the smile broadened self-deprecatingly. "And I'm late," he added. "I'm sorry. I've interrupted your dinner. You must be Anne. I've heard a lot about you, but I can't say you're what I expected."

Grant, she thought numbly. He had to be the missing member of the party, Ashley's current companion. Damn, double damn, she fumed silently. What a waste.

But that smile was not to be resisted. She answered it, basking in its warmth. "You may be late, but everyone's later. I finally gave up waiting for them. They're next door skating, and God only knows when they'll be back. If you like, I can give you directions."

"Would you mind if I waited here with you?" he questioned easily, and that voice was like silk running down her spine. "Unless you'd rather be alone."

Triple damn, Anne thought. He's nice, too. She stepped back from the door. "Welcome, stranger. I'll even feed you, if you're hungry. Heaven only knows what shape the chicken will be in by the time the others return."

"Thank you. I thought you'd never ask." He followed her into the hallway, his magnetic presence seeming to fill the large hallway, making Anne far too aware of him and that easy, damnably sexy grace of his.

"Where would you like to eat?" Her voice came out admirably level, a fact that pleased her. Not a soul would be able to tell that half her mind was at the moment involved in the most convoluted sex fantasy of her life.

"Where were you going to eat?" he countered, that voice still melting her.

Damn, the man was putting her hormones in an uproar, and it was all for nothing. Ashley was luckier than he knew. "I was heading down to the kitchen."

He raised his eyebrows over those searching blue eyes. "What are you, the scullery maid or something?" he drawled, but there was a curious light in those eyes.

"Hardly. I just love to cook." Now why did she feel defensive? She was about to go on, explaining her familial situation, and then stopped short. There was no need to explain her life story to a total stranger. As long as she didn't feel ill-used, then she wasn't. It was that simple, she had always told herself, and did so again. "But I'm willing to be flexible," she added. "Kitchen, dining room or library?"

"Does my nose deceive me, or is there a fire in the library?"

"There is."

"And you'll join me?" The eyes were intent on her upturned face, and Anne had the flashing feeling that Ashley might get very angry with her indeed.

Smiling up at him, she nodded. "I will." Let Ashley be jealous, she thought defiantly. When it comes right down to it, she was perfectly safe with this charming man. More's the pity.

Five minutes later they were seated on the floor in front of the fire, companionably discussing Anne's work for Jolles. Curious as she was, she deliberately refrained from asking him any questions about his own life. Ashley's friends usually didn't bear too much scrutiny.

"So you're the chief cook and bottle washer, an editor, a dress designer—"

"And a handyman, an electrician, a mason, a pianist, a quilter, a painter of inadequate watercolors, a decent contralto, a dutiful daughter and supportive sibling, even a part-time plumber. In other words, I'm a hopeless dabbler. Jack-of-all-trades, master of none." She sighed, staring into the amber dregs of her cognac.

He swirled his meditatively in the Waterford snifter, the last one of the ancient set. Without hesitation Anne had offered him the good stuff, a silent vote of approval, despite her reservations about his life-style.

"You may be a dabbler," he said meditatively, his voice that low, delightful drawl. "Or you may be a Renaissance woman. Ever look at it that way?"

She laughed, genuinely pleased. "How tactful! But I don't excel at any of those things."

"Not true. I have incontrovertible proof that you are a very great cook, even when the dinner has been sitting for hours. And your taste in cognac is nothing short of divine."

"How do you know I didn't just ask the liquor-store clerk for the most expensive kind?" She curled her feet under her, enjoying this, enjoying him and the quiet companionship of the night. And the spice of danger that was only an illusion.

"You knew what to ask for," he said, that wonderful voice succinct. Leaning back against the chair, he stretched his long, jeans-clad legs out in front of him, stretching his arms overhead. The movement drew the heavy sweater tight against the leanly muscled torso, and another wave of lust swept over Anne, one she foolishly allowed full rein. After all, what was the harm in it? She was perfectly safe from any danger of consummation—she could sit here and lust to her heart's content, build the most delicious fantasies that had no chance of fulfillment, and face Wilson and Ashley with innocent eyes.

"What's that expression supposed to mean?" Grant's voice was lightly amused, and Anne allowed her eyes to play over the wide but not too wide shoulders, the blue, blue eyes, the mouth that curved in a smile.

"Just thinking," she murmured. He was very close, but she told herself she had nothing to worry about, even as her heart began beating faster and faster and her palms got damp. She could smell the crackling pine logs, the fumes of the cognac mingling with the faint trace of a woodsy after-shave. "This is a very pleasant way to spend an evening," she added, her voice coming out surprisingly husky.

"I agree." His voice was low, caressing, and Anne swallowed nervously. "An excellent meal, a fire, a great cognac and a beautiful woman. I couldn't ask for more." And before she could realize what he was doing, one arm slid around her, pulling her close, his head bent down and that smiling mouth met hers.

She could taste the cognac on his lips as they gently brushed hers. She was so bemused that her own lips parted beneath the soft pressure, and his tongue snaked out, delving behind her teeth to fully explore the sweetness beyond. She sat there in a kind of passive delight as he slowly, gently, thoroughly kissed her, more completely than she had ever been kissed before. When he finally pulled away, it was only a fraction of an inch, his arm still around her, his eyes smiling down at her. "Shell-shocked?" he inquired pleasantly, his breath warm on her face. "I would think you'd be used to being kissed." And his mouth descended again.

This time all passivity left her in a rush, her mouth opening beneath his, her tongue tasting and exploring his mouth as thoroughly as he had hers. She twined her arms around his back, dimly conscious of the brandy snifter still clutched in one hand. His tense, strong body started, then relaxed as he moved closer still, his body burning against hers. He was easing her back onto the carpet when reality finally intruded with a rush and the sound of voices from the hallway, and reluctantly he let her go, his blue eyes still dark with desire.

He rose with one fluid movement, reaching a hand down to her. Staring up at him dazedly, she finally placed one slim hand in his large strong one. As it closed around her, pulling her to her feet, her eyes met his, cloudy with confusion.

"It reeks of cognac in here," she said finally, for lack of something better to say.

He laughed then, humor and something else lighting his eyes. "That's because you poured your cognac down my back," he said pleasantly.

"I didn't!"

"You did. But don't worry—it soaked through my sweater and no one will notice. Though I do admit it's a little damp." His smile lit his dark face. "It's just as well—I need something uncomfortable to concentrate on." He reached out a surprisingly tender hand and pushed a silky dark strand of hair away from her flushed face. "I imagine you'd rather your family didn't know what we were just doing."

It took all her willpower to keep from nuzzling against that hand like a starving kitten. Never again, she warned herself sternly, would she have the mistaken notion that any man was safe to lust after. It was going to take a fair amount of effort to shake the effect those blue eyes were having on her. "I don't believe Ashley would be too happy," she murmured caustically, hoping to see him show some trace of remorse, or even discomfort.

"Ashley?" His forehead wrinkled beneath the curly mop of hair, then cleared. "Oh, you mean your brother. Is he the protective type? I'll be sure to watch my step around him." With a sudden, lightninglike movement he kissed her on her upturned lips, which were parted in amazement. "You know, you're nothing at all like your sister," he added as a clincher.

"Noah!" Holly had appeared in the doorway, her blond curls rioting around her angelic face, her cheeks flushed from the cold, her eyes sparkling, her mouth curving in delight. "We'd almost given up on you." Racing across the room, she flung herself into his arms.

Anne was too horrified, miserable and guilty to notice that her dinner companion accepted Holly's enthusiastic welcome with a restrained if tolerant embrace.

"We wondered whether you'd fallen through the ice," he murmured, looking down at Holly and reaching behind his neck to unclasp her hands.

"We?" Holly looked around, spied her sister and immediately launched herself into Anne's arms in her usual demonstrative fashion. "You took good care of Noah while we were gone, didn't you, darling? We didn't expect to be gone so long. Is dinner completely ruined?"

"Dinner's on the warming trays, Holly." Her own guilt had eradicated any last traces of irritation on Anne's part.

"And she took very good care of me indeed," Noah said in that caressing voice of his, sending a warm flush over Anne's pale countenance.

"Holly, who is this fabulous man?" Ashley had appeared in the doorway, a Harris tweed overcoat flung casually across his narrow shoulders, the blond young man who had made an earlier appearance hovering anxiously behind him.

"Ashley, this is Noah Grant, a friend of mine from New York." Holly made the introductions with a haphazard vagueness. "Noah, this is my brother Ashley and his friend, Steve Piersall."

"The protective type?" Noah Grant murmured wickedly at Anne, who only succeeded in looking more miserable.

"Well, darling, I must say your taste is improving," Ashley Kirkland drawled, sauntering into the library and proffering one surprisingly large, capable-looking hand. Naturally tall and slender, Ashley had long ago learned to capitalize on his willowy looks, dressing in dove grays that emphasized his will-o'-the-wisp quality.

His long horse-face was dominated by a large nose, a rather small mouth and uncomfortably sharp blue eyes. They took in the tableau in front of him, and he smiled with a touch of malice. "Hello, Anne," he added, almost as an afterthought. "Been enjoying yourself?"

As the middle child of the family, Anne had long ago learned how to deflect both her elder brother's wicked tongue and her baby sister's winsome ways. She did so now, with her usual calm efficiency. "Of course, Ashley. Don't I always?"

"I wouldn't know, darling. I'd hardly think so, with that upstanding gentleman you're engaged to. But then, there's no accounting for tastes."

Anne felt rather than saw Noah Grant's start of surprise. Casting a surreptitious glance at him, she found Holly standing as close to him as humanly possible. Noah was smiling absently down at her, but the look in his blue eyes was enigmatic.

"Could we please eat?" Eldridge Kirkland appeared in the doorway, looking cranky and overtired, and concern swept over Anne. Their father hadn't been well since the mild heart attack that had slowed him down last fall, and standing about in chilly weather and eating at strange hours were scarcely the best thing for a man in compromised health.

"Of course we can, Proffy," Holly soothed with the charm that always managed to calm the professor's outraged sensibilities. "As soon as I introduce you to my beau." Again Anne felt Noah's start of surprise, and she could find a small trace of pity in her heart for him. She had yet to meet a man who could prove a match for Holly's feminine wiles. "This is Noah Grant. Noah, this is my father, Eldridge Kirkland, but we all call him Proffy."

"How do you do?" Noah managed to escape Holly's

pretty clutches long enough to shake the professor's hand. Proffy glared at him, as he did at any suitor for his younger daughter, and managed a semicivil grunt before turning and heading for the dining room with the regal assurance that all would follow.

"Aren't you coming, Noah?" Holly got no more than two feet before she realized that Noah wasn't following.

"Your sister and I have already eaten. I'll keep you company in a moment, but first I'd like to change my shirt." The words were casual enough; the amused look he sent a still-numb Anne was anything but.

"Well, I'm not really hungry," Holly said hastily. "I'll show you to your room." She started back toward him eagerly.

"No, you go on ahead. Anne can show me. We were in the midst of an interesting conversation when you got back, and I wanted to finish it."

Was that a threat or a promise? Anne raised worried green eyes to his face, but his expression was unreadable. "We'll be down in five minutes," she said firmly as Holly still hesitated. "You won't even miss us."

Holly cast a languishing look at Noah. "Want to bet?" she said soulfully before trailing into the dining room.

"I may have to lock my bedroom door tonight." Noah's voice was rich with humor, and a small, reluctant smile appeared on Anne's shadowed face.

"I don't think the lock works," she murmured, leading the way up the angled stairway, unaware of Noah's appreciative gaze behind her. "You can always put a chair under the door handle."

"Where does your sister sleep?" he queried as she opened the door to her beautifully proportioned bedroom.

"Next door. But there's no connecting door."

"And where do you sleep?" She couldn't tell whether it was a casual question or not, and her heart began to pound again as her mouth tingled with sudden remembrance of his cognac-laden kisses.

"I'm sleeping in my studio," she said, moving aside to allow him to precede her into the bedroom. She hovered at the door, reluctant to follow him inside, reluctant to leave him without some sort of explanation.

He was the first to bring it out in the open. "I suppose I should say I'm sorry about what happened in the library." His mobile mouth quirked upward in a rueful grin.

It took all Anne's willpower to keep from responding, "Are you sorry?" Instead she said, "I'm partly to blame. I didn't realize who you were."

He was tossing his suitcase onto her bed, snapping it open with quick efficiency and pulling out a fresh shirt. He paused to stare at her for a moment before stripping off the wool sweater. "You didn't?" He tossed the sweater onto the bed, and to her embarrassment the wide stain of cognac was a dark patch between his shoulder blades. He seemed more curious than anything else, and as he unbuttoned his shirt and pulled it out of his pants Anne wished she had escaped when she still could with a modicum of grace. But to run now would be ridiculously coy, and it was important that she be sophisticated and unmoved by that all too brief moment of passion by the library fire.

"You said your name was Grant," she explained, unable to tear her gaze away from his chest. He had tossed the stained shirt onto the bed and was taking an achingly long time in putting the new one on, giving Anne more than enough time to memorize the beautifully sculpted expanse of his chest, the lean, wiry strength, the golden skin with its faint trace of hair that seemed made for...

Anne cleared her throat. "Steve Piersall arrived earlier and I assumed he was Holly's Noah. So when you arrived and said your name was Grant, I naturally thought you were Ashley's latest... friend." She wondered vaguely if he'd be insulted by her false assumption, but she was still too distracted by that body to care.

He pulled a blue corduroy shirt on, and Anne watched all that lovely skin disappear with mingled relief and regret. "You thought I was Ashley's latest," he repeated, amused. "No wonder you seemed so comfortable—I haven't been used to being treated as quite so safe. Well, suffice it to say I'm not Ashley's friend." He moved across the room, tucking his shirt in around his lean waist, his tread light and purposeful. "And, as you discovered to your everlasting guilt, I'm not particularly safe. And I'm not Holly's Noah, either. Does that make you feel any better?" That last question was in a deep murmur as he stood directly in front of her, not touching her, his blue eyes warm and smiling down at her.

Those smiling eyes were hard to resist, but resist them she did. "It's none of my business," she replied coolly.

"Liar." He laughed, but it was a gentle laugh, with no mockery to be heard. "Am I going to get a chance to meet the upstanding gentleman?"

"Who?"

"That was Ashley's term for your fiancé," he explained gently. "Where is he, by the way?"

"Wilson will be here for dinner tomorrow," she said. "I'm sure you'll like him." Actually, she was sure he wouldn't, but she couldn't think of anything else to say.

"That remains to be seen." Both his face and his voice were enigmatic as he casually took her elbow in one strong, capable hand. The warmth of his flesh burned through her loose chamois shirt, and Anne wanted to yank her arm away and race down the hallway. She also wanted to turn and drag him back into the bedroom, but of course she did neither, forcing herself to remain unmoved as they went back downstairs. But all she could think of was the strong hand on her elbow, the thumb caressing her with a light, almost absentminded touch; and for a moment she allowed her fantasies a final free rein before clamping a firm hand down on them, summoning up the disapproving ghosts of Wilson and her sister to drive the guilt homeward.

Noah seemed to have an almost eerie ability to read her mind, for he stopped her at the bottom of the stairs, looking at her with a wry expression. "There's no need to feel so guilty, Annie," he said softly. "It wasn't your fault, you know. You're only human. I'm sure Wilson will forgive you." He chose that moment to bring up his other hand and gently brush a stray wisp of silky black hair from her face.

Anne's thoughts were far removed from her erstwhile fiancé and wholly concentrated on the man in front of her. Holly was right, she thought miserably. He very well might be the sexiest man alive.

She managed a bright, no-nonsense smile and deftly pulled away from him. "I think I'll survive the disgrace," she murmured, preceding him into the dining room and moving to sit beside her father, determined to keep as far out of his reach as possible for the rest of the night. He was just too damned distracting.

To her intense disappointment, a determined Holly and a meddling Ashley made that all too easy, so that

Chapter Three

Noah shut the heavy white-painted door with a silent, well-oiled click. The crystal doorknob winked at him in the dim bedroom light, and for a moment he considered following Anne Kirkland's half-facetious advice and propping a chair against it. Holly Kirkland didn't really give a damn about him, but she was bored and obviously unaccustomed to taking no for an answer. It had taken all his not inconsiderable reserves of charm to escape her with his long-lost virtue still reasonably intact, and even so he couldn't be sure he'd distracted her permanently. She was definitely the type to sneak into his bedroom and his bed sometime in the middle of the night if the mood struck her, and the mood seemed to be hovering about like a dangerous cloud. And normally he would have welcomed that midnight excursion with wry forbearance and a great deal of physical pleasure.

But not tonight. Definitely not tonight. He'd gotten involved with this as a favor to his father-in-law, and pretty, easy Holly Kirkland was supposed to be a side benefit. A side benefit he no longer wanted. He hadn't particularly liked what he was being asked to do, but it had seemed no worse than a dozen other chores he'd had to perform since he'd passed his bar exams. And they were nothing compared to the deal-making and sleazy scuffling that had fallen to his lot as a law clerk. It was no wonder that he wanted out. It was only a wonder that he'd stood it so long.

It was well past midnight already, and the house was silent. Noah turned and leaned his back against the door, surveying the bedroom with interest. He had the very strong suspicion that this was more than just a spare bedroom. There was a subtle scent in the air, a delicate hint of flowers mixed with something sharper. A grin slashed his face as he recognized the smell of the spilled cognac on his discarded shirt, and for a brief, dangerous moment he let his thoughts drift back to that moment by the fire.

It had been irresistible. She'd sat there, cross-legged on the faded Oriental carpet, her green eyes shyly flirting, her mouth smiling, her entire manner treating him as if he had the combined sexuality of Old Mother Hubbard and Mister Rogers. And while he didn't consider himself possessed of an overwhelming sexual vanity, he wasn't used to being treated like an eunuch. And when she'd looked up at him with that innocent, sexy face of hers he'd given in to the temptation to show her just how uneunuchlike he was. And had enjoyed every moment of it, from her sudden, astonished response to that clutching, unexpectedly heated need that had spread between the two of them like wildfire.

But it had been a stupid mistake. He had complicated an already unbearably complex situation, and there didn't seem to be anything he could do about it. He was here to do a job, a last favor for his father-in-law, and then his debts, emotional and professional, would be paid in full, and he'd be free. And he needed that freedom very badly. He couldn't afford to let an impulsive attraction for Anne Kirkland deter or distract him.

Pushing away from the door, he crossed the room, absently unbuttoning his shirt as he went, sniffing the air with an appreciative delight. It smelled like roses. Innocent, with a touch of full-blown passion beneath the fragile petals. Anne Kirkland chose well when she chose her scent. He could still remember the faint trace of it against the soft skin of her neck. And what was he doing, standing in the middle of what must be her bedroom, having erotic fantasies about a woman he was going to hurt very badly? Through no fault of his own, through no desire of his own, he was going to be the instrument of the destruction of her security. And standing there thinking about her delicious skin wasn't going to change matters.

It had all seemed so easy just three days ago. Wendell James had outlined the situation, leaving Holly Kirkland to fill in the details. The Allibet Foundation was very interested in purchasing an estate on the New Jersey side of the Delaware, just across from New Hope, as an artists' colony and retreat. Negotiations were delicate—three of the four owners wished to sell. It was up to Noah to find out just how suitable the Kirkland house was for their purposes, just how likely they'd be to knock down the price a bit, and what sort of encumbrances, including the recalcitrant fourth owner, stood in the foundation's way of purchasing the property.

Holly Kirkland had been exactly as he'd expected when he met her Wednesday night at her preordained singles bar. He'd heard her play once, years before, when Nialla was still alive, and been favorably impressed with her facility and her light, lilting touch. Nialla had insisted she lacked depth, but Noah had argued that age and experience would remedy that. Nialla had disagreed, accusing him of being bemused

by her prettiness, and they had spent the rest of the
night fighting, as they spent so many of their nights in
the year before she died. Fights that would resolve in
the passion that neither of them could get enough of.

Part of him had dreaded meeting Holly, remembering those interminable fights and their unforgettable af-
termath, but her light flirtatiousness had managed to
push Nialla's memory into the background, and he'd
been grateful. It was too much to hope that Nialla's
reproachful ghost would disappear entirely.

Holly had leaned across the tiny table at the bar, her
strong hands with their short, serviceable nails pressed
together, the low-cut front of her flame-colored silk
dress dipping to expose most of her small, high breasts.
Noah knew enough about women to recognize the gesture as practiced and deliberate, a fact that amused him
without lessening the desired effect.

"The problem, Noah," Holly had murmured in a
confiding tone that could barely be heard above the
thumping strains of Joe Jackson, "is my sister."

"Your sister?" he echoed politely, sipping at the
dark whiskey in front of him.

"The fourth owner. You have to understand, the
house is an albatross. It's simply too large for us to afford anymore. We just keep throwing money at the old
monster, and no matter how much we give, it still demands more. It's falling down around us, and Anne
can barely keep up with the repairs. It's running her
life, blinding her to everything, and there's no way to
make her see reason."

"You've tried?"

"Of course we've tried," Holly replied, her concern
not interfering with her ability to bat her eyes. "She's
got a fixation about the place—she won't leave till she's
forced out. That's why we've got to lie about why

you're coming with us. If Anne had any idea we were planning to sell the house, she'd do anything she could to stop us."

"Could she?"

"Stop us? Possibly. Not legally. Wendell James has already checked that out. We only need three of the four owners to agree to sell. But she could make things very difficult, delay things. We've all agreed—the only thing we can do is present her with a fait accompli."

"Who's 'we'?" he inquired pleasantly enough over the din, covering the instinctive feeling of distaste that filled him at the idea of more trickery.

"My father, my brother and me. We've accepted the facts of life even if Anne can't. Wendell is taking care of the legal aspects of this whole mess—he just needs you to check out the local ramifications."

"So I gather. He trusts me to make sure it's what the foundation really wants."

"I don't think there's any question of that," Holly said confidently. "You'll fall in love with the place— everyone does." She toyed with the dregs of her drink. "We'll have to think of some excuse for your presence this weekend. I think we should just tell Anne that we're lovers."

That trace of diffidence in her voice was admirable, he thought distantly. Just a shy peek from her blue eyes—there it was—and a self-deprecating little smile. He knew his cue and replied with an ironic suavity that was lost on her. "I'm sure I'll manage to be convincing."

There was no question about it, her answering smile had been breathtaking. And it had been a respectable interval since he'd spent the night anywhere but in his solitary bed. Holly Kirkland was exactly the sort of woman he liked. Bright, pretty, talented, with a shell around her heart like a chocolate-dipped ice-cream cone. They could pleasure each other's bodies without endangering any emotions, which was just what he wanted. But not that night.

It wouldn't have taken much to move the relationship into bed. Holly's bright-blue eyes had made it more than clear that she found him attractive. And he had had every intention of taking her up on her unspoken offer, once they got to the old house. But that night her calm plans had turned him off as much as her pretty body in that luscious silken dress had turned him on, and he'd made a plausible excuse.

And now he was practically hiding out in a solitary bedroom, having done everything in his power to deter her. And he couldn't quite understand why. Unless it was a belated regret over what they were doing to her sister.

It was a beautiful old house, there was no question about it. And that it was falling down around the genteelly impoverished Kirkland family was equally apparent. Anne Kirkland was fighting a losing battle; sooner or later she would have to accept defeat. He just wished that he wasn't going to have to be part of that defeat.

Taking off the rest of his clothes, he climbed into bed, wishing for the first time that he owned something as mundane as nightclothes. They usually made him feel that he was suffocating, but they'd provide at least a measure of protection if Holly felt like doing a little night walking. Would it be a different matter if it was Anne Kirkland? Probably. And yet it was Anne who was trouble, not Holly. He had to remember to keep his distance from both sisters. He had enough trouble in his life.

Turning off the light, he lay back in the narrow bed, resting his head against the pile of feather pillows. The

sheets were crisp and cool against his body. He liked
the idea of Anne Kirkland sleeping in this bed. Maybe,
with great good luck, he could fall asleep thinking of
her. Even those dangers were preferable to his usual
nocturnal companion.

But he should have known. The fitful moonlight
shone in the window, cutting a wide swath across the
bed. There was just the beginning flutter of pale snow-
flakes filtering down. And with the inevitability of
death and taxes, he remembered Nialla.

ANNE WAS AWAKENED at a little past seven by the blinding sunlight streaming in her wall of windows. With a
small moan she burrowed back under the quilt in a vain
attempt at shutting out the merciless glare. Punching
up a small corner to let in a tiny amount of oxygen, she
shut her eyes once more. But the quilt soon collapsed,
Anne started smothering, and within five minutes she
threw the cover back with a hearty curse. Swinging her
bare feet onto the floor, she tried a glare at the brilliant
sunshine, a glare that immediately dissolved into a delighted smile. It had snowed during the night, a good
four inches, and the trees, the yard, the hillside were a
fairyland of white.

It was impossible to be bad-tempered on such a day,
she thought, pulling on her best jeans and her favorite
silk blouse before topping it with a less-than-baggy
sweater. Why she eschewed the loose-fitting flannel
shirt was something she didn't care to consider, and
the only blot on her horizon was the fact that the
showers in the house were all on the second floor. The
last thing she wanted to do was to run into a passion-
sated Noah Grant, fresh from a night in her sister's
voracious arms. It didn't matter that she had no right
to care, both because of Wilson Engalls and her sis-

ter's prior claim. She simply didn't want Holly to have
him.

Within minutes the smell of freshly ground coffee
was filling the underground kitchen. To Anne's amazement the late-night glasses had all been washed and put
in the drainer, the counters cleaned off, and everything
left spotless. It was impossible to believe either of her
hopelessly impractical siblings capable of the act or the
motivation, and her father would have broken more
dishes than he washed. *Perhaps Steve Piersall was the
housewifely type,* she thought with a trace of her brother's malice. But she knew perfectly well who had
washed the dishes.

"Is that coffee for anyone?" She didn't have to turn
to see him. Indeed, she had known all through the
night that he'd be the first one up.

She turned from the sink in her best casual manner,
inwardly breathing a sigh of relief. "As soon as it's
ready," she murmured. "I didn't expect to see you so
early."

"I had a good night's sleep," he replied, a small grin
lighting that dark face, and Anne caught herself staring, fascinated. He looked like a tall Celtic Gypsy, with
that dark skin, the blue, blue eyes and the wildly curl-
ing black hair. And she had read too many romances,
she thought with disgust.

"You were able to fend off Holly?" She shouldn't
have said such a thing. It was less than loyal to her
sister, but she had always had trouble controlling her
thoughtless tongue.

"So far, so good," Noah said with a laugh. "I'm
counting on you to protect me."

"I think you're more than capable of taking care of
yourself," she said. Pulling down two of the ceramic
mugs she had made several years ago, she poured them

both full of the thick, richly scented brew. Fussing with sugar and cream for Noah took another few moments, and then she perched herself on the counter by the sink, her favorite seat, one that she assumed would keep her at a safe distance from the sexy, rumpled man with her in her basement kitchen with only the silent snow for company.

She assumed wrong. With the effortlessness due to long legs he climbed up beside her, one jeans-clad thigh almost touching hers, and took a sip of the hot coffee.

If she edged away from him, she'd end up in the sink, a spot both undignified and uncomfortable. Taking a sip of her black coffee, she promptly burned her tongue.

"Though if you're not interested in Holly," she added, her mind still working, "then I don't understand why you accepted her invitation. My sister is hardly subtle—I would have thought she'd made it clear what she had in mind. If you wanted to avoid it I don't see why you agreed to come."

There was a fleeting guilty look that crossed his face like a passing cloud, and then he smiled that impossibly charming smile that effectively banished suspicions. "I like your sister," he said—not really an explanation. "And I admire her tremendous talent. I was also at loose ends this weekend and the idea of being maneuvered into a weekend affair seemed like a pleasant enough way to pass the time. Quite frankly, I wasn't interested in much more than that from Holly, but then I knew she wouldn't be willing to give any more. That's the problem with great artists—they're incredibly selfish from necessity."

Having grown up sandwiched in between two brilliant artists, Anne could scarcely refute that statement.

"What made you change your mind, then?" she questioned, taking another cautious sip of her coffee.

"Change my mind?" He was staring down at her, a curious expression in his eyes.

"About a passionate weekend with Holly," she prodded.

He was silent for a long moment, a fact Anne could only be grateful for. "I don't want her to think I'm too easy," he said finally with a twisted grin. "I want her to respect me." Before she could push him further he changed the subject. "What kind of coffee is this?"

"Sumatran beans. Freshly ground." At least coffee would be a safe topic of conversation.

She was wrong. "Do you realize how rare a truly great cup of coffee is?" he countered severely. "Will you run away with me?"

"I thought you weren't easy," she murmured, a slight smile in her eyes. "Besides, I don't think Wilson would like it."

"Wilson?"

"My fiancé. You remember, the upstanding gentleman," she prodded, feeling that all too familiar flash of guilt. "This house would fall down around us if I left. I think you'll have to run away with Holly."

He was watching her out of blandly curious eyes. "No way," he said finally. "She makes instant coffee."

Anne was startled. "How did you know that? I thought you hadn't succumbed to her myriad charms yet."

"I haven't. I succumbed to her offer of coffee after you deserted us last night, and that was mistake enough." He shuddered expressively. "Powdered milk wasn't much help, either."

"I could almost find it in my heart to pity you."

"I was hoping you would. Don't abandon me to my

fate tonight, I beg of you." He was suddenly very close, and the coffee on his breath mingled with hers. Unconsciously she leaned toward him, her lips parted breathlessly, once more falling under his spell.

"Noah," she murmured breathlessly, "don't do this."

"Don't do what?" he whispered, his lips brushing hers. "You're feeling the same way I am—don't deny it." One hand reached out and deftly removed her half-full coffee mug from her hand, setting it down on the counter. "We'd better put this out of harm's way. I didn't mind brandy down my back, but I draw the line at hot coffee." And his mouth caught hers again, tasting of the rich sweetness of creamed and sugared coffee. Anne made a little moaning sound in the back of her throat, and she raised her hands to push him away from her. A shared kiss by a fire was one thing, and she could always blame the brandy. Right now it was broad daylight, and she had absolutely no excuse, much as she wanted one. And she wanted him. The hands pushed for a moment against his chest, then curled around his shoulders, the fingers kneading the tightly muscled flesh, as she slowly, languorously tipped back her head beneath his searching mouth.

The clatter of footsteps down the narrow kitchen steps pulled them apart, and a moment later, when a somewhat disheveled Holly appeared in the door, Anne was again staring down into her coffee, only the telltale flush on her usually pale face attesting to her recent activity.

"Good morning!" Holly said cheerily. "This certainly is the most ghastly time of day to get out of bed."

"Then why did you? I don't think you've gotten up before noon since you were eighteen," Anne shot back, her smile taking the sting out of her words.

"Artistic license, darling. We great talents have to have our beauty rest. But today I made the supreme sacrifice so that I wouldn't miss a minute of Noah." She peered around the kitchen. "Have you got any more coffee? Instant will do."

Despite herself Anne met Noah's expressive grin, and she burst out laughing. "Holly, it's a shame to waste good coffee on you. It's on the stove."

"You know, sis, there's nothing worse than a coffee snob," Holly rejoined cheerfully. "There are a great many things more important in life than a cup of coffee."

"Name one," Noah said promptly.

"Oh, not you, too." Holly sighed, her blue eyes narrowing suddenly as she took in their proximity at the counter. "Well, you two are certainly getting along like a house on fire," she murmured above her coffee. "I wouldn't have thought you'd have much in common."

"Apart from coffee and cognac we don't," he murmured, sliding down off the counter and strolling to the door to peer out at the snow-covered countryside. "I wonder if it's snowing in Vermont."

Holly's pout was attractive, but Noah missed it entirely. "Aren't you enjoying your stay, Noah? I hadn't realized we'd be boring you already."

"I'm enjoying it immensely." His eyes met Anne's for a brief pregnant moment before smiling blandly at Holly. "You have to realize that the sight of snow sends any skier's blood racing."

"Oh, is that what did it?" Anne murmured provocatively under her breath from her perch on the countertop, and he grinned at her.

"What did you say, Anne?" A tiny bit of a whine was added to the dimpled pout, and her wide blue eyes slid from her sister to Noah with sudden suspicion.

"Nothing, darling. Are you ready for breakfast?" Anne stretched luxuriantly, yawning. "Excuse me, I'm not used to having company so early in the day."

"You'd better complain to Wilson about that. It's up to him to get you used to it," Holly snapped, and Anne's head shot up, her green eyes troubled as she surveyed her sister's angry face. Holly continued on, undaunted. "You haven't met Anne's fiancé yet, Noah. Ashley hates him, but Proffy thinks the match is made in heaven. He's much more tolerant of old Wilson than he is of any of my men friends. But then, Anne is thirty-four, and I guess he figures she knows what she wants by now."

Noah leaned against the oak table, more amused than anything else. "Thirty-four, are you? My, you are ancient! I'm surprised you don't need a cane to get around."

"I can still manage pretty well," Anne replied lightly, her eyes concerned as they took in Holly's obvious distress. She had known for years that Holly hated to lose. But why should she feel threatened by Noah's harmless charm, unless he meant more to her than one of the brief encounters she'd enjoyed over the years.

"Yes, she's two years older than you," Holly added with all the deftness of a sledgehammer. She had been blessed with neither Ashley's malice nor Anne's slightly mocking humor, and her attempts at acerbity fell flat.

"So she is," Noah said mildly, taking in the tension with a wry smile.

Finally Anne forced herself to move. "Look, why don't you two go on up to the dining room and I'll get a start on breakfast? If you're feeling noble you might even set the table." She slid off the countertop and began rustling around the stove.

"That sounds like a good idea." Noah refilled his coffee mug, getting one for Holly while he was at it. The anger and suspicion were gone from the younger woman's eyes—instead they were filled with belated guilt and misery.

"Anne, I'm..." Words seemed to fail her, and Anne could very well guess why. She could hardly admit to being jealous of her elder sister—Holly could never admit to any insecurities at all.

"Don't worry about it, cranky," she said in a low voice, accompanying it with a forgiving smile. "I can see now why you sleep till noon."

Holly smiled back, obviously relieved, as she caught Noah's arm in a lightly possessive grip. "Two eggs, over easy, with sausage and English muffins," she demanded blithely. "What would you like, Noah?"

He stared down at Holly, his easy smile nowhere to be seen. "First of all, I'd like you to stop treating your sister like a short-order cook and honored serf," he drawled, the sting in his voice faint but present. "And for breakfast I'll have whatever she's making, or better still, I'll make it myself and save her the trouble."

Anne swallowed, waiting for the explosion, and Holly's eyes flashed dangerously for a moment. And then the tension left her, and she laughed, a light, unaffected laugh that was a major part of her charm.

"You're right; I was thoughtless, and I'm sorry. Anne, you go on upstairs and set the table, and Noah and I will make breakfast."

"Now that sounds like a good idea," Noah seconded, his eyes warm with approval. "Even better, why don't you take your coffee, go into the living room, and put your feet up? Read the paper, take it easy. Holly and I will set the table, too. You deserve a morning off."

"Yes, darling, you look like you've been under a lot of strain," Holly added, and for the first time Anne wondered if Ashley's malice had really passed her by.

"All right, I'm going," she acquiesced. "But you have to clean up any mess you make."

"Cross my heart!" Holly promised. "I'll put Noah in charge of KP."

"Hey!" he protested.

"Women's lib," she chirped back saucily. "Go on, Anne. You can trust us in your precious kitchen."

As she climbed the narrow stairs to the second floor, Anne was conscious of a queer feeling of isolation. Their laughing voices drifted up to her, and more than anything she wanted to be a part of that laughter, share in the lighthearted banter. But Holly had made it clear that banter could only include two people.

Curiouser and curiouser, Anne thought as she ensconced herself on the frayed sofa in front of the now cold fireplace, propping her feet on a pile of magazines atop the cherrywood butler's table. Never had she seen Holly so snappish, and there could be little doubt as to the cause of it. Hadn't she said Noah Grant was the sexiest man alive? Without question he was definitely in the top ten, and it was little wonder Holly had set her sights on him. What was a surprise was her jealousy of Anne. She suspected that Noah's flirtation was second nature to him—that she meant no more to him than Holly.

But Holly was no challenge; she was his for the taking. Not that she had put up much of a fight, either, Anne thought wryly, staring into the empty fireplace. It would be a very good idea if she spent the day in her studio, working on the Chinese manuscript, and then have Wilson come over early. A good dose of Wilson's steady charm would drive these absurd fantasies from her mind in short order. Never mind the fact that she'd been having second thoughts about Wilson these last few months. There was still no room in her well-ordered life for a charming, overgrown leprechaun like Noah Grant, and there was certainly no room in his for the likes of Anne Kirkland. It would be an extremely good idea if she didn't forget that again.

Chapter Four

The political ramifications of the Ming dynasty, written in Harvey Etling's turgid, academic prose, were hardly conducive to keeping Anne's mind off the distracting presence of Noah Grant. Shortly after breakfast she disappeared into her studio, equipped with a box of ginger snaps and her third cup of coffee, leaving strict instructions with Holly that she wasn't to be disturbed. She'd had little doubt Holly would manage to keep intruders from her studio, particularly a certain one, and during the next six or seven hours she slogged through just over half of the five-hundred-page manuscript. Unfortunately Etling's urge to sound erudite quite often circumvented grammar, necessitating rather tedious line editing, and by the time Anne finally looked up from the manuscript scattered around her on the bed, her head and eyes ached, her muscles were cramped, and her temper hovered between depression, exhaustion and definite snappishness.

The faint rich aroma of coffee filtered through the narrow door to her haven, the smell tickling her nostrils and bringing a latent resolution to her tired body. Straightening from her reclining position, she started pushing the scribbled-on manuscript into some sort of order when the door opened and the doorway filled with a distracting male body.

"So this is where you've been hiding all day," Noah observed casually, looking around him with interest as he ducked into the room. The door cut into the solid rock wasn't suited for people more than five feet eight.

"I haven't been hiding; I've been working," she said irritably, angry at the sudden quickening of her pulses. "And looking for some solitude."

He held up the tray holding two mugs of steaming coffee. "I come bearing gifts. Surely you can't kick a messenger out who comes equipped with coffee?"

"You seem to have an uncanny ability to find all my weaknesses," she said with a sigh, reaching an eager hand for the mug. She took a tentative sip. It was slightly stronger than she usually made it, but divine nonetheless. "And you must have made this. No one else in the house knows how to make coffee, unless Ashley's friend has hidden talents."

"I'm sure he must." Noah slid down to sit on the floor, his long legs stretched out in front of him, and Anne could only be thankful he didn't choose the bed. "But I'd guess Ashley would know that better than anyone else. They've been off somewhere all day." His blue eyes surveyed the twilit room before coming to rest on her. "I like your studio."

"So do I. It's a great place to escape to when my family's demands get overwhelming."

"I can imagine so. Your family seems to be the type to get overwhelming quite frequently. This does look a little unfurnished for a bedroom, though."

"Oh, this isn't usually my bedroom," she said blithely, then her unruly tongue ground to a halt.

"I didn't think so. You usually sleep next door to Holly, don't you?" He grinned at her.

"Did you go through my drawers?" she questioned curtly, unable to hide her discomfort.

"Didn't think of it. Though that's a good idea. No, I can recognize that delicious smell of roses that permeates the room. And I can recognize your taste. No one else in this house would have such a strange collection of books. Your mind fascinates me."

"Why? Because I like steamy romances and Doris Lessing?"

"Not to mention Dick Francis, Dorothy L. Sayers and Charles Dickens."

"Acquit me of the last!" she begged. "Dickens found his way up there while I was looking up something. I disapprove of him heartily—he's tedious and sexist."

"So was almost everyone back then." He took a sip of his own coffee. "He has things to recommend him, though. You ought to try him again."

"Forget it. He had his chance and he blew it with *A Tale of Two Cities*. Did you say you had a message for me?" She tried to keep her mind off his lovely long legs, the sensual curve of his mouth, that mop of thick black curls, and how much she liked having him stretched out comfortably in her inner sanctum, arguing about Dickens.

"Wilson's car is broken down."

"No!" She was immediately panic-stricken. Noah Grant was already playing havoc with her fantasies— she needed Wilson around to make her see some sense, or heaven only knew what might happen. She hadn't been prey to this kind of nervous schoolgirl passion since she was seventeen.

"Don't worry, he'll be there to protect you from me," Noah said with a grin. "Holly went to fetch him, which explains why I'm momentarily free. Did you tell her to cling to me like a burr all day, or was that her idea?"

"She didn't need much encouragement, I'm afraid. I'm sorry, has she been intolerable?" Anne knew still another pang of guilt.

"Almost. I know I have myself to blame as much as anyone. I realized what I was getting into." His clear blue eyes caught hers for a long, silent moment, and Anne was suddenly, belatedly aware of the encroaching winter night. The sun had set, and the room was filled with blue shadows reflecting off the snow. There was a bright sliver of moon already in evidence, casting eerie shadows of bare limbs onto the wide oak floor, across Noah's face, reaching out ghostly fingers to touch Anne's restless body.

"I should start dinner," she said, not moving, and her voice came out low and breathless.

He ignored her inane comment. "Are you afraid of me, Annie love?" His voice was low and beguiling. "I wouldn't hurt you, you know."

"Wouldn't you?" she found herself saying caustically, then gave herself a mental and physical shake. "And why should you? This is an entirely ridiculous conversation, Noah. You're not in a position to hurt me."

"Aren't I?"

"No!" Her voice was stubborn and a little too loud in the quiet room. "And I think we'd better retire to the kitchen before Holly comes back and slits our throats."

"Not Wilson? Isn't he the protective type any more than Ashley?" Slowly, casually, Noah rose to his full height, stretching his lean, lithe body indolently.

"Wilson, as you'll soon discover, is eminently civilized. Holly's more emotional." A frown crossed her face. "And surprisingly jealous."

"Maybe I bring out the worst in her," Noah offered lightly. "Though I never fancied myself as irresistible."

Anne let that pass. "No, it's been going on longer than that. She's been edgy around me and Wilson for the past eighteen months, and I can't imagine why."

"Past eighteen months?" Noah echoed, suddenly very curious. "How long have you been engaged?"

Anne looked at him without batting an eye, daring him to mock her. "Eighteen months," she replied briefly.

"Don't give me that fierce look, Annie love. It's none of my business if your fiancé is a little slow on the uptake," he murmured. Before she could protest he caught her hand, pulling her off the bed to stand beside him, and for a moment Anne could smell the faint trace of spicy after-shave he used, mixed with the coffee. She took a sudden step away from him, toward the door, and he laughed.

"And I wouldn't worry about Holly doing us in," he said, following her out into the kitchen. "I think I've finally found the perfect distraction for her. She lit up when she heard your fiancé on the phone."

"Holly and Wilson?" Anne dumped her coffee mug in the sink and headed for the refrigerator. "Don't be ridiculous. She thinks he's a stick-in-the-mud and he thinks she's an impertinent baby. He calls her 'brat.'"

"How endearing. Maybe that's what Holly needs." Noah deftly removed the salad fixings from her hands and headed toward the chopping board.

The sudden temper that had been plaguing her of late flared once more. "Well, that's too bad for her. She's not going to have him, too."

"Too?" he echoed, fascinated. "Who else has she

commandeered? Or did you mean because of her obviously favored position in the household? Your father does seem to dote on her."

"Yes, he does, and I learned long ago not to let that bother me," she said frankly. "A lot of men prefer their women to be charmingly scatterbrained and helpless. Gives them a sense of superiority. Holly's very good at appearing helpless, when actually she's capable of just about anything she puts her mind to. She wouldn't be where she is in her profession if she couldn't. Brilliant talent isn't enough. You need discipline, determination, ruthlessness...."

"And that selfishness we talked about earlier," Noah added, shredding the lettuce in large, capable hands before tossing it in the bird's-eye maple salad bowl. "Selfish with their time, their energy, their emotions, their love."

"Not to mention their money," Anne added wryly, remembering the cost of the cognac. "You sound like you've been through it before. Have you known many artists?"

"I was married to one." The words were short, clipped, the expression on his face shuttered. Anne stared at him for a long, silent moment, trying to still the absurd rush of jealousy that had swept over her at his terse words. There was no doubt in her mind that he didn't care to talk about his marriage, no doubt that if she did pursue it he would abandon her in the kitchen. And even if that was a very sensible idea, she couldn't bring herself to do it.

"Well, then, you know as well as I do what it's like. And it's even worse growing up with them," she said easily, slicing onions. "I hope you like *carbonnades à la Flammande*?"

"What kind of beer do you have to go with it?"

"German and Dutch. I wanted to find some Flemish beer but I couldn't think of any."

"I can't either." There was still a note of strain in his voice, and he whirled on her suddenly, his lean, strong body taut. "Do you know what the definition of blemish is?"

He looked so very serious, the smile wiped from his dark face, and all sorts of things ran through her mind. The scarring of a bad marriage, the wounds left by petty jealousy? "No, what?" she questioned, her voice as tense as his.

"The language they speak in Felgium."

"Damn you!" She collapsed against the sink, weak with laughter.

"I thought you'd like that," he said with a smirk. "Do you know how they torture seasoned criminals?"

"They make them listen to your jokes?"

"No, Annie love. They torture seasoned criminals on a spice rack."

"Oh, no," she moaned. "Go away. I'd rather do the salad myself."

"Sorry, but I haven't found a willing victim for a long time. I was almost kicked out of law school for that last one."

"I'm not surprised. You should be ashamed of yourself, Mr. Grant."

"I can't help myself, Ms Kirkland. It comes over me sometimes, this dreadful compulsion to tell bad jokes. I need help."

"You do indeed. I think you should corner Holly and tell her. Then she'd leave you alone for certain."

"And then I could spend the rest of the weekend backing you into dark corners." There was a dangerous gleam in his eyes. "That sounds like an excellent idea."

"On second thought, maybe you'd better spare Holly the disillusionment. She told me you were the sexiest man alive—I'd hate to see her illusions shattered so completely."

"You think telling bad jokes diminishes my sexuality?"

She paused midway through her third onion. "It quite effectively unmans you," she said, gesturing with her knife for emphasis.

"If you didn't wave that knife around I could very easily prove you wrong," he murmured, the gleam in his eyes more pronounced. "That's not a challenge I can let pass by."

"Too bad. I'll defend my virtue at all costs."

"Then I'll have to wait until I can catch you without a knife," he replied, undaunted.

"And when Wilson and Holly are out of the picture, and when I'm as addled as I was last night and this morning," she added sternly. "That's a tall order, and one I don't think fate is likely to fill."

"Addled, were you?" he queried, much interested. "I wonder why?"

"How could I help it with the sexiest man in the world bent on adding me to his list of conquests?" Anne replied, her voice wry.

He started to say something, then changed his mind. "I don't have a list of conquests," he said quietly.

"That's not what Holly said." She was concentrating very hard on the onions, but she could feel those mesmerizing blue eyes watching her, feel the heat from him as he moved closer to her slender body by the sink.

"I'm not a monk," he said finally. "I have normal, healthy urges that I try to fill in normal, healthy ways. And having to bed every woman in sight isn't a healthy, normal way as far as I'm concerned." Abruptly he changed the subject. "Why don't you have a food

processor? Any cook as good as you deserves one."
Reaching deftly around her knife, he took half-a-dozen
onions with him to aid in her slicing.

"Don't I know it." She sighed covetously. "At this
point we can't afford it. Every penny goes into this old
house." She looked around her with mingled exasperation and affection. "I'm afraid a new roof is going to
have to come first. I only wish we could afford to replace the slate."

"It must be rather expensive—the upkeep of a
house this size," he observed casually.

"It's like pouring money into a hole in the ground
that never gets filled," she admitted. "But I love it—I
don't begrudge a penny of it."

"Do the others feel that way?"

Anne shrugged. "Not really. But then, very little of
their money ever makes it to New Jersey. Their lifestyles eat up almost every cent they make."

"So who supports the house?"

"I do. Proffy's half-salary just about covers food and
gas—most of it goes into his retirement fund. And then
there have been the medical bills this year, not to mention that the foundation is crumbling." She gave herself a tiny shake. "So no food processors for me for the
time being. Let's talk about something more cheerful
for a change. Do you think we'll get more snow?"

"Some people wouldn't find that so cheerful—especially the road crews and people who have long commutes to work. But yes, I think we're going to get some
more tonight, and then with any luck the storm will
move up the East Coast and dump a foot or two on
New England."

"Won't the road crews and commuters dislike it
there, too?"

"I'm sure they'll hate it. But the skiers will be in
seventh heaven."

"And that includes you?"

"That includes me. Why? Don't you approve?"

"I think it's insane. Why would anyone want to slide down a mountainside on two sticks? It's beyond my comprehension."

"I guess I'll have to change your mind." He dumped the chopped onions into the bowl with hers, and Anne wrinkled her nose.

"I don't see why. I've made it to the advanced age of thirty-four without liking skiing—I imagine I can get through another thirty-four or so the same way."

"Not if I have anything to say about it."

"God save me from a missionary," Anne said, sighing. "Damn."

"Damn?" Noah echoed.

"These onions were so mild I thought they wouldn't get to my eyes. I'm afraid this last one was more than I could take." Laughing, she lifted watery, reddened eyes to his, the tears streaming down her face.

He moved swiftly toward her, placing one strong, warm hand on her shoulder as he lifted the other to her tearstained cheek. His smile was wary.

"Very affecting," he murmured. "I wish all women laughed when they cried." His head bent slowly down, and she knew he was going to kiss her; and once more, like a besotted teenager, she was going to let him. Before his mouth met hers, however, he pulled back, slowly, without a trace of guilt. And directly behind her she heard the kitchen door open. Turning, she met the distinctly displeased and surprisingly similar expressions of her sister Holly and Wilson Engalls.

IT WAS HARDLY an auspicious beginning for the evening, and things went steadily downhill from there. The instant antagonism that sprang up between Wilson and

Noah, barely restrained, was bad enough. Holly's intermittent bad temper and remorse only exacerbated the situation. But the absolutely crushing blow, the real stunner, the knockout punch, was when Anne looked up at Wilson's tall, sturdy figure as she dusted the snow off his broad shoulders, broader than Noah's lean strength, her eyes wandering over the strong, handsome face, the firm chin, warm brown eyes and finely molded mouth and realized she felt nothing more than sisterly affection.

"Hello, darling," he greeted her in his even, mellifluous voice, coming over to give her a perfunctory kiss on the cheek. "How are you feeling? You look rather pale. Has Edmund been working you too hard?"

"I'm fine." Her voice came out slightly hoarse as she struggled to regain her composure. "You've met Holly's friend, Noah Grant?"

Holly had already claimed Noah's arm, beaming up at him like a proud mother hen. The barely civil nods that passed between the two men didn't aid the palpable tension in the kitchen.

"Grant," Wilson acknowledged coolly. "Holly's been telling me a great deal about you. I imagine we have a fair amount in common."

"Really?" Noah murmured, his eyes sliding to Anne's troubled face for a moment before meeting Wilson's bland gaze. "I wouldn't have thought so." His brilliant smile took the offense out of the words, but Anne wasn't fooled.

Neither, apparently, was Wilson. He smiled thinly in response to that glorious smile. "Wouldn't you?" Wilson wasn't giving anything away, even his temper. "We're both lawyers, both more than fond of a Kirkland."

Once more Noah's blue eyes slid over Anne's pale

face, and she tensed, waiting for the next outrageous
statement. When it came, however, it was relatively
mild. "True enough," he murmured, patting Holly's
hand, which rested on his arm with seemingly absent
affection. "Do we have an appreciation of Scotch in
common?"

"It is about that time, isn't it?" Wilson replied easily,
and Anne felt the tension drain from her. No longer
did the two men seem like dogs circling each other,
their hackles raised. Their studious politeness might
mask hostility, but Anne was suddenly secure that that
hostility would stay under wraps. "I'd prefer bourbon,
however. Can I bring you something, Anne?" he
asked, ever the solicitous gentleman.

"No, thank you, Wilson. You three go on up. I'll
make do with the cooking sherry." Her need to get
them away from her bordered on desperation.

"Or you could always start in on the beer," Noah
suggested in dulcet tones. "I think there's a nice Blemish one in the refrigerator."

"Don't you mean Flemish?" Holly questioned with
a frown as Anne choked.

"Of course." Noah's face was as blandly innocent as
Wilson's. "Let us know if we can help you, Annie."

"You've helped enough." The slight edge to her
voice was missed by two-thirds of her companions.
Noah's blue eyes gleamed appreciatively.

"So tell me, brat, what have you been doing with
yourself since I last saw you?" She could hear Wilson
query as they disappeared up the narrow steps. Holly's
voice floated lightly back to her, and then she was
alone.

Her knees felt like water as she slowly sank to a chair
by the oak table and dropped her head in her hands.
What in heaven's name was happening to her? And

how could she ever have been so stupid, she demanded of herself. Had she been living in a complete fog for the past few years not to know the difference between affection and love? And she couldn't even congratulate herself on finally coming to her senses—it had taken a man of Noah Grant's considerable charms to make her see reason.

She didn't love Wilson Engalls, hadn't ever loved Wilson Engalls except as a friend. He was handsome, kind, protective and slightly domineering in a manner that could be extremely comforting when one was overworked and overstressed and unable to make another decision. The few times they had made love had been pleasant though not earth-shattering experiences, and Anne had always felt genuinely comfortable with him. But comfort didn't equal love, and she knew with a sudden depressing certainty that she would never marry Wilson Engalls, even if doing so would save her house for her.

She also had to remember that lust didn't equal love, either, even if she appeared to be suffering from an advanced case of it. Noah Grant was a very attractive, very appealing man who was two years younger than she, and he came fully equipped with a barely perceptible plate of armor around him. He was obviously used to life in the fast lane, to women like Holly. He'd proven more than useful in making her realize the idiocy of her arrangement with Wilson, but that was as far as it went.

Of course, she added dreamily to herself, he had also managed to demonstrate to her that there was a great deal more to kissing than she had previously supposed. There was a world of difference between Noah's kisses and Wilson's closed-mouth salutes. So far sex had been a pleasant, comfortable experience, though that experi-

ence had been surprisingly limited for this day and age.
She could count on both hands the number of times
she'd made love. Wilson was a definite improvement
over the hurried fumblings of her college classmates,
but the earth had failed to move. Anne had always supposed the steamy descriptions in novels were euphe-
mistic exaggerations. Now she wondered.

But Noah Grant was not going to be the one to enlighten her, much as he'd doubtless be willing to. He
might have been in the mood for a weekend fling—
that was the last thing she needed. She would do her
best to keep out of the way of temptation. And temptation it was—an overwhelming one. And sometime
soon, when the memory of Noah Grant was banished
from Wilson's jealous brain and Anne's restless heart,
she would calmly, politely sever the too long engage-
ment.

Like the coward she was, she stayed hidden in the
kitchen during the two hours it took for the dinner to
cook. The motley assemblage had only gotten through
the first part of the meal before Anne was searching
desperately in her mind for an excuse to leave the
table. She could always feign an upset stomach, but
considering they were all devouring her food that
might not be politic. Her miserable eyes surveyed the
table, and she took another healthy gulp of her Heine-
ken.

Ashley was at his very worst, sitting back at the foot
of the table, toying with his food, surveying the others
with that malicious glitter in his eyes. He had disdained
the beer that was a traditional accompaniment to *carbonnades*, preferring to bring his rum-and-tonic to the
table. It must have been his fourth, Anne estimated by
the flush around his eyes, the sneer on his mouth and
the slight belligerence in every spoken word.

Stephen Piersall didn't look much happier, and Anne couldn't blame him. Ashley, when he was in a mood like that, was no one's treat. Quietly the blond man addressed himself to his food, shoveling in massive amounts, his eyes slithering nervously to Ashley's sullen face at various intervals.

Holly was chattering, loudly and nervously, with not a soul listening to her but a studious Wilson. Proffy was morose, Noah silent and Anne ready to scream. Her only recourse was to the beer, and she kept on drinking.

When one of the far too frequent silences fell as Holly stopped long enough to nibble at her now chilled beef, Anne finally spoke up. "What did you and Stephen do today, Ashley?"

"I doubt you really have the stomach to hear, sister mine," Ashley sneered lightly, casting a mocking glance at Piersall's subdued face.

Not the best choice of subject matter, Anne realized with a sense of fatality. She shrugged apologetically at her brother, but it was too late.

"And how are your wedding plans coming, dear heart? I do hope you're planning to tie the knot before you're eligible for Social Security."

"We were thinking in terms of next fall," Wilson said, unperturbed.

"Such unseemly haste!" Ashley scoffed. "You will have been engaged almost two years by then. Aren't you afraid people might talk? When you rush into things like that, people might think you had to marry her."

"We'll be having children as soon as we can," Wilson announced firmly, and Anne cast him a startled glance. Much as she wanted children, they'd never so much as discussed the subject, and his decision struck as being both arbitrary and smug.

"How nice!" Holly chirped. "I can't wait to be an aunt. How many will you have, Wilson?"

"Two," he pronounced. "I would have liked three, but Anne is getting a little far along in her childbearing years, and I think we'd only have time for two."

Elderly Anne choked on her beer, sending an angry glare at her imperturbable fiancé, but Holly bounced on blithely. "I think that's marvelous! I can't wait to see Anne big as a house."

"And where will this happy, fecund family be living?" Ashley murmured delicately. "Anne is used to having lots of space—I don't think she'll care for that rather spacious apartment you have in New Hope. Not if she has to share it with squalling infants."

"And I wouldn't ask her to. Any more than I'd ask her to give up this place. We all know how much it means to her."

A peculiar, guilty silence fell over the table, darkening everyone's face except Steve Piersall's. Even Noah looked strangely uncomfortable, Anne realized belatedly, and a sudden premonition of disaster washed over her.

"No," Wilson continued, oblivious to the tension. "We've agreed that we'll live here. Proffy has given us his blessing." He nodded majestically toward the head of the table, and Proffy avoided his eyes. "And heaven knows there's more than enough room in this rambling old place. Of course, I'd contribute a bit toward the housekeeping expenses."

"I'm afraid it will have to be more than a bit, Wilson, old boy," Ashley drawled with his usual malice, well aware that Wilson was notoriously tightfisted. "The upkeep on a drafty old house like this would bankrupt a Rockefeller." For some reason his pale, slightly protuberant blue eyes sought out Noah's impassive ones for a moment, then moved onward. "If things keep up the way they are, you and your child bride might find yourselves on the street, the house sold out from under you."

"No!" Anne's voice was raw with pain and anger. "You'll do it over my dead body!"

"But Anne, my precious, you know as well as I do that it won't have to come to that," Ashley murmured. "The house is in all our names, with the stipulation that if the majority of the heirs wish to sell it, they may. So if Proffy, Holly and I decide we could use several hundred thousand dollars a bit better than a crumbling pre-Revolutionary War farmhouse there won't be a damned thing you can do about it. You know it's going to have to come to that, sooner or later. It's inevitable."

Anne fought back the panic that threatened to engulf her, and she managed a stiff smile. "You are a nasty wretch, Ashley," she said in an unconcerned voice. "You love to pick out someone's vulnerable spots and then stick pins in them. Stick away, brother dear. This house has belonged to Kirklands for over a hundred years, and it will for a hundred years more."

"That's a lovely thought, darling, but impractical. Granted you'll pop out the requisite two point three babies, but they'll be Engallses, not Kirklands. And I'm afraid my life-style and preferences do somewhat preclude procreation," Ashley said lightly, casting a contemptuous glance at his companion's flushed face. "So it will be up to Holly, and unless she chooses to do it out of wedlock, they'll have their father's name also. So why bother to hold on to the old ruin?"

Anne set her glass down with a snap. "All right, Ashley, enough. You got to me. I give in. Choose some other hapless victim, will you?"

"Besides, I probably will have my children out of

wedlock," Holly interrupted saucily. "I don't know if
there's a man I could bear to put up with for even nine
months." She cast a sneaky glance at Wilson to gauge
his reaction.

Wilson didn't disappoint her. "You may think that
kind of pertness is appealing, brat," he said heavily,
"but there are some of us who find it in extremely bad
taste. Don't we, Anne?"

Anne was aware of Noah's curious eyes on her.
"Wilson, you should know by now that Holly doesn't
mean half of what she says. She likes to shock people,
so she says outrageous things for effect, and I'm afraid
that over the years you've proven to be one of her favorite victims. You shouldn't rise to the bait."

Wilson seemed to be listening to her with only half
an ear, his brown eyes disapproving, with some other
hidden emotion in their depths. "Her favorite victim,
am I?" he murmured. "I think I'll have to teach you
respect for your elders, brat."

"Try it." Holly stuck out her tongue at him.

"I think I'll get the dessert before you resort to
throwing food at each other," Anne said lightly, pushing back her chair and refusing all offers of help. She
needed a moment or two alone, and for more than one
reason. She needed to get over the shock Ashley's malicious words had given her, and she needed time to
ponder the startling possibility that Noah had hinted at
and suddenly seemed all too likely. That hidden emotion in Wilson's usually bland brown eyes when he
surveyed Holly was a great deal warmer and livelier
than when they surveyed her. Impossible as it might
seem, Anne had the sudden suspicion that his feelings
for Holly might be just a trifle more heated than that of
a disapproving older-brother type.

And Holly's pertness had reminded her of nothing

so much as adolescent flirting. If you couldn't get the boy's attention by being sweet, the next best thing was being a brat. Even if he scolded you, at least he knew you were there.

But heavens, what an absurd mismatch that would be, Anne thought, fetching the strawberry Bavarian cream from the refrigerator. Neither of them would be likely to change for the other, and they'd doubtless fight like cats and dogs. And anyway, it was probably all a figment of her imagination. Nothing would have been quite so neat and comfortable than having her fiancé and Noah's pursuer fall in love. It was just too convenient to be remotely possible.

"Do you need any help?" Speak of the devil, Anne thought with a sigh of acceptance.

"No," she said resignedly. "But now that you're here you can carry the liqueur glasses; I forgot to put them on the table earlier."

"I knew I'd come in handy for something," Noah said with an engaging grin. "Your sister and fiancé have an interesting relationship, don't they?"

So he'd noticed it, too. She smiled blandly. "Do they? They've known each other forever, of course. And they've always fought like cats and dogs, I'm afraid. Not very comfortable at the dinner table, but then, we're used to it. And anything's better than Ashley's tongue." A sudden shadow darkened her usually pale face. "Actually, Wilson and Holly are just like brother and sister. Despite her teasing she was delighted when we got engaged."

"Eighteen months ago," he said impishly. "About the time you said she started acting jealous. Well, they don't look like any brother and sister I've ever seen. I'd be willing to bet she wasn't as delighted as she said she was."

"And I'm willing to bet you that you're just hoping she'll be distracted enough to let you escape," Anne shot back, ignoring her own suspicions.

"Perhaps," he said, unconvinced. He started toward the narrow kitchen steps and she followed him, the Bavarian cream in her hands. When he stopped short, blocking the doorway, she nearly careened into him, flattening the Bavarian cream on his back. Luckily she was adept enough to catch herself in time, and she contented herself with a mild curse.

"Do you really care so much for this house?" He had turned back and was looking at her out of troubled blue eyes.

She didn't hesitate. "Yes. This house means more to me than anything."

"More than your family?"

"It depends what you mean. If one of them was ill, or really needed something, then they would come first. But if it's a question of Ashley and Holly wanting an extra thousand to keep up their extravagant lifestyles and not wanting the considerable bother of a house this size, then yes, the house would mean more to me than them." She took a deep breath. "I can't expect you to understand, but this house is part of my family. It's my child, my mother, my security and my happiness."

"And you'll sacrifice everything for it?" Despite the lightness in his voice there was no mistaking the dead seriousness behind his question.

"I haven't made any sacrifices I haven't wanted to," she said, firmly believing it. "And I never will."

"I wish I could believe you," he said enigmatically. And then he turned and continued up the stairs, leaving her staring perplexedly after him.

Chapter Five

Noah Grant stretched out in front of the fire, reveling in the unexpected solitude of the moment. Though he could have wished for one certain companion, the silence was nevertheless welcome. He warmed the brandy in his hand, taking another small sip as he stared meditatively into the flames. The Kirkland family was not at all what he had expected, and he could feel himself being drawn in against his will. It was hard to remember that he was here to do a job, not to get involved in the various emotional entanglements that ran rampant. And that included the wistfully beautiful woman who'd run and hidden in her room the moment her younger sister drove off with that pompous idiot.

Not that Wilson was really that bad, Noah conceded. A little stiff, a little unimaginative, but definitely not a stupid man. Except for the fact he didn't seem to have noticed that he was in love with the younger sister, not with his fiancée, he was really quite astute. It hadn't taken him long to figure out why Noah was really there, even if Annie still remained mercifully in the dark.

As for Holly, she'd certainly forgotten her determination to seduce him once Wilson appeared on the scene. It was a good thing his masculine ego was reasonably secure, he thought wryly, remembering her haphazard attention throughout the evening. Looking into Holly's distant, unhappy blue eyes, Noah had little doubt that she knew the depths of her feelings. It was no wonder she was such a brat—she couldn't help but suspect Wilson's feelings might be warmer than he let on. It must be incredibly frustrating for her—no wonder she was eager to take out all those untapped sexual energies on the first willing man. Except that he wasn't particularly willing.

He had always chosen his sexual partners carefully, for their invulnerable hearts as much as for their various attractions, but his ego did draw the line at being someone's substitute in bed. Even if he deliberately steered clear of any sort of commitment, he still wanted some level of honesty in bed, and Holly Kirkland wasn't going to provide that. Her sister was another, far more dangerous matter.

Leaning back, Noah wondered idly whether the kindest thing he could do would be to leave Anne strictly alone. No, perhaps the kindest thing would be to distract the voracious Holly. He wouldn't put it past her to ignore any sisterly loyalty if Wilson gave her encouragement. And if Anne really loved the man...But she couldn't, he told himself. It would still come as quite a blow to her pride, if not her heart, when Wilson finally recognized what he was really after. Noah could only hope it happened before the long-postponed wedding and not after.

Of course he could be noble and disinterested and point it out to her. He'd already dropped a few hints, but she'd turned that pale, distant face on him and shrugged her shoulders. Those deep-green eyes of hers could be so deliberately bland. Until he kissed her, which he'd done far too often and not anywhere near enough in the past twenty-four hours. And then her eyes would widen and stare up at him, all vulnerable and yearning, that clever mouth of hers would soften and tremble, and...what the hell was he doing, sitting here having erotic fantasies? He should have outgrown that by now. Maybe he should reconsider the far too willing Holly.

But the dangerous fact remained that Annie moved him more than any woman had in years. Since Nialla. And he was here under false pretences; in effect, lying to her. He'd better keep his damned roaming hands off her. Apart from the deceit involved, she was exactly the sort of woman he always steered clear of. Vulnerable, loving. Clearly wanting children, despite that oaf of a fiancé's dictatorial pronouncements. And there was nothing he could offer her but pain.

Would she be asleep already, he mused, taking another sip of the cognac, lying curled up on that ridiculously narrow daybed, with the moonlight streaming in that wall of windows, silvering her sleeping body and throwing the rest of the room into shadows? Did she wear anything when she slept? And if he went for a midnight stroll around the back of this rambling, tumbled-down estate, would it be ridiculously perverse to find himself outside her window?

"That's a damned strange expression on your face, Grant." Ashley's lightly affected voice broke through his erotic fantasies, and Noah glanced up at him with a distinct lack of welcome. "What are you doing here, dear boy? Mooning over my sister? I wouldn't have thought it likely." He sauntered into the room, his pale eyes shadowed, his mouth discontented. "Where is she, by the way?"

Noah could play games, too. "She's driven Engalls home."

"I wasn't referring to Holly."

"Weren't you? And what makes you think it wouldn't be Anne driving her fiancé home? Wouldn't it be more logical that she'd be the one?"

"Much to Holly's dismay. And don't give me that innocent look. You know as well as I do what's going on in that particular ménage."

"I don't know if anyone actually does, particularly the principals. To answer your question, Anne disappeared into her bedroom the moment Wilson and Holly left."

"Jealous, do you suppose? Maybe she's finally catching on." Ashley slouched into a chair by the fire.

"She's certainly not unobservant. But I don't think that's why she went to her room. She's hiding from me." Now why did he say that? Noah cursed himself. Ashley Kirkland was the last person he should be frank with. He forced himself to laugh lightly. "She doesn't trust my reputation."

Ashley wasn't fooled. A light filled his pale eyes. "Oho. Sits the wind in that quarter? I'm surprised at my cloistered Anne. I thought she had taken a vow of celibacy. The only thing that ignites her passion is this damned house."

"Why?" Despite his distrust of the man, Noah couldn't control his curiosity.

"Why the house, or why the lack of men?" Ashley countered. "The first is easy. Our mother died when Anne was twelve—a very impressionable age. Proffy never was terribly practical, even twenty-some years ago, and he'd always pretty much ignored her. I was the golden, talented firstborn son; Holly was the darling baby girl. We must have been pretty overwhelming siblings for anyone to have. Anne was rather solemn and awkward, almost a changeling, and I'm afraid Proffy treated her as such. So she turned to the house for comfort, and when Mother died she became the perfect little mother and housekeeper. She's a very strong woman, you know. She mothered all of us, Proffy included, and the house became a minor obsession. The only time she's ever left for any extended period of time was during college." He paused, cocking an eyebrow at the fascinated Noah. "Any more of that cognac? It looks a bit better than the stuff Anne usually forces on her seedy older brother."

"It is," he replied shortly. "But I'm afraid I just finished it." The lie came easily—for some reason he didn't want Ashley swilling Anne's precious cognac.

"Oh, well. I suppose I've had more than enough to drink. Anyway, as I was saying, Anne might have succeeded in breaking away from this house and her voracious family if she'd only chosen a bit more wisely."

"Chosen what?"

"Her first love, dear boy. But I'm afraid her taste—as always, when it comes to men—was execrable. She developed a mad crush on some mindless jock, allowed herself to be seduced and pretty much abandoned when something more desirable came along."

"And she developed a pathological hatred of men and a demented devotion to this house ever since?" Noah mocked. "Sorry, Ashley, I'm afraid it just won't wash. Anne's too wise and warmhearted to fit the picture you've drawn."

"I didn't say she hates men. She just keeps them in their place, and keeps her heart secure. Which is a neat trick—I wish I could master it. Her involvements in the last dozen years have been abominably civilized—I think she deliberately chooses the most boring men she can." Ashley crossed his ankles with elegant preciseness. "Of course, it could be that she doesn't want to compete with me. I rather like that notion."

"Don't count on it," Noah said dryly, draining his cognac and wishing there was some way he could sneak some more without Ashley's pale eyes discovering him.

"Well, then, we can simply accept the fact that she prefers to live a boringly mundane life. I'd watch myself if I were you, Grant."

"What do you mean?"

"I may remind you that I know as well as anyone exactly why you're here. And it wouldn't do for you to get either emotionally or physically involved with my older sister. Holly's a different matter, she knows the score. Leave Anne alone." All mockery had left his voice, and Noah looked at him curiously.

"You are a protective older brother after all," he mused.

"Only when I don't have to exert myself too much," Ashley replied with an airy wave of his hand, taking up his decadent persona once more. "Anne's going to be hurt enough as it is; I don't want to see it made any worse than it has to be."

Noah looked up from his abstracted perusal of the fire. "Why does she have to be hurt? Have any of you really tried to talk with her about the house? She's a very bright lady—surely she can see as well as the rest of you that the house has become unmanageable. I can't believe she wouldn't listen to reason."

"Can't you? Then you haven't tried to discuss it with her. You heard her reaction at the dinner table tonight, you saw the blind panic. This house is her entire life—all her myriad other talents she relegates to minor status."

"Other talents?"

"Anne has more ability in her little finger than the rest of her family put together. Holly's a brilliant cellist, I'm a magnificent painter, Proffy was a great teacher. But Anne can do just about anything. She runs this house single-handedly, doing all the repair work; she paints, quite well, as a matter of fact, plays the piano. You've noticed Holly's rather dashing dresses? Anne designed them and made them. I've been trying to get her to do something for me but she's been too busy so far."

"And those things aren't enough to fill her life without the house?"

"She won't let anything fill her life. I think she deliberately picked a dull stick like Wilson because he wouldn't interfere with her precious house. But she'll have to face reality sooner or later. The sooner the better. Nothing would be worse for her than to let this current state of affairs continue for another five years. By then I don't think she could leave." Ashley sighed.

"But you think she'll leave now, if she has to," Noah prodded.

"She'll have to. She'll hate us for a while." His eyes met Noah's, an enigmatic expression in their pale depths. "She'll especially hate you. I trust that doesn't disturb you?"

Noah shrugged. "Why should it?"

"I don't know. Just an impression I got. That you may be somewhat enamored of my quiet little sister."

Noah grinned. "I don't think so, Ashley. I'm sorry Anne is going to get hurt, but it really has nothing to do with me."

Ashley was unconvinced. "No, I suppose it doesn't.

Still, I'm not often wrong in matters of the heart. I could have sworn that there was something going on between you and Annie. But I suppose I'm just becoming sentimental in my old age. Aren't I?''

Noah met his pale eyes across the room, and said nothing at all.

THE MOONLIGHT SHONE BRIGHTLY in her eyes, and not for the first time Anne regretted the fact that finances had prohibited curtains for the expanse of windows. Usually there was no need for them—it was the rare combination of moonlight reflecting off the snow and the presence of Noah Grant in the house that was effectively destroying her peace. Not to mention the surprising situation that seemed to have sprung up with her sister and her fiancé. It would require very clever handling, much tact and a fair amount of subterfuge to gracefully transfer Wilson to Holly's eager arms. She was too tired to figure out how to do it and too restless to keep it out of her mind. Indeed, it was preferable to lying there in bed, thinking of Noah Grant's blue, blue eyes.

A drink and some company might help, she realized belatedly. Perhaps she'd been too hasty in refusing a late-night cognac. After all, Proffy had only just gone to bed, and doubtless Ashley and Steve would still be wandering around. Add to that Holly's imminent return and she would have been completely safe.

Of course, Holly had already been gone more than an hour on a drive that should normally take fifteen minutes. And Ashley and Steve were involved in their own little scene, whatever that was. Anne had the uncomfortable feeling that she didn't want to know. And there was Noah. When he looked at her out of those Celtic Gypsy eyes of his, he could be trusted about as far as her own determination went. Which wasn't very far.

It didn't even go far enough to keep her in bed, safe behind a locked door, she realized with a sense of fatality as she threw aside her quilt and swung her bare feet to the floor. She was going to calmly dress, go up to the living room and drink a glass of cognac. And if Noah happened to be there, alone, she might very well sit with him for a while, waiting for Holly to return. After all, he wasn't that dangerous—she'd never even tried telling him no. He'd probably back off immediately if she pulled away. More's the pity.

The rose-colored silk caftan floated around her body like a cloud, and the mass of blue-black hair was a perfect frame for her pale, excited face. She didn't bother with shoes, or with underwear for that matter. Why should she bother, she told herself righteously, when she probably wouldn't see anyone?

The cognac was on the kitchen countertop where she'd left it. Pouring herself a small snifter, she started up the stairs toward the living room, her bare feet silent on the steps, the only sound the faint swish of the silk as it swirled around her body.

She paused with her hand on the doorknob when Ashley's voice drifted faintly to her ears. Damn, she thought. He and Steve have taken over the living room. Maybe Noah's in the library.

She turned toward that room, no longer fooling herself as to her intent, when Noah's low, beautiful voice answered Ashley. Anne halted, motionless, her ears straining against her will.

"I leave it up to you, dear boy," Ashley was saying. "I only hope you know what you're doing."

"I do." That usually melting drawl was clipped.

"I'd like you to remember my sister can be very vulnerable. It would be a very good idea if you were to concentrate on why you're here, and not get distracted by Anne's undeniably lovely charms."

Without further hesitation Anne turned the doorknob, ashamed of herself for eavesdropping, her curiosity overpowering any urge to retreat quietly.

"I don't think anyone's going to drown in my myriad charms, Ashley," she said coolly, her dark-green eyes sweeping over the two of them. She expected them to shift guiltily, like the conspirators they sounded like through the closed door, but she was doomed to disappointment. Noah smiled that charming smile at her and Ashley waved an airy hand in her direction.

"I wondered where you'd gotten to," her brother murmured. "Dressed for bed already, darling? I'm sorry if we disturbed you."

"I wondered if Holly had gotten back yet." It was a lame enough excuse but the best she could think of at the moment.

"You'd hear the car first, love."

"I suppose I would," she agreed, hesitating by the door. "What were you two talking about when I came in?"

"Eavesdroppers rarely hear good of themselves, Anne dearest," Ashley said gently.

"Is that what you were talking about?" She kept her voice cool. "You mentioned something about why Noah is really here. I'd be interested to know why that is."

Neither man showed the slightest trace of uneasiness. "I would think that's more than obvious, Anne," Ashley said easily. "He's here to entertain our dear Holly, and to keep her from jumping your fiancé's bones."

Had everyone recognized the situation before she

had? How could she have been so obtuse for so long? "I think she'll run into some opposition from Wilson," Anne replied, outwardly unmoved. "He's a very honorable man."

"Not to mention passionless," Ashley cracked.

"Oh, I wouldn't say that," Anne murmured, more out of duty than truthfulness.

Noah set his brandy snifter down with a decided snap. Rising with a lithe grace, his wiry silhouette outlined by the glowing embers of the fire, he turned and met her calm gaze with an equally impassive expression. If his nostrils flared slightly at the sight of her body outlined by the light from the hall and that smiling mouth tightened somewhat, it was almost imperceptible. "Do you want me to go out looking for Holly?" he queried. "She might have run into a seasoned criminal."

For a moment all discipline left Anne, and a rich chuckle escaped her as she remembered his horrible joke. "Damn you," she said genially. "Wilson would never tell jokes like that," she added as an afterthought.

"No one's perfect," Noah replied, his blue eyes warm with shared laughter.

"What are you two talking about?" Ashley, now that his level of alcohol had receded, was becoming increasingly bad-tempered, and he disliked above all things to be excluded.

"Private joke, Ashley," Anne explained, her laughing green eyes still gazing happily enough into Noah's. "Trust me, you wouldn't want to hear it."

"You're at the point where you have private jokes?" Ashley inquired acidly. "How will Holly and Wilson view that?"

"I have absolutely no idea, nor do I care," she said

sweetly. "And thanks for the offer, Noah, but I'm sure
Holly will be back soon enough. I'll talk with her in the
morning." With a last tentative smile she disappeared
back down to the kitchen, her bare feet silent and
speedy on the wood floors.

"Dear Noah," Ashley said lazily, "my hat is off to
you. I think you missed your calling—you should have
been a secret agent rather than a lawyer. You have a
real talent for subterfuge."

"Subterfuge seems to become more and more nec-
essary for a lawyer," he said shortly, thoroughly an-
noyed with himself and with Ashley's mockery.

"Goes against your noble grain, does it? Then you
must be enjoying the torments of the damned every
time Anne smiles up at you." Ashley laughed to himself, a soft, unpleasantly mocking sound. "Cheer up,
old boy. Even if Anne never forgives you, what have
you really lost? You'll make a rather massive commission, I expect, and there are always other women."

"I bow to your superior knowledge, Ashley." Noah
could be just as malicious if he chose. "Good night."

Ashley watched him leave with sad, surprisingly
sympathetic eyes. "Poor, dear fools," he said softly.
And catching up Anne's forgotten brandy snifter, he
drained it.

THE FLAGSTONE FLOOR WAS ICY COLD beneath her bare
feet, and her toes curled upward in protest. Anne
paused outside her studio, her hand on the old brass
doorknob as her eyes scanned the silent kitchen. There
was a dim light left burning over the sink for any late-
night glutton, the bottle of cognac was still gracing one
tiled countertop, and the quiet dripping of the kitchen
faucet made a soothing sound in the stillness. New
washers again, Anne thought resignedly, moving back

to pour herself another glass of brandy. She must have left hers upstairs. Well, there was no way in hell she was going back up there, even with such a solid excuse. She'd thrown herself in his way enough, when she knew full well she should keep her distance.

There were no more brandy snifters—indeed, all the glasses were in the dishwasher. With a rueful shrug she poured herself a generous splash into a cracked handle-less teacup, draining the bottle before wandering back to the kitchen door. She stood there, sipping delicately at her cup of cognac and staring out into the still night. It was snowing again—great fat silent flakes drifting aimlessly down over the white landscape. Wrapping her arms around her, she leaned her forehead against the frosted glass of the door, dreaming childhood dreams.

She didn't move when she heard him come down the narrow kitchen steps. She knew how he'd move without turning to look, with that graceful economy of motion, all fluid muscles and lean, wiry strength. His blue eyes would hold an unfathomable light in them, and his dark, Gypsy face would be intent. He knew she was there; there was no need for silly words of false surprise and coy hesitancy.

She felt the heat from his body directly behind her, and then his arms reached around her, pulling her gently back against him. Doubts and denials sprang to her mind and her lips, only to be silenced as his hands gently moved her arms away from their self-protective grasp, and one hand reached up to cup her breast through the barrier of her silk caftan.

She could tell herself it was the cold that hardened her nipples against the slowly rotating massage of his fingertips, the pad of his thumb brushing wickedly against the peak that shone darkly through the thin material. And she could tell herself it was the cold that made her lean back against his warm, strong body as if to absorb some of his heat.

But it wasn't the chill that made her push her soft, straining breast up against his teasing hand, it wasn't the cold that had her pressing her rounded buttocks against the iron-hard arousal directly behind her. And it wasn't the cold that made her turn readily in his arms at his gentle pressure.

Those Celtic blue eyes were solemn as they stared down into her wide, vulnerable ones. He gave her more than enough time to move, to duck, as he calmly took the almost empty teacup from her nerveless hand. His mouth quirked up in a small, endearing smile as he realized the contents were far from the warm milk he'd envisioned. Placing the cup on the kitchen counter, he turned his attention back to her.

They stood there, inches apart. Her bare toes were brushing against the tips of his Frye boots, her hands hung uselessly at her sides, and her mouth opened to make some last token protest.

"Don't say it, Annie love," he whispered hoarsely. "Not just yet." Reaching down, he caught her narrow wrists in his strong hands, pulling them up and around his waist. Her slender body flowed against his; hip, thigh and breast pressed close to his suddenly trembling body. His mouth slanted down over hers, taking possession with a beneficial ruthlessness, his tongue a welcome invader, slowly seducing her.

One strong, warm hand had slipped beneath the neckline of the caftan to capture her breast, and the feel of that rough, slightly calloused skin against her soft, protected flesh sent a flame of desire through her. Instinctively her hips pressed up against his in mute response, and a slow trembling began from deep inside, building and spreading as his tongue and his hand continued their demoralizing work. She could feel his arousal harden against her, feel the tension threaded through his back as she clung to him, tilting her head back gladly beneath the sensual onslaught of his kiss. And she kissed him back, her tongue taking from him with savage delight the taste of the cognac, the rough texture of his tongue against hers bringing forth a small, acquiescent moan.

He moved his head back, still keeping her locked against him. His breath was coming rapidly, fanning her face with the sweetness of the cognac. "You know," he murmured, "it's even better when you help." And his mouth sought hers again.

The caftan she had thought so alluring was proving more of a hindrance than a help. The neckline was too high to give him the access he wanted to her firm, rounded breasts, and there was no way he could dive under the full-length skirt with any amount of suavity. Besides, given her lack of underwear, he was bound to get distracted on the way up her trembling, pliant body. Maybe they could move to the daybed in her studio and lock the door.

No sooner had the thought entered her mind when she stiffened with sudden panic and self-loathing, the white flame of desire dying a slow, lingering death. Noah felt her withdrawal, and immediately his hold loosened, just enough to give her the semblance of freedom while still keeping her in reach, and his mouth released hers to travel along her flushed cheekbone to the delicate structure of her ear beneath the curtain of silky black hair.

"What happened, Annie?" he asked gently, moving away, and there was no anger, only sorrow and a mirrored guilt in those passion-dark eyes.

She shook her head in misery, trying to pull out of

his arms, but his grasp, for all its gentleness, was binding. After a moment's struggle she gave up. "I don't do this," she said in a small, broken voice.

"Don't do what, Annie?" he prompted patiently, his hands slowly massaging her tense upper arms even as they held her captive.

She kept her eyes on the flagstone floor, refusing to look at him. "I don't kiss my sister's men in the kitchen while she's driving my fiancé home. I don't fall into strange men's arms, I don't sleep with strangers. I can control my emotions and my libido; I don't go sneaking around necking with house guests," she said bitterly. "In another minute you could have had me on the bed in the studio, and I wouldn't have stopped you."

"Actually, I thought on the kitchen countertop might prove more interesting," he drawled, and she looked up at him then, surprise and outrage warring for control. His hand shot out to catch her chin, holding her face still for his perusal, and a rueful smile twisted the mouth that had just done such devastating things to a usually levelheaded Anne Kirkland. "That's better," he murmured, his voice, his hands, his eyes gentle on her lacerated soul. "You didn't do anything wrong, Annie love. I just seem to have trouble keeping my hands off you. And you, being a normal, healthy female of the species, have been reacting in a normal, healthy way. If anyone's to blame, it's me. But believe it or not, I'm not usually like this."

His hand beneath her chin was inexorable, and she had no choice but to meet his completely frank and open gaze. "Not like what?" she mumbled.

"On the make," he said bluntly.

"Is that what you are? On the make?" she questioned, his frankness alleviating some but not all of her nervousness and guilt. What his matter-of-fact behavior was calming, his nearness was still roiling up, and she stood there, still held firmly by his strong hands and his even stronger will.

His eyes lightened as he considered her question. "No, I guess I'm not," he allowed. "When you're on the make you're out to get any decent-looking female into bed. The only person I want to get in bed is you."

She stared at him, openmouthed in surprise, and his grin broadened. "Does that surprise you? I thought I'd been more than clear as to my intentions."

"Your intention is to seduce and abandon me?" She matched his mocking tone perfectly.

"Oh, Annie love, if only I could," he sighed, reluctantly releasing his hold on her. "But I think you're not a woman a man easily abandons. And I think if I were wise I'd keep my distance." He took a small, symbolic step backward, and she felt a chill pass over her at the withdrawal of his body heat.

A shadow blocked the light from the stairs, and Anne jumped guiltily. Noah didn't even turn—he must have been far more aware than she was of the approaching footsteps.

Her sigh of relief was audible when she met the knowing eyes of her brother. "I thought you two might like to know that Holly just drove in," Ashley said in a bored tone of voice. "I didn't fancy you two being caught *in flagrante delicto*. Holly always had a fiendish temper and the shrillest voice." He shuddered in theatrical dismay.

"Thank you, Ashley," Anne said quietly.

"Don't mention it, my dear. Anything for peace and quiet. Come along, Noah." Despite the lazy tone, there was steel beneath Ashley's banter, a steel to match Noah's resolve.

But Noah's resolve was no match for Anne's dark, pleading eyes and his own better judgment. Running a harassed hand through his thick black hair, he managed a resigned shrug. "Heaven spare me from fiendish tempers and shrill voices," he said calmly. "Good night, Annie. See you tomorrow."

Tomorrow, she thought dismally. *Not if I can help it.* "Good night, Noah, Ashley," she managed coolly. And retrieving her teacup, she retreated into her bedroom.

"I thought I warned you," Ashley said sotto voce, his high forehead wrinkled with disapproval.

Noah stood there, his eyes enigmatic as he stared at the closed door. "You did," he said briefly.

"You don't seem to be paying any attention, dear boy," he remarked plaintively.

Noah turned to look at him then, and Ashley recoiled from the totally unexpected depths of pain there. "I'm trying, Kirkland," he said roughly. "I'm trying."

STUPID, STUPID, STUPID, he told himself savagely. Stupid to have gone after her, stupid to have given in to that irresistible temptation, stupid to have gotten involved. And there was no doubt of it—involved he was. Even a self-absorbed dilettante like Ashley Kirkland could see it. Noah Grant was on the edge of making still another mistake, and God only knew who he would hurt this time.

And there was no damned way he could get out of it, no way he could be honest. For a moment he toyed with the idea of waiting till Ashley finished his midnight prowling and went to bed. He could do a little midnight prowling of his own, beard Anne in that small, cozy little lair, and do something lawyers tried their best not to do. He could tell her the truth.

"Listen, Annie love, I'm here to steal your house away from you," he could say, and watch the light go out of those green eyes of hers. "Your family doesn't care about the house—they'd rather have the money. And if they hurt you in selling it, they've already told themselves that it's all for the best.

"Oh, and I thought while I was here doing this I'd help your sister steal your fiancé, and maybe try and get you in bed myself. I can't seem to keep my hands off you, even though I'm so tied to the memory of my dead wife that I'm hardly even aware of other women. All I know is that I want you, and what I'll give you in return is absolutely nothing. But let's have sex anyway."

What would she do? Would she hit him? Would she scream the house down, do everything she could to stop the sale of the white elephant she loved so dearly? Anything she did would only be nuisance value, but as such it could be substantial. And there was nothing he wanted more than to finish this last little favor for his father-in-law and leave. And maybe then Nialla would stop haunting him.

And he needed that far more than he wanted to spare Anne Kirkland. He knew with sudden self-loathing that he wasn't going to tell her what was going on. And he knew with even deeper disgust that chances were he wasn't going to leave her alone. He'd do his best, but sooner or later something was going to happen between them. And knowing that it would cause nothing but pain to her, he was still going to let it happen. Even help it along.

It was no wonder Nialla haunted him. He deserved it, just as he deserved Anne Kirkland's eventual hatred. If he had any claim to decency he'd leave first thing in the morning, keeping well out of Anne Kirk-

Chapter Six

The house was mercifully, disappointingly silent when Anne woke up, just after the early-morning sunlight blazed into her windows. It had been hours before she'd finally fallen asleep, and she didn't need to look at her small travel alarm clock to know that she'd have to make do with a very few hours of sleep. She lay there for a few moments more, until suddenly the very silence of the house seemed to press down upon her, and she jumped up, determined to escape.

The last thing she needed was a repeat of yesterday's tête-à-tête. She made her escape in record time, dressing, grabbing her manuscript and sneaking out the kitchen door without even the solace of a cup of coffee. Half an hour later she had made her way along the newly plowed highway and was comfortably ensconced at a back table in the almost deserted all-night diner that was a home away from home, already well into her second cup of respectable coffee, Professor Etling's pontifications on Chinese history coalescing into some sort of sense before her tired eyes.

"Crowded house again, Anne?" Mrs. Mendoza had greeted her serenely. "Take your pick of tables and I'll send some coffee straight over. Not too many people out in all this snow."

"Bless your heart," Anne had said in relief. If she hadn't had this one refuge she might very well go mad. "How's Elena doing?"

"Don't ask! She's just about to present me with another grandchild. You'd think she'd learn a little moderation. Stop at four, I told her. But would she listen? Who listens to a mother, anyway? I only hope her five little ones do the same to her."

Anne stifled the little pang of jealousy that always filled her at news of Elena Mendoza Richardson's proliferation. "She's a better woman than I, that's for sure. How she can manage the children and keep her practice at the same time is beyond me."

"Let's thank heavens she's an obstetrician—at least her patients know she's got plenty of experience."

Anne's mind wandered from the Ming dynasty to that conversation. Elena was two and a half years older than she—almost thirty-seven, and she was still having babies. At least Anne and Wilson had agreed on that one thing, even if he hadn't bothered to discuss it with her. But if she wasn't going to marry Wilson, when was she going to have her babies?

She took another sip of her coffee, staring out the windows at the slush-covered highway with its sparse, Sunday morning traffic. Noah had been married. Had he had children, too? She didn't dare ask him—the closed expression on his face last night as Wilson outlined their plans had made an indelible impression. Besides, it was really none of her business. Still, she couldn't help but wonder if he had beautiful babies with curly dark hair and those incredible blue eyes. Were they little Gypsy children, or did they look like his wife? Or like the two of them?

She set the coffee down, spilling a bit into the saucer, and determinedly turned her attention to the manuscript. She had escaped from the house to concentrate on her work and to put Noah Grant out of her mind. She wasn't being particularly successful at either task.

And there was no question but that Noah Grant had to be banished from her daydreams and night dreams. For all the warmth in those laughing blue eyes, the gentleness of his full mouth, there was a touch-me-not quality to him that came through even in his masterful flirtations. Involvement with a man like him would be disastrously heartbreaking. She didn't need the sexiest man alive to sleep with on a weekend and wonder then if she'd ever see him again. To wait desperately for a phone call or a letter that never came, or even worse, suffer through a stilted meeting when he had lost all interest. Besides, a woman with her limited experience would hardly be able to hold a man like him. He needed a Playboy bunny to warm his bed, not a cloistered saint.

"As a scholar, the Ming dynasty means a great deal in terms of..." She forced herself to read out loud in the small, deserted diner. For a moment the sheer grammatical horror of the sentence distracted her, and she made a vicious little mark on the page. Unfortunately, in her intensity she broke the tip of the pencil, and with a sigh she slammed down the stub. There was no way she was going to be able to concentrate until Noah Grant was safely back in New York and out of her life. That would be sometime this afternoon, and doubtless Holly would have the day's activities carefully planned. She could count on her sister to make it easy for her to avoid those activities. Church could take up most of the morning, and it only required that she be fast on her feet to avoid being alone with him again. And that was exactly what she had to do, no matter how much she wanted to be maneuvered into a dark corner, as he had threatened, or rather promised, yesterday. Just a few more hours and she could go back to thinking with her head instead of her emotions. And her loins.

The house was still quiet when she finally returned. Church had run long—never had she been so grateful for a lengthy sermon. She had stalled further, chatting with every silver-haired parishioner she had even the mildest acquaintance with, so that it was past one when she tooled her noisy Volvo up the rutted driveway, with its rapidly melting layer of slush, admonishing herself on the long drive home that she must be cool, calm and friendly. He certainly didn't take those kisses half as seriously as she did. He couldn't be feeling like a passion-starved adolescent every time she walked into the room.

The kitchen was a shambles when she let herself in the back door, but for once she greeted the mess with equanimity. It could take up to two hours to make it spotless—two hours that would keep her effectively away from Noah Grant. The distant chink of glassware and the murmur of voices drifted down from the main floor, and Anne hesitated, a small, craven part of her wanting to run back outside into the rapidly melting snow and sunshine.

But Anne Kirkland was made of sterner stuff than that. Plastering a bright smile on her face, she strolled up the narrow stairway to the dining room.

"There you are, Anne," Proffy greeted her with a marked lack of enthusiasm. "You might have let someone know you wouldn't be around for breakfast this morning. We hadn't the faintest idea where you were."

"Really?" She smiled sweetly as she poured herself a glass of sherry from the sideboard. It certainly wasn't the most amenable house party she'd ever seen seated at the big table. Ashley's eyes were shadowed and bloodshot, Steve Piersall looked, if possible, even more unhappy than last night, and Holly was staring at her with undisguised curiosity tinged with resentment. Only Noah looked reasonably at ease and happy to see her. Which he had no right to be, after last night. She quickly looked away from that bone-melting smile of his.

"I'm sorry if I inconvenienced you, Proffy," she said, lying in her teeth. Proffy was in one of his querulous moods she could do without. "You should have known I'd be at church."

"Church," Noah echoed curiously, still trying to get her to look at him. "You should have woken me up— it's been a long time since I've been to church."

Her eyes skidded back to his, then slid away. "What makes you think we'd share the same religion?" she countered.

He grinned, that endearing grin that had the unfortunate tendency to make her knees turn to Jell-O. "I'm flexible."

"How ecumenical of you, dear boy," Ashley drawled, and Anne could tell from the slurring in his light voice that he had already had far too much to drink. "Anne, my sweet, we're going to attempt sledding, of all things, before the snow melts completely. The stalwart Wilson has promised to meet us at Robinson's Point in half an hour. I trust you'll accompany us?"

Leaning against the doorway, Anne sipped her sherry, trying and failing to keep her eyes from straying to Noah's curly dark head. "'Fraid not, Ashley. I've got to finish this manuscript or Edmund will strangle me."

Ashley nodded sagely, knowing as well as she did that Edmund Jolles worshiped the ground she walked on. "Then we won't see much more of you this visit," he murmured, passing the much-needed information with the infinite tact he was sometimes capable of. "Stephen and I will be leaving at four, and Holly and Noah expect to go shortly thereafter. Isn't that right, Holly?"

Holly nodded. "Of course, it's up to Noah—after all, it's his car. But it would be helpful if I could get back before it's too late."

"But what about your car, Holly?" Anne blurted out, that cursed and unfamiliar jealousy flaming forth again. Noah smiled gently at her from across the room, doubtless seeing straight through her.

"She's lending it to Wilson," he replied before Holly could speak. "Apparently his car will be out of commission for at least a week."

"That's very kind of you, Holly," Anne forced herself to say smoothly, blocking out the cozy vision of Holly and Noah sharing the cockpit of some sleek little sports car. "But when will you pick it up again? Don't you have another tour coming up fairly soon?"

"Not for ages." Holly sighed happily. "I've just managed to persuade Noah to bring me back in several weeks, when spring is a little more on the way. I don't have any use for my car when I'm in the city anyway, and I'd like the excuse to be here when the crocuses are just beginning to come up."

So she wasn't to be quit of Noah Grant that easily, Anne thought, feeling her stomach do an indelicate lurch and her spirits do a spiral. "How nice," she said quietly, and, turning on her heel, she disappeared back down into the kitchen.

"These are the times that try men's souls," she murmured to herself as she drained the sherry and hopped up onto the cluttered counter. A butter wrapper stuck to her dove-gray skirt, and she plucked it away, staring at the greasy spot with listless eyes. A pair of long legs appeared in her vision.

"I wish you wouldn't do that," she said grouchily, looking up into Noah's blue, blue eyes. "I always see you before I hear you."

A fleeting smile lit his dark face. "Church didn't seem to have a very beneficial effect on you. Why are you looking so hassled? I'm sure it won't do any harm for your sainted Wilson to borrow Holly's car. After all, she won't be in it."

"I'm not worried about that," she replied, avoiding his gaze by turning to stare back out the window at the melting snow. "You're going to get pretty wet if you go sledding."

"Don't change the subject." His hand reached out and caught her stubborn chin, forcing her to turn and face him. "You don't want me coming back here, do you?"

She didn't even hesitate. "No, I don't."

"Why not?"

"I think you know perfectly well why not. You have a dangerous effect on me, one you're fully aware of and probably cultivate," she said sternly. "You distract me and upset me, and you'll cause nothing but trouble for both of us."

There was a long, breathless silence. "You're right, of course," he said. It was the last thing she expected or, in truth, wanted to hear.

"I am?"

"Absolutely. You're a forever-after kind of woman, and I'm more into hit-and-run," he said with a self-mocking little smile that didn't quite reach his eyes. "You want children and a husband and commitment. I can't provide any of those things."

"Can't or won't?" she asked quietly.

"Won't." The single word was cold and sharp in her stomach. "The best thing I could do for either of us is to leave you alone."

"And are you going to?" If her voice was husky, she hoped he wouldn't notice. He was standing so damned close she could see every thick, beautiful eyelash that fanned out over those extraordinary eyes.

He stared at her for a long, silent moment. "Yes," he said finally, and Anne felt her heart sink with a thud and her watery knees turn to ice.

"Well, then," she said briskly, unaware that her green eyes were dark with pain, "that should work out very well."

"It should." He stared at her for a timeless moment, then moved a few paces away from her, effectively withdrawing. "Would you like some help cleaning up this mess or would you rather I went sledding with Holly?"

"I'd rather you went sledding with Holly," she lied. But he took her at her word, nodding absently as he left her alone in the cluttered kitchen.

She watched his retreating back out of mournful eyes. Obviously he was made of sterner stuff than she was, to be able to turn his back so easily on the rampant attraction between them. But then, it could hardly have been that novel an experience for him—he must be strongly attracted to women wherever he went. He wouldn't even imagine what it was like to be prey to such an overwhelming longing that all morality, judgment and even sanity went out the window. He'd be unlikely to even think of her again, while she would remember him every time she read a love scene, smelled cognac and coffee, drank German beer, thought or breathed.

"Damn," she whispered.

"Are you all right, Annie?" Ashley popped his head in the door, concern for once overlaying his usual ennui.

"Of course I am," she replied, smiling briskly as she jumped off the counter.

"You're sure?" he persisted, coming into the kitchen to stare at her out of his slightly bloodshot eyes.

"Then what's this?" He reached out one blunt fingertip and brushed away an escaping, self-indulgent tear. "You don't usually cry, my Annie. You're made of braver stuff than that."

She sighed, keeping the smile tightly affixed to her lips. "This mess is enough to send anyone weeping and wailing," she replied firmly.

He stared at her for a moment longer. "You want me to keep him out on the hill until the last moment?"

They had always understood each other very well, Anne thought with a rush of affection. "That would be very helpful," she said, her voice slightly husky.

"I'll do my best, darling," he promised, kissing her lightly on the cheek. "Love is hell, isn't it?"

She didn't even bother to deny it, as she knew she should. "Yes," she said grimly. "It is."

IT TOOK HER MORE THAN two hours to clean the kitchen, and by the time she was finished there wasn't a speck of dirt anywhere in sight. Anne stared about her, hot and sweaty and still incredibly frustrated. All that energy expended and she still felt like screaming from the rooftops. And at that point she had absolutely nothing to do. If she took one more look at the Chinese manuscript, she would really scream. The rest of the house was relatively neat, and she could hardly tear into the guest rooms before their occupants had formally departed. There was even a dearth of old movies on the

Sunday afternoon television schedule. A long hot shower seemed the only alternative, and if the thought of Noah Grant intruded she could turn the cold water on full blast. A little shock treatment might prove effective.

The hot water was amazingly reviving. As Anne stood in the shower and let the steaming water pour over her upturned face she felt at ease for the first time since Friday night, and her natural optimism began to reassert itself. It looked as if she might recover after all. When it came right down to it, what did she have to recover from? A few stolen kisses, an alarmingly attractive man smiling at her with a certain light in his eyes. Enticing as it was, it hardly constituted love forever after. It simply needed to be put in the proper perspective. And even if those kisses rated quite high on her own personal Richter scale, he certainly couldn't be the only man in the world to affect her that way, could he? Probably with a little training Wilson could perform just as effectively. And the moon was made of green cheese.

It wasn't a bad body, she thought, surveying herself in the steam-covered mirror as she towel-dried her thick black hair, trying to see it from Noah's point of view. The legs were nice and long, the hips overfull but not badly so. The waist was small, the breasts full and high, and the arms slender and lightly muscled. Deceptively so—she had beat Wilson at arm-wrestling a few weeks ago. It had given her great pleasure to do so— perhaps too much, she remembered with some regret. Wilson's considerable dignity had been affronted, even though he had done his best to hide it. Would Noah Grant mind if she beat him at arm-wrestling? Not that she could even come close—she had felt the strength in those wiry arms.

"Stop it," she ordered herself, shaking out her still-damp hair and turning to reach for her bathrobe. She stared at the empty hook in horror, then at the laundry chute that had heretofore been so convenient. All her clothes had slid down that chute into the basement, and there was nothing, absolutely nothing in the huge old bathroom for her to put on that was larger than the bath mat.

The word that came from her mouth at that point would have deeply offended the proper Wilson, though Noah would have probably laughed, Anne thought rue-fully. What the hell was she going to do? The longer she hesitated, the worse trouble she was going to be in. She had spent a long time under the shower—the others would be arriving back at any moment. The sooner she moved, the better. But where in heaven's name could she move to?

Of course she never had any choice. The bathroom was directly across the hallway from her bedroom. In that bedroom, along with Noah Grant's paraphernalia, were her clothes. She could either dash across the hall to her room, praying to an impassive God to keep Noah Grant out on the hillside at Robinson's Point, or she could race through the entire house in a mad dash for the studio two flights below. The choice was obvious.

Opening the door a tiny crack, she listened for a moment. Not a sound in the old house—everything was a deep, heavy silence. Holding her breath, she flung open the door and ran across the hallway to her bedroom, the threadbare towel wrapped inefficiently around her tall body, her bare feet making wet foot-prints on the faded Oriental runner. She resisted the impulse to slam the door behind her, closing it instead with a silent click. She leaned against it, dizzy with relief, her heart racing, her breath coming in shallow pants. So intent had she been on escape that she failed to notice the tall, silent figure at the top of the stairs, the deep-blue eyes that had watched her mad dash with mingled surprise and amusement.

He stood there for a long moment, leaning against the wall. He should go back downstairs, he told himself, and leave her strictly alone. He wanted her, but he was also adult enough to be able to leave her alone when he knew it would only be disaster for both of them. Wasn't he?

She was standing just inside her closet door when she heard him outside. Instinct swamped rational thought, and she jumped inside, pulling the door closed behind her. Grabbing the first thing her hands could reach, she pulled the threadbare chenille robe around her trembling body. The tie was long gone, and all she could do was hold it tightly around her, praying that he'd go away without looking in the closet.

There was absolutely no sound from the bedroom. Pressing her ear against the closet door, Anne concentrated fiercely, but there was nothing but silence. Had she imagined the sound of footsteps, the turn of the doorknob? It was more than possible—she had been so concerned with getting caught she could have conjured him up. She waited another minute, her heart pounding, her palms damp as they reached for the doorknob. Slowly, silently she turned it. Still no sound from the bedroom. She pushed it open a crack, then a tiny bit more, peering into the darkened room. There was no sign of him. Surely he would have turned on a light against the gathering gloom. Suddenly brave, Anne pushed the door the rest of the way open. And came face to face with Noah Grant.

He was standing in the middle of the room, completely relaxed and unsurprised. She clutched her robe closer around her body, shocked into temporary silence as she felt those Gypsy blue eyes travel slowly over her. "Not that this isn't a charming surprise," he murmured, "but I thought we decided to keep away from provocative situations."

"This is an accident," she said. Her face flushed with embarrassment, and her wet hands gripped the robe more tightly.

"I'm not going to tear it off you, Annie," he said mildly enough, his eyes not missing any of her movements. "You're just as safe with me as you want to be."

"I never doubted it," she said, a trace of regret in her voice. "I hadn't expected you all back so soon. I didn't mean to invade your privacy; it's just that I forgot to bring my robe when I took a shower, and—"

"We all are not back." He cut in to her stammered explanations.

"I beg your pardon?"

"I came back early, despite your siblings' best efforts. I got soaked during the sledding and I didn't really fancy the idea of driving back to New York in wet jeans. A hot shower and a cup of coffee seemed very appealing." His eyes were still unreadable in the twilight.

"There's still plenty of hot water," Anne said nervously, edging away from him. "And I'll be glad to make you some coffee. Why don't you go on ahead and I'll just—"

"Annie love, you're babbling," he said gently.

She forced herself to relax. "I am, aren't I?" she admitted with a rueful smile. "I'm not used to this, I'm afraid. I'm completely unsophisticated. It's a good

thing you decided I'm not your type—you would have
been bored to death in a matter of hours.''

"I didn't say you weren't my type," he corrected her
patiently. "I decided it would be wiser to leave you
alone. There's a difference. And I don't think you
could ever bore me."

"That's because I'm a mysterious older woman,"
she said with a trace of her old impishness. "I'll go
make the coffee."

She was halfway to the door when his voice stopped
her. "Wait a minute, old lady," he said, the deep,
warm voice having its usual mesmerizing effect on her.
She turned to look at him questioningly, and he
crossed the room in two long strides. His hands reached
up and cradled her face, his thumbs gently outlining
her lips. "I've changed my mind." And his mouth
caught hers, his warm lips brushing hers.

Desperately she sought control, holding herself rigid
in his arms, her lips closed as he teased against their
stiff contours. He moved his mouth a fraction of an
inch away, his eyes burning down into hers with
warmth, tenderness and desire. "Don't be afraid of
me, Annie, love," he whispered, his breath hot and
sweet on her upturned face. "Open your mouth." And
when his lips met hers again she gave up her last attempt at withstanding him. She let go of the death-grip
on the frayed bathrobe and slid her arms up his body
and around his neck, opening her mouth beneath his
and giving entrance to his questing tongue.

"That's it," he whispered against her teeth, his
tongue tracing the trembling outline of her lips. "I
won't hurt you. I was always taught to respect my
elders." There was a breathy note of laughter in his
voice as his hands moved around her waist and pulled
her closer against him. She could feel the damp jeans

against her ankles, feel the tangible evidence of how much he wanted her against her hips. And then as her tongue met his the last vestige of mental acuity vanished, and she felt herself drowning in sensation.

The cool air as it hit her body wasn't even enough to bring sanity back. The robe slipped from her shoulders and landed in a pool at their feet, and Anne paid it no mind as she felt her body scooped up effortlessly into his strong arms. A moment later she was lying on the bed, her bed, where she had spent so many solitary nights. But this time she wasn't alone. His mouth left hers, to travel along her petal-smooth skin, down to capture one rosy-tipped breast. Her body stiffened in reaction, and her fingers dug into his shoulders convulsively, before moving to his thick curly hair, to cradle his head against her breast. The roughness of his clothes against her naked body was both frustrating and incredibly erotic, and she moaned, deep in her throat, as his hands gently, carefully traced random patterns of desire over her skin. And then he moved up to claim her mouth again, almost as if he couldn't get enough of the taste of her.

"I must be out of my mind," he whispered against her lips as her hands reached up to fight their way through the buttons of his rough corduroy shirt.

"Me, too," she murmured. His skin was heated against her fingers, the chest smooth and muscled with that tantalizing dusting of hair. Wilson was covered with a thick mat of hair, she remembered dazedly. You could barely feel his skin. The touch of Noah's silky-smooth flesh beneath her fingers melted the last ounce of her resistance. Her hands moved down to his belt buckle with a boldness that should have shocked her.

Noah murmured his approval as his hand sought the delicate skin of her inner thighs. His lips were trailing light, nibbling kisses across her face, distracting her from the inexorable destination of that questing hand. Until he found her, the soft damp center of her desire, with a touch sure and knowledgeable.

She arched against him, a low moan in the back of her throat. "That's it, Annie love," he whispered gently. "I thought you'd like that." His hands left her reluctantly as he rose up above her, his figure dark in the twilit room. His hands went to his belt to help her, and she closed her eyes as she heard the chink of the belt buckle, the sound of leather being slid through his belt loops. And then another sound intruded, the sound of voices, and her eyes flew open.

"Oh, no!" she moaned, her eyes dark with despair.

Noah swore, short and sharp, and pulled her trembling body into his arms, cradling her protectively against his bare chest as he lay on the bed beside her. "You don't have a lock on this damned door, do you?" he whispered, and in mute misery she shook her head.

He kissed her then, long and hard and deep, and once more her body responded, racked with tremors of long-dormant desire. When he moved away she looked up at him beseechingly, her lips trembling, her dark-green eyes filled with unshed tears.

"Damn," he said again. And pulling her tightly against him, he moved his hand down between her legs again, his touch sure and practiced. She stiffened in protest, but he ignored her, pressing her face against his shoulder, as he quickly, carefully, brought her to the edge of fulfillment. And then beyond, as her body exploded in a daze of ecstasy. He pressed her face against his shoulder to muffle her involuntary cry, and as wave after wave of mindless pleasure swept over her she wept into his shoulder.

Slowly she drifted back to earth, back to her bed and

the man whose arms she was lying in. As he felt her body relax he loosened his grip on her, letting her head fall back into the cradle of his arms. His eyes were warm and tender as they looked down at her, and his lips were curved in a gentle smile before they reached down and brushed hers.

"Noah! Are you up there?" Holly's voice was damnably close. With lightning speed Noah was off the bed and at the door, guarding it with a surprising ferocity as Holly's slender fists beat against the other side. "What are you doing, Noah? I thought you wanted to leave by four. It's four-thirty already." She rattled the doorknob, but Noah's full weight was pressed against the door, and she couldn't budge it. "Can't I come in?" Her light voice held just a trace of a whine, and Noah winced.

"No, you can't come in. I'll be right down—I'm just about ready to go."

"I'm staying right here until you come out." Holly's voice through the thick door was petulant. "I don't want to go back downstairs without you. I think Anne's mad at me, and I don't want to have to face her without you to protect me."

Noah's eyes met Anne's enigmatically across the room. "I don't know what protection I'll be," he murmured, half to himself.

"I'll wait for you out here." Anne knew that tone of voice far too well, and with a silent moan she buried her face in the pillow.

Gentle hands wrapped the bathrobe around her curled-up body, gentle hands stroked the damp hair away from her flushed face.

"Annie love?" he whispered, but she shut her eyes tight, refusing to look at him. She heard him sigh, a deep, worried sound, and felt the almost imperceptible

brush of his lips against her tightly closed eyelids. And
then he was gone, shutting the door and the room's
lonely occupant firmly away from Holly's prying eyes.

NOAH WAS DRIVING FAST, too fast, the New Jersey Turn-
pike disappearing beneath the radial tires of his aging
VW Beetle. Holly sat next to him, her mindless chatter
finally dying away in the face of his preoccupied mono-
syllables. Her head was averted, her eyes trained on the
countryside with its rapidly melting snow, the advanc-
ing sunset gilding the gray-white landscape with a
golden-orange glow. Noah allowed himself a brief, cur-
sory glance in Holly's direction, and for a moment he
thought he could see the elusive resemblance between
the two sisters. It was subtle—the line of her jaw, the
curve of her cheek, a certain set expression to her
dreamy mouth. In the darkened interior of the small
car he could pretend it was Anne Kirkland sitting next
to him, and for a moment he let himself go with it,
imagining those wonderful green eyes turning to him,
that curious melting expression as she tried to fight
him off. But she hadn't been fighting him when he last
saw her. She was lying curled in on herself in that narrow bed, and he didn't know whether to hate or congratulate
himself. He lifted his hand off the steering wheel, moving to take the hand that lay limply in her lap.

Before he could touch her she turned, and the illusion was shattered. Bright blue eyes looked up into his,
startled, instead of those limpid green ones he'd hoped
to see. The blond curls seemed brassy and artificial in
place of the black silky mane, and her face looked
young and petulant and discontented.

Noah dropped his hand back on the wheel and
pressed down harder on the gas. "What went on this

weekend?'' Holly questioned in a blandly curious voice.

"You showed me around the house,'' he answered flatly. "I talked with your father about a tentative schedule, we argued a bit about money and I made my decision. You know all that.''

"I was talking about what happened between you and my sister.''

Noah kept his eyes glued to the highway. "What in the world makes you think something happened?'' he countered.

Holly laughed. "I've known Anne all my life, Noah. I'm not obtuse. Self-centered, yes; obtuse, no. There was something going on between you and Anne or I know nothing about men and women. And I assure you, I know a very great deal. What was it—love at first sight?''

Noah counted to ten, tapping his long fingers against the steering wheel. "You'd like that, wouldn't you, Holly?''

"Not particularly.'' She slid down farther in the bucket seat, eyeing him with a mischievous glance. "I don't like being turned down in my sister's favor. And you did turn me down, didn't you, Noah? No matter how tactful you tried to be.''

"I didn't sleep with your sister, Holly.'' He carefully avoided answering her question.

"Of course you didn't. I told you, I know my sister very well. She's always so good, so pure, so strong.'' The bitterness in her voice sounded like that of a spoiled child. "I don't think she'd recognize a less than noble impulse, even if she was decadent enough to have one. Saint Anne of Lambertville.''

Noah sent her a curious glance. "Why are you jealous of your sister? On the face of it, you have everything and she has nothing."

Holly laughed, an unhappy little sound. "All that's true. Do you think I'm going to deny it? But things are never as they appear. Anne never makes foolish mistakes. Anne can do anything. And Anne..." Her voice broke, and she turned her profile back out toward the countryside.

"And Anne has Wilson," Noah completed gently. This time he did move his hand from the steering wheel, reaching out to take her unresisting one in a comforting grip.

"Yes," Holly said. "Anne has Wilson. Stupid, isn't it? I can have any man I want." She shot an apologetic glance at him. "Well, almost any man. And for the last ten years I've been desperately in love with a stodgy banker who disapproves of me and is unimaginative enough to think he's in love with my sister."

"And you don't think he is?"

"Of course not. Anyone with eyes could see that it's me he loves, not Anne. Anne's more like a sister to him. I never thought he'd be foolish enough to ask her to marry him. I thought I had enough time. I thought he'd wait." She gave herself a tiny shake, flashing her brilliant smile at Noah. "My mistake, I suppose."

There was a long silence. "You know that if you take her house away all she'll have left is Wilson," he said finally.

"I know."

"And from what I've seen of Wilson he's a perfect little gentleman. Even if he discovered he was in love with you after all, he won't abandon her when she loses the house."

"I know," Holly said again. "But I have to take the chance. Anne can't hold out against the ravages of time much longer. In another few years the house will collapse about her ears."

Noah managed a forced grin. "Maybe the foundation should offer less."

"We won't take less," Holly said firmly. She turned back to face him. "So what did happen between you and my sister?"

Once more he avoided a direct answer. "Do you think I'll take her off your hands and assuage your conscience? You picked the wrong man, lady. I won't be seeing her again."

"You finished your work?"

"I found out what I came to find out," he said.

"And what will your recommendation be?" she asked in her breathless voice.

"I'm going to recommend that the foundation offer your asking price," he said flatly, trying to ignore the feeling of betrayal that swamped over him.

"And will they?"

"They wouldn't have sent me down if they didn't trust my opinions," Noah drawled. "They'll buy your house."

Holly nodded, leaning back against the leather seat, averting her profile once more. He stared at her in the gathering dusk, once more giving in to the dangerous fantasy. That gold hair looked dark in the shadows; the slightly voluptuous breasts were smaller and prettier. He could imagine her voice, husky, without that breathless little giggle that Holly affected most of the time.

But that mass of curls could be dark-brown, couldn't it, he thought suddenly, unwillingly. Those averted eyes could be warm and brown and reproachful, and the full mouth could tell him how he'd failed her. It could be, should be, Nialla there beside him. What was he doing there, driving with one woman, dreaming of another, with no place for his guilt-ridden memories of Nialla? Once again he'd failed her.

"Are you really not going to see her again?" Holly's voice broke through his sudden, tortured thoughts.

"Who?"

"My sister," Holly said impatiently. "You said you'd finished your work and wouldn't be seeing Anne again. Did you mean it?"

He could imagine Nialla still, watching him out of those lost eyes of hers. "I meant it," he said.

"In that case," Holly said lightly, "why don't you spend the night with me?"

He pulled himself out of his abstraction with a shout of laughter. "Forget it, Holly."

"Why?" She was undeterred. "We've both had a celibate weekend. How about a nice bit of recreational sex to take the edge off?"

And suddenly the feel, the sound, the scent of Anne came back to him as she lay curled up in his arms, and a surge of frustrated wanting swept over him, a wanting so strong that he was almost tempted. In the dark it would be easy enough to pretend she was her older sister. The long drive back had taught him there was at least a minor resemblance. He could ignore the fact that she doused herself with some heavy, musky fragrance instead of the sly, delicate scent of roses that clung to Anne's skin. And he knew from bitter experience that it was only when he was in bed with another woman that the memory of Nialla left him alone.

But he couldn't do it, tempted though he was. "I think," he said, "that you're going to have to cut back on your recreational sex if you want to win Wilson."

"I was going to pretend you were him," Holly said, unabashed.

"I'm sure you were," he said with a resigned grin. "And I would have pretended you were...someone else. But that's not a healthy way to enjoy recreational sex, Holly. At least, not as far as I'm concerned."

"But you don't want me?" she pursued, and he could hear the thread of anxiety in her voice.

He responded like a gentleman. "Of course I want you," he lied, then wondered if it was a lie. Those few minutes on Anne's narrow bed had left him in a damnably frustrated state. Holly would be more than adept at relieving that situation. "But it would be a mistake for both of us," he continued doggedly.

"I suppose so." She leaned back, subsiding, her momentary insecurity assuaged. "And you're not going to see Anne again?"

"I'm not going to see Anne again," he agreed. And this time he knew he lied.

IT WAS A QUIET NIGHT in the old house. Proffy had fed himself, amid much grumbling, and gone to bed early. There was an echoing, peaceful stillness as Anne wandered through the empty rooms. She could hear the steady drip of the snow melting off the roof, and knew she should go up to the attic to check the leak above the bathroom. And she knew for the first time in her life she was going to let her responsibility to the house lapse. She was too tired and too disturbed after the upheaval of the weekend—she needed a small bit of time to herself. The roof would have to wait.

For the thousandth time she thanked heaven that she'd had her mother's spinet moved to the tiny room off the kitchen. The Bechstein grand in the library was a better instrument, but it sat directly below Proffy's bedroom, and the wood-paneled walls served as sounding boards to carry the rich sound throughout the house. The small antique spinet suited Anne perfectly, and if the rough plaster walls bounced the sound around, she didn't mind. She had every intention of playing for hours that night, with none of her perfectionist relatives to suggest or criticize, to point out a fumbled note or a blurry passage. She was going to pound and thump and soar, she was going to play Chopin with all the sentimental flourish her mediocre talent could command, and as she played she had every intention of indulging herself in a good, hearty fit of tears as she thought about the loss of Noah Grant.

And tomorrow morning she was going to return to work, putting all distracting thought of a Celtic Gypsy face out of her mind, and play only cheerful, mathematical Bach in the small hours of the morning. But for now she was going to cry.

Chapter Seven

"Damnation!" The plate slipped out of her grasp and went sailing onto the stone floor in a tangled mass of broken china, scrambled eggs, toast, butter and jam. Bits of food spattered Anne's bare ankles, and it was all she could do to control the uncharacteristic urge to burst into tears.

"Was that the good china?" Proffy inquired grumpily from the doorway, his full plate of breakfast in his hand. He preferred to have it delivered to him in the dining room, not to have to fetch it like some damned maid, but Anne had been increasingly demanding the last few weeks. If things kept on this way, she'd have him washing his own dishes and making his bed.

"It was." Her tone of voice encouraged no further discussion, but Proffy had always been obtuse with his middle child.

"Let's see, that would give us approximately four plates left out of a service for twenty," he announced, his voice heavy with sarcasm. "That was my mother's Wedgwood, Anne."

"It gives us three plates out of twenty-four, and I know perfectly well where it came from," she said, her voice a combination of weariness and temper. It was a tone she'd found herself using far too often in the past two weeks, but she couldn't seem to help herself.

Proffy's bushy white eyebrows rose in surprised dismay. "You've been in the foulest mood lately," he complained. "I don't know what's gotten into you these past few weeks. You never used to be so touchy."

Anne surveyed her father with jaundiced eyes, then relented. "Sorry, Proffy. I think it must be cabin fever."

"I thought people only got that when they're snowbound," he argued.

"Or housebound." Anne sighed, squatting down to pick up the larger pieces of plate mashed in with the food. "It feels like I've been here forever. I think I need a vacation—it's just too bad I can't afford it."

With her head bent she couldn't see the hopeful light that leaped into Proffy's bespectacled eyes. "You should get out more," he said gruffly. "You've spent far too much of your time devoted to this old pile of stones. It's not healthy, Anne. You should be out enjoying yourself, not slaving away trying to keep a roof over our heads."

"Speaking of roof, the south side is getting worse," Anne said shortly. "I may have to reapply for a loan if it gets much worse. You'll have to cosign, of course, and so will either Holly or Ashley."

"You may run into some trouble there."

Anne looked up from her position on the floor. "What do you mean? The roof is leaking, it needs fixing, and I haven't saved enough money. No bank will give me a loan unless the legal owners of the house sign for it. You know as well as I do that any three of us constitute legal ownership."

Proffy put his plate down on the oak table, and his voice was unusually kind. Dangerously so, Anne thought. "You can't keep pouring money into the place, Anne. It's a losing battle—you'll have to face it sooner or later, and the sooner you do, the happier a life you're going to lead. Holly and Ashley have accepted it, and I learned long ago that we wouldn't have the old place forever. You can't stop the ravages of time, Anne."

"Are you quite finished, Proffy?" Her voice was cool, studiously polite and quite furious.

Her father shrugged. "You won't listen, of course. You are as stubborn as your mother was. Heaven protect me from such difficult women. I'm going out for breakfast." He fixed a disapproving glare at her blank face. "And if you want to know where I'll be today, you can find me at a place that offers peace, quiet and convivial companionship."

A reluctant grin broke through Anne's worried expression. "Oh, the Merry Widow. Give Mrs. Morgan my love. Will you be back in time for dinner?"

"I've told you children I don't like that nickname," he fretted. "And no, I won't be back for dinner. I may not even be back till tomorrow morning." He said it with a little boy's defiance, and Anne's amusement temporarily banished the last of her worries.

"Heavens, she is living up to her nickname!" She laughed. "You'd better be careful with such a wanton, Proffy."

"You wouldn't know a wanton if you saw one," he said stiffly, his dignity much affronted. "You've been a sore disappointment to me as a daughter, Anne."

All of her amusement fled. "Why? Because I haven't been properly wanton?"

"Now is neither the time nor place to go into it," he said ominously. "But you're going to have to change your attitude, young lady. You can't always have it your way. Your comfortable little life is going to have to go through some upheavals, and it's the best thing that could happen to you."

Anne eyed him steadily. "So you're not about to enumerate my failings as a daughter?" Her voice was deceptively cool.

"Look at the talent in this family!" he burst out unwisely. "Look at Holly, look at your brother! Wonderful artists, with international reputations! Your mother was a concert pianist. Even I was the foremost expert on Baroque quartets in my day. You come from a line of such talent, such accomplishments, and what do you do with your life? Devote it to a rotting old house."

Anne had heard all this many times before. For the first time she felt like fighting back, trying to explain some bit of her choices to him. "Did it ever occur to you that I might not have inherited the amount of talent the others did?"

"Nonsense! Of course you did."

"Everyone can't be brilliant, Proffy," she persevered. "There always has to be at least one loser in the litter."

"You didn't even try! You refused to continue studying the flute when you were twelve, gave up the piano by fifteen, and threw away your paints. You had promise, Anne, and you refused to follow through. You tossed it all away."

Anne stared at him blankly. Her studio was off limits to her family—none of them knew of the delicate, hopelessly romantic watercolors that lay neatly under the daybed. No one heard her playing the piano late at night—strange, haunting melodies of her own creation amid the thundering classics she had committed to memory during her years of study. And if she had her way, they would never see or hear them, the children of her creativity that she knew could never compare with her siblings' magnificence.

"Promise wasn't good enough, Proffy. I simply refused to be mediocre in a family of greatness." She shrugged, managing a rueful smile as she dumped the broken plate and the food into the trash. "I've made my life and I'm happy with it. Why can't you accept that my way is different from the others'?"

"Because I wanted to be proud of you, just as I am of the others. I didn't expect you to reach your brother's and sister's heights, I just expected you to make use of your talents. But you refused. You're so strong, Anne. And yet you're a coward and a quitter. And I'm ashamed of you." Turning on his heel, he stalked out of the kitchen.

Anne stood there, listening to his footsteps die away, a curious numbness settling in around her heart. Picking up his full plate, one of the last three Wedgwoods, she started automatically for the trash bin. She looked down at the plate, then out into the rainy spring morning. Whirling around, she flung the plate against the kitchen wall, the crash of the china and the wet slap of the eggs easing a small part of the knot in her stomach.

"Damn you, Proffy," she said aloud, calmly enough. "Damn you to hell for being right." And ignoring the mess all around her, she stepped carefully around the broken china and went into her studio, slamming the door behind her.

HER HANDS WERE SHAKING, Anne realized wearily as she propped herself up on the sofa and surveyed the mess her studio was in. It had been a rough two weeks, and that final confrontation with her father had been the last straw. A quitter and a coward, he'd said, judging her as he'd always judged her and found her wanting.

Well, he was right, as usual. Except that she wasn't
nearly as strong as everyone supposed.

Her room was littered with half-finished projects, a
sign of her preoccupation since that damnable house
party. Not a single project had she finished in all that
time, with the lone exception of the cursed Chinese
manuscript. For the past ten days she had been trying
to plow through an incredibly technical treatise on
tropical diseases, and the words flew at her fast and
furious, with the unlikely names of schistosomiasis,
trypanosomiasis and yaws. She could only manage a
few pages at a time without her head aching, yet she'd
promised Edmund it would be done by Tuesday. And
never had she felt less like working.

Well, she wasn't going to spend her weekend worrying about Proffy, worrying about her own failings, and
most of all, worrying about Noah Grant, who had vanished from her life with what ought to be reassuring
dispatch. She had her work cut out for her. First, the
damned manuscript. Add to that the absolute necessity
of doing something about the huge hole in the south
side of the roof, and she could look forward to falling
into an exhausted sleep. Which was something she
hadn't enjoyed in quite a while. No sooner would her
head touch the pillow than thoughts of what she could
have done, should have done, filled her brain, keeping
her wide awake into the early hours of the morning.

Catching up the manuscript in unwilling hands, she
tried to avoid the reproach of her studio. No less than
three unfinished watercolors littered the table, the
small spinet was pulled apart, half tuned, the instru-
ments lying forgotten on the bench. Yards and yards of
brightly colored Italian silks lay tossed in a pile by her
sewing machine, with one vivid swath tied loosely
around the dressmaker's dummy. Holly needed a com-

plete new wardrobe for her next tour, starting with Ashley's opening next weekend. Anne's duties were clear; her inspiration, however, was at low ebb. With painful determination she slogged through another ten pages, then tossed the manuscript aside to stare out into the gloomy late morning.

It didn't look as if the rain was going to let up in the slightest. It came as a heavy drizzle, soaking into the already drenched ground, dripping through the hole in the roof and widening the stain, rotting the already weakened timbers, probably overflowing the bucket she'd put beneath it. The weather report hadn't even held out the faintest promise of clearing—the rain was supposed to continue all weekend long and into Monday. Whether she liked it or not, she was going to have to face the roof in the pouring rain, and the wonders of schistosomiasis couldn't keep her from it.

Well, the longer she put it off the worse it would be. Better to get it out of the way before the whole roof fell in. It was an easy enough spot to reach—all she had to do was climb out the dormer window in the back bedroom and edge along the roof no more than a couple of yards. Whether or not the slate would prove slippery in the rain was a complication; not to mention the fact that she had already proven singularly inept when it came to patching the slate roof. More slates usually broke beneath her too enthusiastic hammering than she needed to mend in the first place.

It was early afternoon when she accepted her fate. The slates were damnably slippery beneath her sneakered feet, and they proved even more brittle than usual with her admittedly nervous patching job. Her wet fingers were numbed with the cold as she worked on the split slates, her black hair was soaked about her head, the rain running in icy rivulets down her back to settle at the base of her spine. She could only be thankful that that particular area of the roof had a fairly mild pitch—every time she tried to shake the rain from her line of vision she felt her tenuous hold on the tile slide a tiny, terrifying few inches. She had almost finished patching the final tile when an all too familiar crack signified that she'd managed to shatter still another. She was too cold, wet, weary and frightened even to curse as she pulled another slate from her workbelt. The slate spun out of her numb fingers, dancing down the angle of the roof and over the edge. Anne watched it go with a sick feeling, then reached for the final slate. If she blew it this time she'd have to crawl back into the house and then once more onto this rain-slick roof. And this time she was going to live up to Proffy's harsh words. Physically as well as spiritually she was going to be a coward and a quitter. For all her usual bravado, she didn't think her nerves could stand much more.

She forced herself to work with painfully slow deliberation, prying up the broken tile and letting it follow its mate over the edge into the boxwood hedge below. To make matters worse, the wind began to pick up, icing her fingers, the constant *whoosh-whoosh* of the giant oaks above her head pushing her inexorably toward a panicked haste.

She was almost finished, the slate still intact beneath her delicate tapping, when she thought she heard the sound of a car through the heavy beat of the wind and the rain. She tried to peer out through the rain-swept afternoon, leaning a bit too far toward the edge of the roof. With a sudden sickening ease she felt her feet slip beneath her, felt her weight propelling her down toward the edge of the roof. She had strong doubts that the two-hundred-year-old boxwood would break her fall from three stories up. It would be a shame to crush those ancient boxwood, she thought dazedly, clawing for a foothold as she slid. And then, amazingly enough, she found it—her foot caught in the aging but sturdy copper gutters that lined the edge of the roof. She lay there, facedown on the wet slate, unmoving as she tried to regain some semblance of control. Her heart was pounding loudly in her ears, so loudly she almost didn't hear the voice call out from overhead through the increasingly violent storm.

NOAH GRANT should have known better than to have turned his battered old car in the direction of Lambertville. He couldn't even begin to fool himself that it was directly on his way from Philadelphia to New York, couldn't tell himself he had any reason to roam over the tumbled-down elegance of the huge old house once more. And with the steady, pouring rain he couldn't even pretend it was a desire to see the rapidly burgeoning spring countryside.

No, he was going to do something incredibly stupid, dangerous and self-indulgent, something that could sabotage all the work of the last three months, sabotage his final hurrah in the world of law. And he was going to do it anyway, because he simply couldn't help himself. He was going to see Anne Kirkland.

That is, if she lived long enough. Speeding along the rutted driveway, splashing through the rain-filled potholes, he kept his eyes riveted to the slight figure clinging to the roof, cursing steadily under his breath. The ancient VW slid in the mud, and quickly, deftly he turned the wheels into the direction of the skid, regaining control almost instantly until he ended up against one of her prized boxwood hedges. He took the steps three at a time, that constant litany of prayer and curse under his breath, then wasted valuable moments trying to find which window she was hanging out of, all the time envisioning her sprawled and smashed on the ground below. It wasn't until he came to the back bedroom, the rain-wet curtain flapping in the breeze from the open window, that he found her, still clinging like an exhausted limpet to the slate roof.

"What the hell do you think you're doing?" His voice was rough, masculine and very angry, but he kept it low enough not to startle her into loosening her grip.

For a dreamy moment Anne wondered whether she had indeed gone over the edge and was now in that delicious state between life and death. What would Noah Grant be doing here, calling her from above? And in such unwelcoming terms? Anyway, shouldn't she be able to see her body lying there in the boxwood, hovering between life and death, and wasn't there supposed to be a bright beneficial light coming from the great beyond? Unless she wasn't heading for the great beyond, but someplace a great deal warmer and less welcoming. Well, no doubt she deserved it, and she could do with some warmth right now.

"Don't move." Noah's voice came again from directly above her, soft and reassuring, and this time she lifted her head to look for him. It was hard to see him through the blinding rain, but he was there all right, perched on the edge of the window, about to follow her out onto the roof.

Summoning all her strength, she pulled herself slowly, tentatively to her knees. He was scarcely a yard away, just out of reach. Three feet had never seemed so far.

"You'd better stay there, Noah," she called back in a calm voice. "It's too slippery out here—you'd just go over the edge yourself." She tested her weight carefully. "If you could hold out your hand for me I think I can make it up to you."

"And if you can't?" His voice was rough with anger and skepticism and something else.

She smiled up at him through the pouring rain. For some strange reason she suddenly, in the face of death, felt blazingly, gloriously alive. "Then it was nice knowing you," she replied, her voice carrying across the slates.

"Damn it, Annie, I'm coming out." He was halfway out of the window when Anne stopped him.

"If you do I won't come in." Her voice was stubborn, leaving Noah little doubt that she meant it.

"Are you trying to kill yourself? I hadn't pegged you as a quitter."

The words echoed unpleasantly in her head. "No, I'm not trying to kill myself. But I'd rather have my death on my hands than yours. And I assure you, these wet slates barely hold my weight—you'd slide off them so fast I'd barely have time to wave goodbye." She gave him a moment to consider it. "Trust me, Noah. If you hold out your arm to me I can reach it. I promise you."

"What if I got a rope?"

"I don't think there's time," she said faintly.

He was a dark silhouette against the open window as Anne watched him hesitate. She could hope it wouldn't take him too long; her numb fingers couldn't maintain their purchase for very much longer.

Slowly, almost in a dream, he leaned out the window and reached his arms out as far as they would go. He was just out of reach, and the few inches that separated the tips of his fingers from her huddled body seemed insurmountable. It would have been so much easier to simply let go, but she had promised him. She wasn't a coward and a quitter, despite what Proffy had said. And she never, never went back on a promise.

The roof cut into the wet knees of her jeans as she edged herself upward. The traction beneath her Nikes was minimal but there, and the hands drew miraculously nearer. Near enough to touch, if she reached above her head. But she needed her hands down lower, to help lever her body upward. Slowly, painfully she crept upward, until she felt his fingertips brush her shoulders. And then she abandoned her last bit of care, reaching up for him as she felt her feet give way beneath her.

The hands around her wrists were like iron as they swung her up through the air with dizzying force, dragging her through the open window. Her knees caught on the sill, catapulting her against his chest, as her feet gave way beneath her, and she felt herself enfolded against a racing heart as they both tumbled to the bedroom floor. She lay there with him, trying to catch her breath and control the idiotic trembling in her limbs. She knew they were too weak to support her as yet, but she also knew she couldn't lie in a heap on top of Noah Grant, no matter how tightly his arms held her.

Using all her meager strength, she pushed against the too comforting grip that surrounded her. To her intense disappointment he let her go readily enough, and she rolled away to end up against the wall, her breath still coming in rapid, shallow gasps.

Propping himself up on one elbow, Noah glared at her. She had never seen him look so fierce, she thought distantly. His Gypsy face looked quite frightening. "What the hell did you think you were doing?" he demanded.

"Fixing the roof." She found she couldn't move away from the wall, couldn't even summon the energy to push the wet curtain of hair back from her face. She could feel tiny tremors begin to rack her body, and tried to stiffen her muscles to hide the betraying weakness.

"Hardly the best time to do it, wouldn't you say?" It was practically a snarl in his delicious voice, and Anne felt her very tenuous control begin to slip.

"I can't think of a better one," she babbled nervously. "The roof was leaking—it had to be fixed. I didn't see how I'd get someone out to do it, and besides, I probably couldn't have afforded it. So I did it myself."

"Damn it, Annie, you could have been killed!" he shouted, swinging to a sitting position. "I thought you had more sense than that."

"I guess not." The tremor was in her voice now, and she could feel the reactionary tears fill her eyes. She had to get out of that tiny room before she disgraced herself completely. Not only was she on the verge of hysterical tears, but she had the sudden, overwhelming urge to be sick. Her muscles refused to obey her, however. "Do you suppose you could leave me alone for a moment?" she managed to ask in a strangled voice.

"Why? So you can climb back out on the roof again? I wouldn't put it past you." The disgust in his voice flayed her already lacerated spirit.

"No," she said. "I think I'm going to be sick."

He got her into the bathroom and to the toilet just in time, holding her trembling body as the spasms racked her, murmuring soft, soothing endearments as one hand stroked the damp hair away from her face. She knew she should be miserably embarrassed, should use the moments between spasms to order him away, but in truth she was grateful for the strong arms supporting her miserable body, for the warm voice and soothing hand. When the final wave of nausea had passed he moved her away, leaning her weak body against the wall again as he rose and wet a washcloth. The cool, damp cloth against her flushed face was blissfully welcome.

All anger had fled from his dark face. "How are you doing, Annie, love?" he asked gently. The worry in his voice was richly satisfying.

"I'll be fine," she whispered. "I guess I was more frightened than I thought."

"I guess you were."

With difficulty she roused herself. "I should thank you."

A brief smile lit his face. "My pleasure."

"Hardly that," she murmured. "But I appreciate it, nonetheless."

"And I would appreciate it if you stayed off wet slate roofs," he said, carefully bringing a light touch back to the atmosphere. "In the meantime, I think you could do with dry clothes, a fire and a snifter of cognac to warm you."

"Sounds divine," she said with a weary sigh. With a supreme effort she pulled herself to her feet, using the wall for support for her trembling limbs. "Why don't you go ahead with the fire, and I'll be right down?"

"And how do you expect to get there—crawl?" he countered, fully aware of just how weak she was. Before she realized what he was doing she felt her body swept up into his arms. The sudden dizzying feeling of weightlessness set her stomach to roiling again, and she controlled the nausea with an extreme effort. Besides, she knew full well that there was nothing left in her stomach to get rid of.

"You're back in your own bedroom, I take it?" he murmured, striding down the hallway to her door. She could do no more than nod, bemused, as he carried her in, dropped her on the bed, and with calm efficiency began stripping off her sodden clothes. She couldn't help but remember the last time she'd been on this bed with him, equally naked, and a hot flush covered her body as he quickly undressed her. She could see the small grin that quirked at the corners of his mobile mouth, but he kept his eyes bland and his hands efficient as he wrapped the threadbare towel around her shivering body.

"You're going to have to get better towels," he said lightly, rubbing her skin briskly. Slowly, surely, feeling began to penetrate her chilled bones beneath his expert ministrations, and she nearly cried in protest when his hands left her.

She wasn't prepared for his equal efficiency in dressing her. Impersonal hands pulled on the cotton bikini panties, the warm faded jeans, the soft silk and cotton shirt. That they hadn't bothered with a bra didn't escape her notice, but she decided to ignore it as he roughly towel-dried her hair, then took a step back to survey his handiwork.

"I think you'll live," he observed, an impish light in his eyes. "Especially once we get something warm and alcoholic in you. I must say, you're the only thirty-four-year-old woman I know who can still blush."

"I'm probably the only thirty-four-year-old woman you know who gets herself into such embarrassing situations," she shot back, feeling braver once she was clothed. "If you want to go ahead with the fire, I promise I can make it downstairs without falling flat on my face."

He wasn't fooled by the lightness in her voice. "And you'd like me out of your bedroom," he added, and his smile broadened as her blush darkened once more.

"All right, but use the banister when you come downstairs. Did we drink all the cognac?"

"I bought some more. I should never have allowed myself to develop a taste for it—it's too expensive an indulgence. I'm afraid this old house is my only allowable indulgence," she mourned.

"Well, tonight you need it. Where do you keep it?"

"In my studio."

He nodded. "I'll see you in the library. If you're not there in ten minutes I'll come looking for you." He was gone before she could say anything. Too late she remembered the mess her studio was in, the watercolors laid out for anyone's prying eyes. Well, there was nothing she could do about it. She could hardly race down there and beat him to it—at this point it would take all her strength to get her down the winding stairway and into the library.

"Stupid, stupid," she told herself sternly, pulling herself together and heading toward the hallway. Slowly her limbs were regaining the strength that panic and stress had robbed from them, and with the return came intense curiosity and a sort of frightened satisfaction. What in heaven's name was Noah Grant doing here, arriving like a deus ex machina, just when she needed him most? That must have been his car she had heard through the keening wind. And he was here, alone with her in this big, rain-besieged house, and heaven only knew when Proffy would return.

A sudden, wretched thought flared into her brain. He had doubtless brought Holly back to pick up her car. Her sister was probably down in the kitchen, raiding the refrigerator at that very moment. And for the very first time in her life Anne wished her sister on the other side of the world.

The fire was blazing in the old fieldstone fireplace

Harlequin reaches into the hearts and minds of women across America to bring you

Harlequin American Romance.™

FOUR FREE BOOKS...
AND FREE TOTE BAG!

Get these Four Books and Tote Bag

FREE!

EXPERIENCE *Harlequin American Romance*™...

with these four FREE books and FREE tote bag.

◀ **SEE EXCITING DETAILS INSIDE**

Send no money. Mail this card and receive these four new full-length *Harlequin American Romance* novels absolutely FREE. Plus a FREE canvas tote bag.

when Anne walked into the library, the wool socks on her chilled feet silent and slippery on the shiny wood floors. It took her a moment to decide the safest place to sit, choosing the far corner of the comfortable couch a moment before Noah came back in, two brandy snifters and the cognac on a tray. Anne peered behind him, but there was no Holly lurking in the shadows.

"You look a little more human and less like a drowned kitten," he observed, pouring her an indecent amount of cognac and pressing it into her hand. "How are you feeling now?" He sat down by her feet, taking his own cognac, the long slim fingers warming the bowl of the glass as he watched her.

"I feel more human," she murmured, taking a cautious sip. "Where's Holly?"

"In New York, I expect."

Pleasure and confusion warred for control, but she remained outwardly unmoved. "You mean, you didn't bring her to pick up her car?"

"No, I did not."

"But then...why are you here?" She allowed her confusion to shadow her green eyes.

"Would it come as such a surprise if I came to see you?" he countered, his eyes playing gently over her troubled face.

She couldn't meet that gaze. The fire proved an excellent alternative, the golden flames licking hungrily on the apple logs. "Yes," she said in a distant voice. "It would surprise me very much."

"Why? You're a beautiful, talented woman. Or has your family beaten you down so much that you don't recognize that fact?" There was a note of harshness in his voice.

"My family hasn't beaten me down," she said flatly. "They haven't done anything I haven't let them do. I don't believe in victims—I think people make their own mistakes."

"I might agree with that." There was a curiously life-less tone to his voice. "Then why are you surprised I came to see you?"

She turned to face him again, and then wished she hadn't. Those blue eyes in his Gypsy's face were so very hard to resist. Particularly when coupled with that mop of curly black hair, the high cheekbones and the thin, sensuous mouth. "Because I thought we decided you were going to keep your distance. Or have you de-cided you're capable of more than a weekend fling?"

He didn't even hesitate. "No."

She could be just as impassive as he could. "And you know that I'm not interested in settling for halfway measures. So it's a waste of time for you to be here."

"Oh, I wouldn't say so," he murmured lazily, lean-ing back against the cushions, his hand straying to her ankle. "And you've forgotten to mention that you've already got a fiancé. I would think he'd be the major barrier to a passionate interlude with me. So why can't he be your forever-after love? That would give you more than enough free time for a weekend fling with me. We might even stretch it to a month."

"Gracious of you." She relaxed somewhat under his banter. She knew perfectly well that there was a note of seriousness beneath his lightness; that he would gladly take her back up those stairs to her bedroom and finish what he started a few short weeks ago. "But you know as well as I do that my devoted fiancé is in love with my sister. That wouldn't augur well for happy-ever-after, don't you think?" She moved her ankle out of his grasp. "I'm not interested in a wedding license for a few years of legal sex. I'm interested in a lifetime."

"You don't ask much, do you?" His hand followed

her, catching her ankle again and slowly, deftly removing the thick wool sock to massage the sole of her bare foot. "Why don't you make it eternity while you're at it? Why stop at something as mundane as death?"

"That's too much of a burden to ask of people, if you really love them," she said slowly. "People die; nothing can change that fact. And they usually die at different times. I wouldn't want anyone I loved to spend the rest of his life mourning me."

"Wouldn't you?" His face was turned away from her as he continued to slowly, sensuously massage her foot. "I don't know if it will be up to you, when the time comes." There was a curiously bleak tone to his voice, and then he turned to her, the full force of his blazing blue eyes scorching her. They were no longer lazily on the make, or softly concerned. They were predatory. "Put your cognac down, Annie, love."

"Why?" Her voice only wavered slightly, and she tried to keep her gaze steady.

"Because I'm going to kiss you, and I don't fancy another bath. The cognac's too good to waste down my back." He took the glass out of her suddenly nerveless fingers, set it on the coffee table, and with a strong, determined grip pulled her off the sofa and into his arms.

Chapter Eight

There was no sweet, gentle seduction in that mouth on hers, no questing tenderness. Only demand, raw and angry and blatantly sexual, as his tongue invaded the stunned interior of her mouth with masculine force, tasting richly of the cognac, demanding a response to his heated desire. A response Anne was at first too shocked and angered to give. She struggled against him for a moment, but he was even stronger than she had imagined. One lean, strong hand held her curled up across his lap, the other cupped her breast, the thumb flicking angrily across the aroused peak, as his tongue continued its almost savage assault of her tender mouth. It was a kiss of punishment, anger and revenge, and it had very little to do with the sexual tension that existed between them.

Anne had her hands raised against his shoulders in a fruitless effort to push him away, when she realized with sudden clarity whom all that anger and hatred was directed at. Not at her, but himself. And if she succeeded in pushing him away, slapped him as hard as he deserved across that dark, Gypsy face, then he would only hate himself all the more.

Her response was simple enough, and something she

had longed to do. Her hands slid up and around his neck, her fingers twining lightly through his thick black curls. Her mouth softened against his, her tongue reaching out to meet him as she moved closer into his hard, lean body. And just as suddenly his anger was gone, and with a low groan of both despair and desire he buried his face in her neck, his breath warm and labored against her skin. She held him there, cradled against her, and this time she spoke the soothing words, smoothing his hair gently back. And then his mouth caught hers again, warm and wet and lingering, his tongue gently exploring all the mysteries that had heretofore been denied him. And it was her turn to groan, with both desire and despair, as she felt him ease her back down against the thick Oriental carpet, his hungry mouth never leaving hers, his hands sliding up under the loosened blouse to cup the untrammeled breasts that had hardened into aroused peaks beneath his ministrations.

It was a kiss of apology, of healing the hurt his earlier kiss had inflicted, and she responded to it joyfully, willingly, her body arching up against his. The feel of his desire through their clothing sent a blaze through her loins, and she groaned again, her arms slipping around his broad back to hold him ever closer. Every doubt vanished, leaving her a willing partner in his practiced seduction. She was his; nothing could stop the inexorable spiral that hurtled them toward completion.

Nothing except Noah himself. With a sudden, shaky laugh he broke off their kiss, rolling away from her to sit back against the couch, his breathing as rapid as hers. "I knew it would be a good idea not to let you wear a bra." His voice was lightly humorous, and Anne took her cue from him. They needed to lighten the situation, and quickly, before it went completely out of their control.

She didn't bother to move away—for the moment she was safe from any further decisions. "You just couldn't figure out how to put it on me," she declared smugly.

He raised an eyebrow. "Oh, you think not? I'd be glad to prove you wrong, lady. As long as you let me take it back off again."

"Never mind!" she said quickly. "I believe you. Anyone with your experience would hardly be slowed down by an engineering trifle like a bra."

"I'm glad you appreciate me," he murmured, rolling back to cover her still recumbent body. His hands cupped her face, holding her so that she had to look up into those intense blue eyes blazing down into hers. How could she have ever thought he was easygoing? There were more depths in those blue eyes than she had even begun to guess at.

She smiled up at him, tenderly, with only a tiny trace of pertness. "Oh, I appreciate you," she said seriously. "Only too well."

He stared down at her for a moment longer, his answering smile distant and preoccupied. And then his head dipped down, his lips brushed hers, lightly, tantalizingly. "You, my dear Ms Kirkland, are a very dangerous woman. Remind me to keep my distance." And with that he rolled off her, jumping lightly to his feet.

Anne felt suddenly chilled with the withdrawal of his strong, warm body, but she told herself sternly it was all an illusion. The fire was putting out more than enough heat, even for such a blustery day. With more aplomb than she felt she swung herself into a sitting position. "I'll remind you," she said quietly.

He was staring out into the rain-swept afternoon. "What makes you think I have such massive experience?" he questioned suddenly, turning to look at her curiously.

"Something Holly said, I suppose." She shrugged.

"And what else did she tell you?" His voice was low, curiously emotionless.

"That you were a widower. And that you hadn't been seriously involved with anyone since your wife died."

There was a long pause. "True enough. I do not, however, get my jollies from sleeping with every available and unavailable female. I haven't been a monk, but I haven't been the playboy of the Western world either. I'm a normal man, with normal urges, but I do my best not to hurt anyone. Do you understand what I'm telling you?"

"No." She was completely mystified.

"I'm saying that I don't seduce vulnerable ladies in tumbledown mansions. When I make love I do it for fun and pleasure, and I do it with women who are good friends, with the same needs and urges I have. I never sleep with someone who needs or wants more."

She should have dropped it, taken the warning and the reassurance in his voice and left it at that, but she couldn't. "And why don't you need and want more?" she questioned in a low voice.

"Because I had it," he said bitterly. He moved to the fireplace, his back to her, staring down into the flames. In the sudden silence she could hear the crackling of the fire, the steady ticking of the grandfather clock in the hallway, the heavy beat of the rain on the windows, and the ever-present sighing of the wind. She opened her mouth to break the silence again, then closed it. He had come to her with demons riding him, riding him hard. If he needed peace and quiet she would give it to him. It was the only thing she had to offer that would be different from his New York City harem.

She saw the tension finally drain from his shoulders, felt rather than heard the sigh leave him. When he finally raised his head to turn and look at her, the smile he gave her was achingly sweet. "Did anyone ever tell you you're a very restful woman?"

"Does that mean I'm boring?" she demanded with light affront.

"Oh, no." He shook his head, and once more those strands of sexual awareness were being strung between them. "You're the least boring woman I've ever met. You should try being trapped in a small car with your sister for two hours. She's quite a brilliant cellist, but when it comes to anything else her conversation is distinctly limited." With casual grace he lowered his lean body into the chair beside the fire, across the room from her. Anne could only be glad he eschewed the couch for the time being—if he continued to look that beautiful in the flickering firelight he might have to fend her off with the fire poker, she realized with a trace of long absent humor. "What are we having for dinner?" he suddenly asked.

That did startle her. "You're staying for dinner?"

"And the night. Surely you wouldn't be so cruel as to send a poor man out into a night like this? Besides, your father will be chaperon enough."

"Proffy might not be back tonight." She tried to keep the troubled note out of her voice.

"Don't look so worried, Annie, love." He stretched his long legs out in front of him. "I've told you before, you're as safe as you want to be with me."

"I'll try to remember that," she said dryly.

"Good. When we finish the cognac I want you to come down to the kitchen with me. I brought you a present. Though when I saw you dangling from the roof I left it in the car."

"I wasn't dangling," she protested, her stomach sinking in remembrance of that tenuous hold. "I was just resting for a moment."

"Sure you were."

"What sort of present?" A sudden chill ran through her, making her voice equally cold.

"I brought you a food processor. Every good cook deserves one, and a great one like you..." He took in her angry expression. "What's wrong? I thought you said you wanted one. Would you rather chop twenty onions by hand? I hadn't realized you were such a purist."

"I can't accept it." Her voice was stubbornly mutinous.

"And why not?"

"Because it's too expensive. If you think you can buy me with a..." Her voice trailed off before his shout of laughter.

"Annie love, you are priceless! What a brilliant idea. I never thought I could entice you into my bed with something as mundane as a Cuisinart. Aren't you putting a rather low price on your favors?"

"I'm glad it amused you. I don't happen to think it's funny," she replied stiffly, glaring at his convulsed figure.

"I'm sorry, angel. If I had thought it would work I'd carry one with me at all times. It certainly saves a lot of time and bother, not to mention money. It costs a great deal to escort a woman around New York nowadays. And I find it a good habit to wait for the third date before I take her to bed. That way she respects me."

He grinned at her, and she glared back, torn between outrage and amusement.

"I thought you didn't take that many women to bed," she shot back.

"So I'll only have to buy half a dozen," he replied blithely.

Amusement finally won. "You're incorrigible," she chided him. "How can you be so calculating when it comes to love?"

"I'm not. I'm only calculating when it comes to sex," he said with a disarming smile.

"Well, I've decided my price is higher than a Cuisinart," she said smartly. "I want a microwave, a mixer with a dough hook, a pasta maker and a sable coat."

"Is that all?"

"And an emerald necklace. It would match my eyes, don't you think?"

"Admirably. Will you keep the Cuisinart on account?"

"I suppose so. But no payment until you deliver the rest of the goods," she warned him.

"Sounds fair enough. As long as you feed me to keep up my strength. I brought some wine and some more cognac, too." He held up the almost empty bottle. "You've been making inroads on this one."

"What kind of wine?"

"A light, dry Vouvray. You'll like it."

"How will it go with sautéed chicken?"

"Very well indeed. Unless you'd rather go out for dinner?"

"I thought the weather was too miserable to venture out?" she shot back. "No, we may as well stay here—I already took the chicken out. Why risk death and dismemberment in a tornado?"

"It might be exciting," he offered, that dangerous

light back in his eyes. "We might be marooned and have to spend the night in the car."

"No, thank you. I prefer the safety and comfort of my own bed."

"So would I," he said blandly.

"No," she said, her firmness directed more at herself than at him.

"No?" he echoed. "I guess we're back to where we started," he murmured, leaning his lean, wiry body back into the chair.

"Not quite. I have a Cuisinart, and you're going to have the best chicken sauté you've ever eaten and a warm bed for the night."

"Not the right bed, though," he said, closing his eyes for a moment. "Almost a fair trade, though." He opened them again, watching her with that sudden, kindling warmth. "I'm not going to stop, I'm afraid."

"Stop what?"

"Wanting you. And I don't give up easily when I want something as much as I want you." His voice was soft, firm and implacable, and a sudden sense of *déjà vu* swept over her.

"I guess you'll just have to learn self-denial."

"Will I?"

"Absolutely," she said, her tone brooking no other possibilities.

"We'll see," he said serenely, closing his eyes again. "We'll see."

RATHER THAN ABATING, the storm picked up in intensity as the afternoon wore on and edged over into the evening. It was past eight when Anne stared out the kitchen window into the rain-swept darkness beyond, and a shiver of apprehension washed over her. Dinner was almost ready—Noah had been banished to the library with the chilled Vouvray and a plate of Brie and freshly baked French bread while she monitored the final cooking moments. She was torn between the desire to whisk the chicken off the stove and carry the dinner upstairs, half-cooked, and the very strong desire to run into her studio and lock the door behind her. He hadn't touched her at all in the last few hours, not since that brief tussle on the library sofa.

For all that, it had been a surprisingly peaceful afternoon. While Anne curled up on the sofa and plowed determinedly through schistosomiasis, Noah stretched out on the floor in front of the fire, content to stare into the flames, turning to watch her out of those blue eyes of his when he thought she wasn't looking. She was acutely aware each time that gaze turned to her, but she kept her eyes downcast on the manuscript, trying to will it to make sense to her. The best she could do at that point was make sure the grammar was kept straight, and the more complex points she could deal with later when she was less distracted.

"What are you working on?" he'd inquired lazily, tucking his hands behind his curly head and looking up at her. "You've got a frighteningly fierce expression on your face."

"Tropical diseases," she'd replied glumly. "Schistosomiasis, trypanosomiasis, yaws." She sighed, stretching her cramped muscles. "It's getting a little tedious."

"What's yaws?" Noah asked.

Anne raised her head, contemplated him a moment, and then said sweetly, "A Swedish shark." She had to move fast to duck the pillow he'd thrown at her, but the memory made her chuckle as she stood undecided over the savory chicken.

In the long run, though, what did they have in common other than an appreciation of terrible jokes? That, and a barely controlled lust for each other. Plus a real sense of peace when they were together as they had been that afternoon, not talking, just sitting in front of the fire, completely at ease. She had listened to his impersonal conversation, his amusing tales of the time he'd spent as a public defender when he was young and idealistic, as he'd put it. Obviously he'd hoped to keep the topic neutral and nonprovocative. But he'd ended up revealing more of himself anyway. Despite his wry humor in describing his inept felons, his real compassion for them came through. And as she recognized that compassion, she felt the strands of attraction wrap tighter and tighter around her.

But when it came right down to it, what did she really know about the man? That he was a widower, still mourning his dead wife. That he indulged in recreational sex. That he disliked being a lawyer and the compromises in integrity it involved. She knew he was gentle and kind and driven. What else had Holly told her during that phone conversation so long ago? That he was the sexiest man alive? That phrase would come back to haunt her, reminding her of her initial skepticism. She could attest to the fact that on that count at least Holly was remarkably astute.

The utilitarian black phone hung on the kitchen wall, a mute temptation to her suddenly insatiable curiosity. She barely hesitated. It took her no time at all to dial Holly's number in New York, all the time hoping that there'd be no answer. She was about to hang up on the third ring when her sister's light, breathless voice came over the phone.

"Darling, how are you!" she cried happily, and a fresh wave of guilt swept over Anne. "Is everything all right? Are you having as nasty a storm as we are? How's Proffy?"

"Proffy's just fine. He's out with the Merry Widow, and he told me he might very well spend the night with her."

"Naughty, naughty," Holly chided with a bubble of laughter. "What are we going to do about such a disreputable example?"

"I don't know. I only hope the widow Morgan isn't playing fast and loose with his affections." Anne kept her voice brisk and cheery. "Speaking of which, how's your love life?"

"Smashing, as always. I've met the most divine man. He's in advertising, if you can imagine anything so completely soulless. But he does have the most magnificent body. He lifts weights, he tells me. And he has the cutest little mustache—he's sort of like a short Tom Selleck." She let out a soulful sigh.

"Uh...sounds wonderful, Holly. But what about Noah Grant? I thought you were interested in him?" She held her breath, waiting for the artless answer.

"Heavens, I gave up on him weeks ago. He was proving amazingly hard to get, considering his reputation, and I decided to hunt for easier game. Not that I don't have my moments of regret every time I see him." Another lusty sigh. "I sure wouldn't kick him out of bed for eating crackers."

"What exactly is his reputation?" She kept her voice casual, but Holly's suspicions were finally aroused. "Why?"

Anne thought fast. "Why?" she echoed vaguely. "Oh, I think he's been in touch with Proffy about something. I'm not sure what, but it made me curious."

Surprisingly enough, Holly seemed satisfied with the explanation. "He's got a reputation as a very astute, knowledgeable and charming man. Excellent at his job, socially very desirable. Discerning when it comes to women, but seldom without a real beauty beside him. He's still mourning Nialla, I think, but that makes him all the more attractive."

Nialla, Anne thought numbly. Somehow knowing her name made it worse. "He's pretty social?"

"Not as much as he used to be. As a matter of fact, he's been practically reclusive the past few weeks. Quite a turnaround for him, but I gather his closest friends aren't surprised."

"Who are his friends?"

"I can't imagine why this is pertinent, Anne," Holly said crossly.

"Humor me, Holly. I'm just curious." Her voice was lightly innocent, and once more Holly swallowed it.

"Actually, he has a rather strange assortment of cronies. I went to a cocktail party at his apartment a few months ago, and he had paroled safecrackers hobnobbing with Wendell James, of all people."

"Who's Wendell James?"

"Head of the Allibet Foundation." There was a sudden nervous rush to her voice.

"Allibet Foundation? What do they do?"

"You *must* be bored!" Holly snapped. "I thought you wanted to pump me about Noah Grant, not about some arts foundation."

"I do not want to pump you about Noah!" she denied hotly. "I was just bored and curious."

"You've never been bored in your life," Holly said with more than a trace of envy. "And you still haven't found out what you want to know, have you?"

"Haven't I?"

"No. And I'm about to satisfy your curiosity, though I can tell you now—you won't want to hear it. Do you know how Noah's wife died?"

"I suppose you're going to tell me he murdered her," Anne said caustically.

"I wouldn't tell you any such thing. Noah adored his wife. They had this absurdly romantic marriage—always holding hands and the like."

The jealousy was gnawing at Anne's stomach like a vulture, and too late she wished she'd never made this phone call, wished she could think of some reason to stop this conversation that had taken a decidedly painful turn. But there was nothing she could do without giving herself away.

"How very nice for him," she said distantly.

"She died trying to have his baby, you know," Holly said slyly, and Anne almost did push down the receiver. She said absolutely not a word, but Holly didn't need any encouragement, taking an almost malicious delight in imparting the information. "They'd always wanted children, and she had trouble getting pregnant. When she finally did they were in seventh heaven. She took off for a long weekend at their cabin in Western New York State while Noah was busy with work. It turned out she had an ectopic pregnancy, it ruptured, and she died there before she could get help. I guess Noah got worried when he didn't hear from her, and he went up and found her."

"You're making this up," Anne accused her flatly.

"I'm afraid not. Of course he's been plagued with guilt ever since. I guess he feels responsible, though I can't imagine why. Nialla was always the most willful woman, according to Wendell. There was no stopping her once she decided to do something."

"And why should Wendell James know all the intimate details of Noah's marriage?"

"Because Noah was married to his daughter."

"Oh." Anne's voice was hollow.

"They've stayed good friends, despite Nialla's death," Holly continued. "So I would think he'd know."

"Poor Noah," Anne said sadly. And poor Nialla. And poor, poor Anne.

"Oh, don't waste your pity, darling. He does well enough—he's hardly taken a vow of celibacy. Though I wouldn't think you'd be his sort at all. For one thing, he goes for tall redheads, with a few blondes interspersed. I gather Nialla had dark-brown hair. Somewhat like yours." Holly paused. "I think you'd better watch your step around him, Anne. He's more my kind of man—I don't like involvements any more than he does. But he'd break your heart." For a moment there was real warmth and concern in Holly's tone, a warmth and concern that had been missing for a long time.

"I don't think I have to worry about it. After all, I'm engaged to Wilson."

"So you are. How could I have forgotten?" Holly's voice turned flat and cold and definitely hostile. "I don't think that will protect you if Noah decided he wants you."

"I think I'm safe, Holly." Anne managed a creditable drawl. "Thanks for the information, though. If I happen to see him again I'll watch my step."

"Oh, you'll see him again. Despite what he said, I have no doubt at all on that score. 'Bye." She hung up without another word, and slowly, thoughtfully Anne replaced the receiver.

"Find out anything interesting?" Noah murmured pleasantly from directly behind her.

She whirled to face him, her face flushed with guilt. The cool expression in his blue, blue eyes wasn't the slightest bit reassuring. She stalled for time. "I beg your pardon?"

"Surely Holly must have given you all the lurid details of my past," he said with deceptive sweetness, the grimness around his mouth the only clue to his anger. "I've already told you that reports of my sexual prowess are greatly exaggerated."

"I didn't realize Holly had firsthand knowledge," she snapped back nervously.

"Is that what she told you?" He shrugged. "Far be it from me to contradict a lady. Is dinner almost ready?"

"Just about." She eyed him warily, but that blank, easygoing mask had shuttered down over his face again. "Noah, I'm sorry. That was a rotten thing to do."

"Yes, it was." His lovely, rich voice was hard and uncompromising. But at last that bland expression had left his face once more.

"Will you forgive me if I promise not to pry again?"

"I might consider it," he drawled, a predatory gleam lighting his eyes, "if you'll sleep with me tonight."

"I'm going to put saltpeter on your chicken," she warned, relief making her slightly light-headed.

"It won't do you any good," he said smugly. "It's been tried."

"I can imagine," she muttered. "You carry the silver and the wineglasses, and I'll be up with the food in a moment."

He took the cutlery from her, his eyes suddenly quite somber. "No more telephone calls?"

"I promise."

He smiled at her, that achingly sweet smile she saw so seldom. "I trust you."

She watched his disappearing back with a strange longing in the pit of her stomach. He knew just how to reach her, she realized with no small amount of alarm.

He had an uncanny knack of finding her most vulnerable spot and soothing it with his gentle, seductive charm. If she knew what was good for her she would forget her promise, call Wilson up and invite him over for supper. A firelit dinner on a rainy night was just a trifle too romantic to be safe, especially in the company of Noah Grant. She stared at the telephone for a long, contemplative moment, then turned back to dish up the chicken. Even if she hadn't promised, Wilson Engalls would be the last person she would call that night. She was going to count on her own pride and sense of self-preservation to keep Noah at bay. The last thing she wanted to do was follow a well-trod path to his bed for a few blissful nights.

And they would be blissful, she had little doubt of that. But it would be too great a price to pay for a weekend or two. If she even lasted that long. With her lack of sexual expertise his interest would undoubtedly pall almost immediately.

Though he didn't seem to tire of kissing her, she thought dreamily as she started up the stairs. He seemed to take an inordinate amount of pleasure in it, almost as much as she did. Perhaps...

There was a huge, rending crash from directly outside the house, the tinkling sound of breaking glass, and the hallway was suddenly plunged into an inky blackness. Anne tripped, the plates went flying for the second time in one day, and she ended sprawled in the hallway.

"Annie!" Noah's anxious voice reverberated through the dark hallway, and she managed to roll out of the way just before he would have trampled on her. She felt rather than saw him squat down beside her, and his hands were gentle as they caught her and helped her up. "Are you okay?"

"Just fine. I'm afraid that was the last of the Wedgwood. And all our dinner," she added mournfully. Struggling to her feet, she tried to peer through the inky darkness. "What happened?"

"One of those old trees, I imagine. The wind was just too much for it."

An irrational panic gripped her. "Do you think it hit the house?"

"I don't know. I heard some windows break, but that might have just been from the vibration of the falling tree. Go on in by the fire and I'll check."

"Check? How?"

"By going outside and seeing what I can see," he replied patiently. "If it brought the lines down we'll have to call the power company. Unless, of course, it brought the phone lines down, too."

"I'm coming with you." She started after him in the darkness, only to have her arms caught in a firm grip, her body turned around and pushed unceremoniously in the direction of the library.

"You most certainly are not. It could be dangerous out there."

"For you as well as me," she argued, but he was propelling her along the hallway with inexorable force. "I know the area better than you."

"I don't give a damn. You stay put until I get back or I'll carry you upstairs and throw you off the roof where I found you." Undoubtedly he was bigger and stronger than she was; undoubtedly he could have his own way if he was determined on it. Subterfuge was the only answer.

"All right," she replied.

"Good." He turned and was gone.

She waited until his footsteps died away, waited until the heavy sound of the door slamming on the windy night reached her ears. "All right, you can throw me off the roof," she added aloud, a stickler for honesty. She stopped only long enough to grab a heavy waterproof poncho and followed him out into the stormy night.

Chapter Nine

The wind whipped the heavy rain into her face as she rounded the corner of the house. It was easy enough to be discreet—the noise of the wind and rain drowned out any possible sound her sneaker-clad feet could have made. Far ahead she saw the beam of the flashlight sweeping through the curtain of rain. Noah must have had one in his car—as far as Anne knew there wasn't a working flashlight to be found in the entire house. Quickly she ducked out of the way of that meager torch, heading out toward the driveway through the inky blackness.

The ground was wet and slippery beneath her feet; the driveway, when she reached it, was a sea of mud. Determinedly she slogged onward, head down, the thick, oozing mud covering her ankles and sucking at her sneakers with each step. The weakest tree was halfway down the driveway. They'd already lost several limbs this winter, and Anne had ignored the fact that most of the trunk was completely worm-ridden. Getting a tree that size cut down was a considerable expense, one that she simply couldn't afford. Not when the very roof over their heads was in danger of disintegrating.

Peering through the rain-swept darkness, she saw in

the distance a massive shape lying across the driveway. It had come down all right. She sighed, moving forward with fresh determination to survey the damage.

At least it was far enough away from the house that a few broken windows were likely to be the only damage. Anne had become more than expert at repairing broken windows over the past years.

The weak beam of Noah's flashlight swept past her to the giant corpse of the tree lying in her path, then moved back to her. Well and truly caught, she accepted it sheepishly, keeping her back turned to him as she plunged onward through the night. She could hear his voice calling her through the pouring rain, but the hood of her poncho effectively muffled his words. Words she doubted she wanted to hear, when she had no intention of going in just yet. Now that the tree was finally down she wanted a good look at the ancient oak, to see whether the tree was rotten through or whether there'd be salvageable firewood. Not to mention the huge sums of money decent oak could bring in, for furniture and the like. She knew from a wood encyclopedia she'd edited that some trees could be worth small fortunes. Maybe the god of old houses would smile on her at last, sending her a toppled tree worth enough to pay for the new roof.

She could hear Noah's voice behind her, much closer, but she ignored him. She was only within a few yards of the downed tree; she wasn't about to let him drag her inside without discovering what she desperately needed to know.

Suddenly the beam from the flashlight behind her began to swing crazily—as if its bearer were running, she realized, moving correspondingly faster. She was almost to the edge of the branches when the light disappeared altogether. A moment later a body hurtled into hers, tackling her and landing them both in the cold, wet mud. Anne went down face first, spread-eagled, as his body landed on top of hers, and she felt a sharp stinging in her face before the cold mud covered her.

A moment later he had rolled her over. It was too dark to see his expression as he loomed over her, but the furious sound of his voice was bad enough. "You criminally stupid idiot!" he shouted at her. "Didn't you hear me calling you?" Cruelly strong hands dug into her shoulders, yanking her into a sitting position for the sole purpose of shaking her.

"I don't like being ordered!" she screamed back through rattling teeth and the strong night wind.

"Would you rather I let you run into the power line that's about two feet away?" he yelled back. "You may have a death wish today but I have no desire to be a witness."

All the fight left her. "Power line?" she echoed.

"I dropped the flashlight trying to save your stupid neck or I'd show it to you."

"Oh, God."

"Oh, God, indeed." He rose to his feet, hauling her shivering body along with him. "Come on." His tone of voice had softened perceptibly, and she followed him blindly, her cold wet hand still clasped in his.

"Where are we going?" she murmured, completely cowed.

"Out of this damned rain. One thing's for certain—no one's either leaving or coming in here tonight. That tree has blocked the driveway, and there's another one down on the far side of it."

"But what if Proffy decided to come home after all?" she fretted.

"He won't be able to get anywhere near the power

line, unless he's a lot more agile than he appears to be."

"He's not. Proffy abhors physical exercise in all forms." Anne told herself that relief should be utmost in her mind, but as she glanced at the lean, rain-soaked figure beside her she found herself wishing that the fates hadn't chosen tonight of all nights to bless them with a power outage and a house cut off from the outside world.

The wet mud was caked to her legs, her arms, had even found its insidious way up inside the loose poncho when he tackled her. "Are you as muddy as I am?" she questioned in a husky voice as they reentered the darkened house.

In answer Noah reached into his pocket and withdrew a pack of matches. He lit one, the flickering light illuminating an expression on his face that was no longer angry, just wryly amused, and Anne could imagine exactly what she looked like. "No one could be as muddy as you are," he declared.

"Then I get dibs on the shower. We've lost our power before—I know from sad experience that there's only enough water pressure for one decent shower. You can make do in the kitchen sink."

"I don't think I'll fit," he drawled.

"There are candles in the drawer by the sink," she continued, ignoring him.

"What about you?"

"I always keep them around in each bedroom, just in case this happens. I'll meet you back in the library when I've scraped off the first few layers of Jersey dirt. I...I'm afraid I dropped the dinner."

"I remember." He shook the match out just as it was about to burn him, and once more they were plunged into darkness. Anne could feel the warmth of his body heat so very near her, the heat of his breath on her upturned face, the very sexy smell of fresh rain and yes, mud, on his skin.

His voice dropped to a lower note in keeping with the intimacy of the darkened space. "I'm sure we can rustle up something from the refrigerator if we're hungry."

She felt his hands on her shoulders, and she flinched nervously. Instead of pulling back he strengthened his grip, the long fingers digging gently into her shoulders, kneading away some of the tension. "I'm not going to hurt you, Annie, love," he said gently.

Oh, yes, you are, she responded silently, resigned as she stared at him through the pitch blackness. She could only make out his outline, but she knew exactly what his expression would be. That achingly sweet smile coupled with the blazing warmth of those magical eyes. It was a good thing she couldn't see his face, she realized belatedly. The darkness was her only defense against a man she wanted far too much.

"Go on up and take your shower," he murmured when the silence between them had stretched almost to the breaking point. And without another word she turned and fled through the darkened house.

It was like a litany murmured under her breath as she quickly undressed in the candlelit bathroom. "Wilson," she murmured. The name failed to conjure anything more than a disapproving glare from his blandly handsome face. Kicking the rain- and mud-soaked clothing into the corner, she ran some of her precious water supply into a washcloth.

"Nialla," she tried, and the sudden vision of Noah's dark-haired wife swam into her mind. A beautiful, dark-haired witch, willful and pregnant with Noah's longed-for child. Dead, leaving him to mourn with only half a heart. The eyes that stared back at her from the mirror were filled with a sadness still touched with her unwilling longing.

She winced as the washcloth danced too roughly across her cheek. Peering through the candlelight, she gazed with awe on the rich purpling bruise on her right cheekbone. She must have hit her face on a rock when she went down, she mused, remembering with unwilling warmth the feel of his body on top of hers. Something she'd felt too many times, and not enough. Not completely.

The shower was gloriously hot and forceful as she stepped under the heavy stream. There was nothing she would have liked better than to have stood there beneath the pounding water until all those sweetly seductive fantasies left her. But the water supply was severely limited during a power outage, and she quickly scrubbed her tingling flesh with the lavender-scented soap that was her major luxury. Her thick black hair had escaped the brunt of the mud, and she contented herself with a quick rinse, letting the hot water stream over her face. She was so involved in the blissful sensation that she didn't hear the bathroom door open, didn't see the dark shadow silhouetted by the wavering candlelight.

The pounding of the water lessened, faded to a trickle, and then stopped altogether, but Anne was finally, blissfully clean. Pushing aside the shower curtain, she stepped onto the bathmat. And looked up directly into Noah's eyes.

HE SHOULD HAVE KNOWN BETTER, he thought, splashing the small amount of water from the sink over his chest and shoulders in the darkened kitchen. He should have known something would happen, known enough to avoid it. He should never have come to New Jersey, should never have detoured by way of Anne Kirkland.

But if he hadn't, would she have tumbled off that slippery slate roof into the greenery below and lain there, a broken mass of bone and flesh in the pouring rain until that bumbling old fool of a father came home and found her?

And if he hadn't, and she'd managed to avoid that first pitfall, would she have run headlong into the live wire stretching across the rain-drenched, limb-strewn landscape? Maybe he was meant to be there.

The Chinese had a belief that once you saved a life, that life belonged to you. He'd saved Anne Kirkland twice in one day—surely he at least deserved the reward of a few hours of that warm, soft flesh. Just her body and only on loan. Not her heart and soul.

But he knew he was only fooling himself. Anne wasn't the sort to give just her body; it came equipped with all sorts of traps and restrictions and needs that he wasn't capable of dealing with. If he gave in to the temptation that had been haunting him for the last weeks he'd only end up hurting her. And she needed to be loved, not seduced and discarded.

It had been a peaceful afternoon, lying with her in front of the fire, listening to the rain pour down on the leaky sieve of a roof, and for a while he'd fallen under the spell of the tumbledown house. Or maybe it was just under the spell of its desperate mistress.

He should rummage around in the darkened kitchen and dig up a few more candles, then see if he could rustle up some sort of dinner. He should put his damp, muddy shirt back on, lean back, and wait down here for Anne to make a reappearance. Give her time to pull her defenses around her, let her keep her distance. He was helping to rip her house away from her; he at least owed her that much.

But he wasn't going to. He was going upstairs after her, stalking her, ignoring any claims conscience or Nialla might have on him. And when he found her he had the dismal feeling that he would never want to let her go.

NOAH WAS LEANING against the sink, clad only in a pair of denim jeans, arms crossed over his bare chest when she saw him. His hair still glistened from the water, and a few droplets clung to his chest and the thin matting of hair dusted across the tanned expanse. At her outraged expression he straightened into an upright position, handing her the towel she'd left by the sink. She took it in numb hands, still speechless with surprise and anger.

Belatedly she pulled the towel around her wet body. "What are you doing here?" Instead of the strong, angry tone she wanted, her voice came out in a whisper, and her eyes as she looked up at his were both vulnerable and beseeching.

"Waiting for you," he answered, his voice sending shivers of delight along her spine. He took a step toward her, that broad bare chest disintegrating all her determination. One strong hand reached up to gently touch her bruised cheek. "Did I do that to you?"

If the sight of him was demoralizing, the light touch of his fingertips was the finishing touch. "You didn't mean to," she said, her voice no more than a wisp. "I hit a rock when you tackled me."

His fingers passed the bruised cheek to curl behind her head, pulling her slowly, inexorably closer. The look in his eyes was intent, allowing no distraction or opposition. "I'm sorry," he whispered, his lips brushing hers, lightly tantalizing.

Anne shut her eyes in sudden despair. "Don't do this," she pleaded softly, her voice full of pain. "Please, Noah, leave me alone."

He moved a fraction of an inch away, his breath still warm on her face, and his eyes were curiously sad. "I wish I could, Annie love," he whispered. "But I can't." And his mouth took hers again, his hands cradling her damp head and holding her still for his questing tongue.

She felt her head tip back beneath his onslaught, her mouth opening hungrily beneath his voracious one. Her hands let go of the scanty towel and pressed against him, her fingers splayed out across that broad expanse of heated flesh. The touch of his skin was fire, burning away her noble resolutions, her better judgment, her last ounce of sanity. With a little moan she let him pull her closer against the warm haven, the towel falling forgotten to the floor as his hands slid down her naked back to press her lightly against his overwhelming desire.

He moved his mouth away, giving her a moment to catch her breath. "Which bedroom has a double bed?" The question was short, abrupt, and common sense began to rear its ugly head once more.

"Noah, I can't—"

"For God's sake, Annie," he cried, his voice hoarse and ragged, "don't play games with me. If you don't tell me which bedroom I'm going to make love to you right here on the bathroom floor." And to prove his point he pressed her more fully against his hips.

The feel of him through the denim sent a shaft of white-hot emotion through her. The last tiny thread of control was gone—indeed, had been gone for weeks. She had made her token protest, defended her honor. Thank heavens he wasn't going to listen.

"There isn't a double bed in the entire house," she said unevenly, her voice a mere thread. "We're very sedate, I'm afraid."

"Sure you are." His mouth began trailing soft, leisurely kisses across the tops of her shoulders as his hands began weaving patterns of desire over her back. Somewhere she found the nerve to respond, and her fingers lightly threaded through the fine mesh of hair that pressed against her soft breasts. Feeling ever braver, she ran her hands down his sides, down to the frustrating barrier of his jeans, and then slid them around his waist and up his leanly muscled back. He shivered in response, his mouth traveling up her neck with ever-increasing determination, until once more he captured her mouth, his tongue diving past the meager barrier of her small white teeth to taste the nectar of her complete submission.

And yet it wasn't submission, Anne realized dreamily. It was, quite simply, acceptance of the desire that lay between them, desire too strong to succumb to common sense and self-preservation. For a long, delicious moment she was content to receive the gift of his kiss, that thrusting, powerful tongue promising a still more powerful thrust. And then she began to kiss him back, her tongue darting into his mouth with far less practiced skill, tentatively sampling the delights that awaited her.

For the second time that day she felt herself swung up into his arms and held high against his chest. His mouth never left hers as he kicked open the bathroom door and headed into the candlelit hallway. She had no idea where he was taking her, and she didn't care. She was content—no, eager—to follow wherever he led.

And he led her down the winding stairs into the library, stretching her out on the thick carpet with only the light of the fire illuminating her pale body. "This is where we started," he murmured, following her down. "I want to be able to watch your face in the firelight, Annie, love."

She didn't say a word, just stared up at him, her black hair fanned out beneath her. In the fitful glow of the firelight Noah looked almost demonic, leaning over her, his body taut and golden, the muscles etched in shadow.

"Shall I give you one more chance?" he murmured, staring down at her with intent eyes. "A five-minute head start? Do you want to leave me, Annie, love? Do you want to sleep alone tonight? In that narrow bed with its clean white sheets?"

"If I said I did, would you let me?" she countered in a husky voice.

"Games again?" he mocked gently. "If you meant it I would." And then he added, "But you'd be lying. Wouldn't you?" His voice was barely audible as his head dipped toward hers. "Wouldn't you?"

"Yes," she said, the sibilant sound long and drawn out. "Yes, yes, yes."

And with her final, complete acquiescence all hurry seemed to leave him. He savored her body, first with his eyes, that blue, Celtic Gypsy gaze of his traveling hungrily over her body with a slow, hot longing that left her shivering with reaction. And then his hands, those clever, practiced hands that had already proven they knew how to pleasure her. They cupped her breasts, the thumbs gently teasing the already aroused nipples, they stroked her stomach, rippling across her pale flesh in the flickering firelight, they trailed up and down her smooth thighs until they opened to his gentle insistence, and they sought and found the heat of her, taking what they already knew so well.

And finally, as she arched helplessly up against those hands, his mouth followed, capturing one rosy-tipped breast and then the other. A low, helpless whimper of longing came from the back of her throat, a whimper of longing and impatience, and he laughed softly against her breast. It was a warm, happy sound, that laugh of his, filled with a pure, sensual joy.

"You're ready, aren't you, Annie love?" he whispered on a note of triumph that she willingly granted him. "You're more than ready, aren't you? Tell me, Annie."

"Please," she gasped, her breathing ragged, his clever, clever hands driving her to the steep cliff of ecstasy.

"Please what?" he mocked gently, and his deep rich voice only inflamed her more. "Please leave you alone? Please don't do this?" he echoed her earlier words, and wordlessly she shook her head back and forth as she reached vainly for the fulfillment his hands promised yet still withheld.

"Please, Noah," she whispered, opening her eyes to look into his, her need deep and pleading. "Make love to me. Now."

The words were no sooner out of her mouth than she regretted them, terrified that she'd see a look of smug victory cover his face. She should have known better. The moment she confessed the need her body had been telegraphing, a change came over him. The final restraints had been lifted, but instead of smug self-assurance there was a blazing tenderness in his eyes.

It took him only a moment to strip off his jeans. Anne listened to the sound of the zipper in the darkened room, the rustling of the clothing as she kept her eyes on his. She wanted to let her gaze wander over his body, let her hands follow and discover the glory of him, but she felt suddenly, unaccountably shy.

"Don't be afraid of me, Annie," he begged, kneeling between her legs. "I won't hurt you. I promise. I'll be very, very gentle.'' He levered himself forward, and she could feel him hesitate, feel the clenched muscles in his arms on either side of her that supported his weight. And then slowly, miraculously, he filled her, reaching deep inside to her very soul. And after the first moments of surprise and discomfort she welcomed him, reaching up with her arms and legs and her body to greet that magnificent invasion.

His control was absolute. Ignoring the cost, he began to move, rocking back and forth with a slow, steady rhythm. And each time he filled her it seemed a little deeper and a little fuller. A light film of sweat covered her skin, and shudders began to shake her body beneath his. And still he moved, seemingly intent only on pleasuring her, as he varied the force and the tempo of his thrusts.

The white-hot flames were building now, licking her body, and she clung to him like a boat adrift in a storm-tossed sea. And then suddenly, unexpectedly, it happened, and she was flung out into the sky in a shower of stars, and in that explosion of glory she felt his body stiffen in her arms, heard his strangled cry, and she wept, for the joy of being alone no longer.

It was a long time before they returned to earth. She lay there beneath him, content beyond words, listening to the crackle of the fire, the distant soughing of the wind, the ever-decreasing pounding of his heart against hers. She lay there, drifting through the sensations, and mused that she felt happy for the first time in her life. She'd never noticed the lack of happiness before, but suddenly, with this overwhelming fulfillment, she realized how bleak and lonely her life had been. And would be again, she thought, testing the pain as one would prod a sore tooth. But she was still too anesthetized with pleasure to let the agony overwhelm her. It would soon enough, she reasoned, nuzzling her head against his shoulder. Only this time she'd recognize just how empty her life could be. Damn him.

Noah finally raised his head, looking down at her from eyes that were dark and unfathomable in the flickering firelight. "You look unhappy," he whispered, kissing her lingeringly and with delicious thoroughness.

She smiled up at him, the tears still wet in her eyes. Tomorrow would be time enough for the pain. "Looks can be deceiving," she murmured, and kissed him back, running her fingers up the lean sinews of his back. She never wanted him to move, she wanted to lie there forever, enveloped in his warm strength.

And indeed, he seemed in no hurry to quit the haven of her pliant body. With lips and teeth and tongue he explored the contours of her face, the tip of her nose, her eyelashes, the small, stubborn chin, the sensitive earlobes, until he once more claimed her mouth, setting his seal on it and leisurely investigating the succulent, honeyed depths.

When he finally broke away they were both breathless, and as he rolled onto his back he took her with him, tucking her under his arm so that her head rested on his shoulder. She could look up and see his face against the flickering firelight, and a sudden chill swept over her body. His face was dark, shadowed, with a hint of trouble in the slant of his eyes and the curve of his mouth. Tentatively she put a hand on his broad, slightly damp chest, letting her fingers trail softly through the thin dusting of hair. His hand reached up and caught hers, stopping the lazy caress. As if by its own volition his thumb began a lazy caress of its own against her slender hand, even as the sensuous lines of his mouth tightened still further.

"I'm not in love with you," he said abruptly, suddenly, the fingers around her hand tightening. "You know that, don't you?"

Anne looked at him, lazily unperturbed. "Whoever said you were?" she countered softly. She was more pleased than threatened by his words. The very fact that the idea of love could be floating through his mind was definitely a good sign.

"I just wanted to make sure you didn't misunderstand," he continued stubbornly.

"You must seduce a lot of women with that line," she murmured, nestling closer against his taut length.

"Damn it, Annie, I'm serious." He let go of her hand, and she immediately began to trail it along his torso again, her fingertips soft and questing and having, she noticed, a decidedly marked effect on him.

"I'm sure you are." Her voice was infinitely patient, gentle. "I don't understand why you might think otherwise. You haven't led me on, led me to expect anything from you. Quite the opposite, in fact."

"But do you really believe it? Did you make love with me on an impulse, a sexual whim? You're not that kind of woman, Annie."

"Isn't that my line?" she replied sleepily, undisturbed. The more troubled and guilty he was, the more it pleased her.

"No games, Annie."

"All right, what do you expect from me?" She opened her eyes wide, staring up at his intent face as he leaned over her, and her wandering hand was momentarily stilled. "Do you want me to say that I fell madly in love with you, that I expect you to feel the same and to make an honest woman of me? I didn't realize I appeared that naive."

"Not naive. Vulnerable." The blue eyes that stared

down at her were dark with guilt and anger, and she wanted to lift her hand and gently soothe that expression from his face.

"Just tell me what you want from me, Noah," she said gently. "And then it will be up to me whether I want to accept it or not."

"I want to make love to you."

"You just did," she said with a trace of a smile. "At least, I thought that's what we were doing."

"That was only a taste of what I want to do with you. I want to spend the next six months in bed with you, making love to you morning, noon and night."

She snuggled closer. "I think that sounds delightful."

His hand reached out and caught her chin, forcing her to look up at him. "That's what I want to do. But that's not what we're going to do."

"All right, tell me. What are we going to do?"

His answer was the last thing she expected. "Nothing," he said shortly. "I'm going back to New York tomorrow, and you're going on with your life. Marry Wilson if that's what you really want, and if we happen to see each other again we'll be polite and friendly. And that's all."

Slowly Anne withdrew from the circle of his arms, pulling herself into a sitting position, withdrawing into herself. There was nothing she could wrap around her nude body, nothing to shield herself from those cold, merciless eyes. Except that they didn't look cold and merciless in the firelight; they looked warm with desire and a torment to match hers. "That bad, was I?" she said flatly, willing the misery to go away, the tears to keep back.

He sat up swiftly, and the hands that caught her hunched shoulders were determined. "No, my love," he said, and the endearment had the breath-destroying ring of truth. "You were that good."

She stared at him, disbelief and pain warring with the last tiny spark of hope that struggled for dominance. And then she was pulled into his arms, cradled against his chest, as his gentle, gentle hands stroked her face, her hair, her body, holding her tightly against him, and his voice was low and anguished as it rumbled beneath her ear. "I can't give you what you deserve, and I'm damned if I'm going to give you less. You need someone to love you with all their heart and soul, someone to marry you and give you babies, a partner and a lover and a friend. And the most I can offer you is a short, sweet fling, and you deserve far better than that."

"Are you going to tell me why?" she murmured against his chest. She could feel his body tense, and hesitate, and patiently she waited.

"Because I'm still in love with my wife," he said finally. Anne didn't even flinch. She'd been expecting and dreading something like this, but the reality of hearing it was mercifully numbing.

"Are you?" she questioned with admirable restraint, willing her body not to withdraw from his tortured warmth. "Don't you think she'd want you to let go?"

"Maybe. But I don't want to let go," he said bleakly.

"Why not?"

"Because I don't deserve to. As much as I loved her, part of me hates her. Hates her for dying, hates her for killing our baby, hates her for going off to that damned cabin where no one could reach her." His voice was low and painfully rasping. "She was always headstrong and willful, and that willfulness killed her and killed our child. And I hate her for that, and I can't let go. And still tied to Nialla, I can't offer you anything.

You're strong and beautiful and brave and clever," he murmured. "And you've settled for too little for too long."

"You've got it all worked out," she murmured helplessly. "So what does that mean for us?"

"It means this is a one-night stand," he said harshly. "I should have kept my distance in the first place. I promise you, I will from now on. You don't need any more complications in your life right now." He released her abruptly, rising to his feet in one fluid movement, reaching for his jeans. His outline against the fire was uncompromisingly beautiful, uncompromisingly aroused male.

Anne looked away, down at the carpet with a great interest belied by the sudden flame of desire that had shot through her at the sight of him. "So that's settled?" she murmured.

"It's settled," he said, his voice firm in the darkness. "Where would you like me to sleep?"

She looked up at him then, her eyes wandering quite shamelessly over his body. The firelight outlined the muscles and sinews in his long legs, caressed the firm male buttocks, and threw his strong chest into relief. He was still holding his jeans in his hand, and his eyes met hers. "In my room," she replied, very calm. "You said this was going to be a one-night stand. The night isn't even half over."

He didn't hesitate. A moment later he was across the room, pulling her into his arms in a grip so tight only his own willpower would be able to break it. "It's your choice, lady," he said hoarsely, his eyes boring down into hers.

"I've made it," she answered, threading her arms around his neck and resting her face trustingly against his shoulder.

His skin was smooth and warm to the touch, and she sighed deeply, caught up between the twin demons of hope and despair. "I've made it," she whispered again, to herself, as he drew her up the winding stairs to her bedroom.

Chapter Ten

It was the sudden glare of lights as the power came back on that tore her from a sound, sated sleep with a rude violence that had her sitting bolt upright in bed. The curtains were drawn against the faintly encroaching sunlight, the digital clock by her bed was flashing with irritating monotony, and she was alone. And then the sound that had been hovering in the back of her sleep-drugged mind intruded again, this time registering on her fully awake brain. It was the sound of a chain saw—several, in fact.

Slowly she pulled herself from the warm, narrow haven of her bed, pulling a robe around her body as she stumbled toward the window. The front of the house was a hive of activity. Telephone trucks, electric company trucks, men with chain saws and ladders and hard-hats scurrying around busily in the fitful sunlight that glistened off the wet grass. Even Proffy's venerable Plymouth was now parked to the left of the house. And Noah's battered VW was gone.

She was in no hurry—there was nothing to rush downstairs for. A long, leisurely shower helped knead some of the aches from her body, even though the water was barely lukewarm. A part of her regretted washing the last traces of his lovemaking from her flesh, wanted to cling to the physical remembrance of their seemingly unique coupling that still left her weak with longing at the very thought. But Noah was gone, never to return, and she had no reason to doubt his resolve.

She certainly hadn't acted very wisely in her choice for a weekend fling, she mused with some bitterness as she pulled on fresh underwear and a pair of jeans. If she wanted a casual affair, a weekend of adventurous sex with no strings attached, why did she have to choose someone she was halfway in love with? She would have been better off haunting a singles bar, or accepting one of Holly's many invitations for a weekend in New York. Holly wouldn't have let her go through a forty-eight-hour period without several attractive men to choose from, particularly with her sublimated passion for Wilson.

The forest green of her cotton sweater deepened her eyes; the wet tangle of black hair made her narrow face even paler to her discerning gaze. It was a fortunate thing Proffy was so unobservant. She'd still have a great deal of explaining to do about the deep-purple bruise beneath her eye.

While not expecting hugs and kisses, she was still startled by the glare Proffy sent her from across the breakfast table. He was making do with instant coffee and burnt toast, and Anne immediately assumed it was her dereliction of household duty that had earned his displeasure.

"Do you realize how much trouble it is to make a cup of coffee in this house?" he demanded by way of greeting. "I couldn't even find the damned beans, much less the filters and the coffee grinder. This instant coffee must be at least two years old."

"At least," she agreed, barely suppressing a shudder. "One of Ashley's friends brought it. I think he used to use hot water from the tap. And I keep the beans in the freezer."

"That's ridiculous. Why would you want to do a thing like that?"

"It keeps them fresher." She was scarcely in the mood for an argument about coffee, and she changed the subject abruptly. "That was some storm, wasn't it? I must say the repair crews have been quite efficient."

"We were the hardest hit. Just our luck," he grumbled, eying her warily. "You know I don't like to interfere in your life, Anne," he began uneasily. "You're old enough to know what you're doing."

"But?" she prompted, resigned.

"Was that Noah Grant I passed when I was driving back this morning?"

She met his gaze calmly enough. "Probably. Why do you ask?"

"Don't you have any sense?" he exploded. "You know as well as I do that you shouldn't have anything to do with him. For one thing, he's a friend of Holly's, and you know better than to try to steal your own sister's men. For another, you happen to be engaged."

"True enough," she said reasonably, busying herself with the coffee beans.

He seemed even further incensed by her calm attitude. "Not to mention the fact that you are completely unsuited to each other," he railed, his tone of voice increasing. "I always thought you were the down-to-earth, practical one in the family. You should realize it can lead absolutely nowhere, that he—"

"I'm not going to see him again, Proffy," she interrupted smoothly.

"What?"

"I'm not going to see him again. Not if we can help

it." The pronoun was a lie, the reality unbearably accurate. "So you don't have to worry."

He scarcely looked appeased. "You forget, he's involved with Holly, too. I don't think he's out of our life, no matter what you might hope."

"There's nothing I can do about that," she said with a false smile, turning on the electric coffee grinder to drown out his conversation. Her equanimity was running a little thin about now, and Proffy wasn't helping.

He was saying something, and with a weariness that reached into her bones she stopped the grinder. "What was that?"

"I said, I'm sorry if I came down too hard on you yesterday," he said, his voice still too loud. "I didn't mean to be quite so harsh."

Anne shrugged carelessly. "I'm sure you had your reasons." She looked up at him, smiling a cool, distant smile that didn't reach her eyes. "If you think I'm a quitter and a coward you have every right to tell me so." With a snap she turned the grinder back on, drowning out his further explanations.

She took as long as she dared, until the beans were a fine, essentially useless powder, and then turned back to the fuming Proffy.

"You won't even let me apologize, will you?" he grumbled. "You're as bad as your grandmother."

"That was an apology?" she queried. "I hadn't recognized it. In that case, it's accepted. Would you like some real coffee?"

"No, thank you. I must say you're in a surprisingly good mood considering what happened last night."

Unbidden, her mind wandered back to the hours lying in Noah's arms, the feel of his deft, strong hands on her responsive body, the hot, sad light in his eyes as he looked down at her. But then she remembered that

Proffy could know none of that. "I thought the repair crews had everything in hand," she murmured.

"Do you mean to tell me you don't know?" he demanded. "You with your obsessive fixation about this old albatross of a house? Did you sleep through the storm? Noah Grant must be even more distracting than I thought, if he got you to forget about your house."

Anne felt a sudden sick dréad deep in the pit of her stomach. "What are you talking about?"

"Didn't you even bother to check the house for damage?" he countered severely.

"The power was off. We couldn't have seen anything, even if we had tried. What happened?" Even to her own ears her voice sounded shrill. Don't let it be the house, she begged silently. Noah's been taken from me; please God, don't take the house, too.

"When the oak fell, half of it shattered and went flying. The roof is partially caved in, the windows on the left side of the house are shattered, the sashes destroyed."

"It can be repaired?" Her voice was desperate, urgent.

"Not by us. We don't have the money, Anne." She could see no grief in his face, no worry. Only a damnably easy resignation.

"We can find the money. I have several thousand in savings; that will be a start. And we can take out a loan—"

"I've told you before, Holly and Ashley won't agree to it. They're already up to their ears in debt as it is. And the two or three thousand you've been hoarding will barely begin to do a patching job. You'll have to face it sooner or later, Anne. We can't afford this house."

"You can give up if you want to," she said stiffly. "I'm not about to." And she stalked from the room, bristling with rage, determination and a small core of anguish that she determinedly banished. If she was going to save her house she'd have to use all her talents and energies—she couldn't afford to spend her time mourning an impossible love.

"YOU'VE DONE YOUR USUAL marvelous job." Wendell James tossed his linen napkin onto the table and leaned back in his chair with the air of a man well satisfied with his meal, his companion and his lot in life. He was a florid, stocky man in his mid-sixties, bearing no resemblance to Nialla's delicate dark-haired beauty. She had taken after his first wife, and though he'd always been proud of her and the bullheadedness he felt was his only legacy to her, he'd never really understood her, any more than he understood the man who had been her husband. "I don't know what I'll do without you, Noah. You have an insight few people possess, and it's worth its weight in gold to me. Are you sure you want to leave New York?"

Noah smiled back at his father-in-law. "It's either leave New York or leave the law. I've spent too much time and money to give up on my career, no matter how disenchanted I've become, so my only choice is to redirect it. Corporate law isn't my thing anymore, Wendell. I need to feel like I'm making a difference, that I'm needed."

"Hell, Noah, I need you," Wendell shot back. "I doubt if my profits will be nearly as good without your insightful touch."

"I think you'll manage," Noah drawled.

"Sure I will. But I'd rather have you with me. And not just for Nialla's sake. We make a great team, Noah.

No, don't flinch every time I mention her name. She's gone, man. You and I both know it, much as we hate the thought. She's been dead for three years, long enough for you to get over it. It was no one's fault, just one of those freaks of nature, and yet you still go around with one of the worst cases of the guilties I've ever seen. It wasn't your fault, Noah. It's time for you to let go.''

"Wendell, I've let go," Noah said patiently. "Have you seen me living a cloistered life?"

"You've been out with some very beautiful women," he agreed. "But I haven't seen any sign of involvement. Noah, you need to find someone, get married, have children."

"No!" His voice was quiet, harsh, and determined. "No children, Wendell. And no wife."

"Noah, it was Nialla's choice. She wanted children as much as you did."

"And it killed her. I'm not going through that again," he said flatly, ignoring the sudden memory of Anne's pain-filled green eyes.

"So you're going to spend the rest of your life in mourning?" Wendell asked. "I would have thought better of you."

"Hell, no." He managed a wry grin. "I just haven't met the right woman." That was a lie, but Wendell didn't need to know it. The right woman was living in a tumbledown, storm-battered mansion just two hours away, and the papers he'd just handed to his ex-father-in-law betrayed her on almost every level. And there wasn't a damned thing he could do about it.

He'd cursed himself the entire trip back to the city. He wasn't content with screwing up his own life; he had to succumb to adolescent sexual temptation and mess her up, too. Except that it hadn't felt adolescent at all. It had been deep and eternal and inevitable. The only way he could have stopped it was never to have showed up there at all. But he had, and now he was paying for it. And Annie would pay even more.

At least he'd managed to resist the final destructive act. A week after he'd returned from the old farmhouse, Holly had come after him. How she knew, he couldn't even begin to fathom, but somehow she guessed that he had bedded her sister. And she proceeded to use every ounce of her feminine wiles and not inconsiderable determination to seduce him herself.

He had almost given in. He wasn't a man used to fighting temptation, and Holly's determination was beyond willingness. But he couldn't do it. If he was planning to betray Annie, to sell her house out from under her, giving her no chance to fight back, at least he could leave her sister alone.

And Holly's competitive need for him was something less than an aphrodisiac. He didn't know whether she simply had to have every man who wanted her older sister or just wanted a surrogate for Wilson, and he didn't care. When it came right down to it, he didn't want anyone but the one person he should never have had. If there was any shred of decency left to him, Anne Kirkland was now off limits. He'd do what he could to salvage the situation, do what he should have done since that first weekend. He would never go near her again.

"That's a helluva look on your face, Noah," Wendell observed shrewdly. "Is there more to this situation than you're telling me?"

Noah roused himself from his abstraction. "We've worked together for seven years, Wendell. Do you think I'd withhold pertinent information?"

"No. I know you wouldn't. I'm just curious about a little impertinent information. Holly Kirkland is a very pretty young lady. Is she complicating the situation?"

Noah laughed. "No."

"You're sure?"

"Positive. Holly Kirkland's in love with her sister's fiancé, and she's just looking for short-term substitutes."

"Sister, eh? I'd forgotten she had one. I thought there was just her and Ashley. What does the sister do? Is she as talented as her siblings?"

Noah considered it objectively, allowing a tiny shaft of pain in on a purely experimental basis. "I couldn't say. She does everything, and she does everything well." He glanced at the damning file beneath Wendell's blunt fingers. "She's the fourth owner."

"The recalcitrant one, eh?" Wendell knew his man far too well. His eyes had caught the shift in Noah's expression, his ear the nuance in Noah's voice. "Well, she'll recover. She's pretty?"

"Pretty enough," he said in a noncommittal voice, giving nothing away. But a cagey old fox like Wendell James had already gleaned the information he wanted.

"I need you to do me one last favor, my boy," he said slowly. "Sort of a last hurrah. Would you do it?"

Noah was wary. He had a great deal of affection for his father-in-law but not much trust. "What?" he said bluntly.

Wendell was unabashed. "See this thing through. The papers will be ready to sign by next weekend, and the whole family will be down in Philadelphia for Ashley's opening. I want you to go along and get the papers signed."

"No."

"Don't be stuffy, my boy. Everyone knows you've

been seeing Holly—no one will think twice about your showing up. It'll take five minutes, the job will be done, and there won't be any great fuss with the sister.''

"No."

"If I go down, or send someone in my place, there's a good chance that things will be a lot worse," Wendell warned. "I'm afraid the rest of us look like lawyers—the sister would smell a rat. There's nothing she can do at this late date, but if you handled it I'm sure you could make it easier on her."

"You're the prince of darkness, you know that?" Noah snapped.

Wendell smiled his satisfaction. "You'll drive down with Holly Kirkland. She's arranged for hotel rooms for you both."

"You have this all arranged, don't you?"

"I try to be thorough," he said modestly.

Noah sat there, knowing he shouldn't give in. The chance that he could spare Anne pain was minor—he'd be far more likely to make things worse. And he knew in the long run that wouldn't matter. "I'll go. But that's it, Wendell. That's the end of it."

Wendell smiled his beatific smile that had fooled more than one opposing attorney into thinking he was a benevolent old man. "That will be enough," he approved. "That should do very well."

IT WAS A HELLISH TWO WEEKS that followed for Anne. Everywhere she turned the answer was the same—no one was willing to lend her the estimated twenty thousand dollars needed to put the house back in passable shape. She went through her savings in a matter of days, just getting the broken windows boarded up and the hole in the slate roof covered with plywood and plastic. The majority of the damage was in the seldom-used east section of the house. With a stretch of good weather the damage might remain at a manageable level, but of course it rained every day, and Anne spent most of her time emptying buckets of leaking rainwater.

She managed to borrow another couple of thousand to supplement her small savings, but there the credit ended. The banks were blandly adamant, Edmund Jolles had just plowed his profits back into the business, including her cursed word processor, and Wilson was smugly indifferent to her pleas.

"Of course I have twenty thousand dollars, Anne. All wisely invested in blue-chip stocks and municipal funds. I am certainly not about to cash it in to lend it to you when I'll never be repaid. I simply can't afford to make that kind of gesture, much as I'd like to."

"But Wilson..."

"The answer, my dear, is no. It's time you faced the facts of life. I've been thinking that we might be better off building our own house. The upkeep on that old mausoleum must be incredible."

Anne had glared at him. "Holly and Ashley will have to help me then," she said stubbornly. "It's time they took some responsibility for the house, too."

"You've never let them before, Anne."

"Don't be ridiculous. Of course I have!" she protested, incensed. "I've asked for their help time and time again."

"Yes, but on your terms. It's always been your house, not theirs. It's little wonder Holly hasn't wanted to get involved in the whole mess."

Anne had simply stared at him, stricken. "You don't really mean that."

"I'm afraid I do. Holly and I have had long talks on the subject. You're obsessed with that house, Anne, and the sooner you leave it behind the better." Much as she wanted to, Anne couldn't ignore the real concern in his brown eyes, or the unpleasant grain of truth in his allegations.

"All right, Wilson," she said finally, subdued but still determined. "I'll just have to do it without your help."

"I wish you luck," he said, and she believed him. Wilson was nothing if not scrupulously fair. And not for the first time Anne found herself trying to regret that one glorious night with Noah, a night that had left her with far too many lonely nights and the uncomfortable sensation of having betrayed the ever-patient if unimaginative Wilson. Tried to regret it, and failed. Better to have risked everything, rather than take the usual safe path. Even if it had all exploded in her face, leaving her curiously numb, it had been worth the chance.

It was only fortunate that Anne and Wilson's relationship had never been an intensely physical one. For the most part they contented themselves with light kisses on proffered cheeks or a gentle pat on the hand. The few occasions they had actually made it into bed had been more in the nature of marriage insurance, to make certain they didn't find each other repulsive. Overwhelming physical need had been noticeably absent from those few civilized couplings.

If Wilson's brown eyes had ever heated up with the warmth they showered on Holly, if his perfectly manicured hands ever reached for her with anything approaching yearning, she would have to tell him about Noah. At the moment she was too caught up with trying to save her house to deal with severing their long-term agreement. Time enough for that after Ashley's opening that weekend.

It was his first major showing in almost eighteen months, and the family was planning to turn out in full force. Ashley had reserved a block of hotel rooms for them, a major party was planned, and even Wilson, disapproving as he was of Ashley's lifestyle, was going to join them. Anne had little doubt that the show would be another huge success, and in the flush of praise and certain money, Ashley would doubtless prove to be a little more openhanded than usual. Holly would have some handsome man in tow, either the short Tom Selleck type or someone even more luscious. Couple that with the provocative dress Anne was fashioning for her, and her mood should be equally sanguine. She, also, could be persuaded to be more generous if approached in just the right way. Especially once she realized that Wilson would soon be available.

By the time Anne arrived in Philadelphia that weekend she was in a reasonably optimistic mood. Ashley had chosen the Elgin Hotel for his celebratory party. Apart from its proximity to his huge old town house, it had a certain seedy charm entirely in keeping with Ashley's somewhat raffish life style. To Anne's surprise the place was packed—a new showing by Ashley Kirkland was a major event in the art world, and representatives from all over the world seemed to have congregated on the small, turn-of-the-century hotel, making it resemble nothing so much as a convention of Hollywood character actors. It took her only a short while to get settled into the double room she would be sharing with Letitia Morgan, the Merry Widow herself.

As Anne hung the two dresses in the small, compact closet with the gently peeling paint, she cast a last admiring glance over them. Even with her usual modesty she knew she'd outdone herself.

For years Holly had counted on Anne to create beautiful, unusual clothes for her performances, clothes combining grace with the airy quality and the touch of sensuality that was her onstage persona. The shimmering emerald green would set off her delicate blond charms to perfection, not to mention that the lines of the dress, seemingly demure in front, plunged to a point well below the small of her back, exposing all the creamy skin. Holly would love it, and look absolutely glorious in it besides, securing all the attention she so needed.

For herself, Anne had fashioned something much more subdued. The purple silk had been rejected by Holly. "I don't know why I bought it—purple makes me pale and uninteresting," she'd complained. But no one could have looked pale and uninteresting in the finished creation. The scooped neckline was much higher than Holly usually preferred, but it suited Anne perfectly, and the long sleeves were gathered at the shoulders and the wrists to give a full, flowing effect. Anne knew with a certain bleak satisfaction that she would look elegant, sleek and almost beautiful in that dress. It was only a shame that the one person she'd had in mind when she'd made it wouldn't be there to see her in it.

No sooner was she settled into the small, stuffy room than she went in search of Ashley. It was a little past five—the rest of her family would arrive at any moment, and she wanted time to put her plea to Ashley before Proffy could influence him. In her gray wool slacks and heavy sweater she looked out of place in a hotel full of peacocks, and the suite of rooms belonging to her brother was empty to her knock. It was probably not an auspicious time to be asking him for money, anyway. Once the show was the huge success she knew it would be, Ashley would doubtless be more mellow. Unless his intake of alcohol contributed to that mellowness, she thought with an added trace of worry.

She turned down her own corridor, lost in her thoughts, oblivious to the lean figure that headed toward her from the other end. That figure hesitated for a moment, then continued onward, and his warm, deep voice broke through her oblivion.

"Hello, Annie."

At the sound of Noah's voice she stopped still, her face pale and stricken, the look in her eyes as they met his vulnerable before she managed to shutter them. He cursed softly under his breath at the pain he saw still lurking there.

"Noah." Her voice was cool and composed, neither welcoming nor unwelcoming. "I didn't expect to see you here."

"I didn't expect to be here. There was... er, some last-minute business I had to take care of in Philadelphia this weekend, so I offered to drive Holly down."

"Business?" she echoed, keeping her voice light and impersonal.

To her surprise, that innocuous topic of conversation seemed to make him even more uncomfortable, and he ran a hand through his tangle of black curls with unaccustomed nervousness. "It's something I'm doing for a friend, so to speak." His blue, blue eyes stared down at her intently from out of his Gypsy face, and it was all she could do to keep from squirming. She couldn't read anything in those eyes—not longing, or regret, or even indifference. "Are you all right?" he said finally.

"Of course I am. Did you think I'd be pining away for you?" she demanded caustically, ignoring the fact that that was exactly what she'd been doing, and that the raw pain in her voice told him so.

"Of course not. I've been worried about you, Annie. I'm sorry I took off without saying goodbye that morning. And I'm sorry I haven't called. Given the circumstances, I thought it would be better if it was a clean break."

"It would be better," she said firmly, resisting the impulse to reach up and run her hands through those tangled black curls, to throw herself against his chest, to thrust her hands up inside his sweater and run them along the smoothly muscled torso that she remembered far too well. "However, I suppose this can't be helped. You haven't seen Ashley, have you?"

"Not recently."

"Damn. I needed to talk to him." She managed a wry smile. "I don't suppose you happen to have twenty thousand dollars you can lend me? The house needs a new roof."

She was completely unprepared for his reaction, the cold light of anger that filled his eyes and the curl of disgust at his mobile mouth. "I don't feel that guilty," he snapped, turning on his heel and stalking back down the corridor.

She stared after him, openmouthed. "Apparently you do," she told herself softly. "How very interesting." She was about to follow him down the corridor, determined to do battle, when Holly's light tones assailed her from behind.

"There you are, darling. I've been looking everywhere for you." Dutifully they brushed cheeks. "I love my dress."

"You've seen it already?" Half of Anne's mind was following Noah down the corridor, and it was with an effort that she turned her attention back to her sister.

"We arrived at the same time Proffy did with the Merry Widow in tow. She was only too happy to let me in your room to get the dress, but I warn you, she wants the bed you chose." Holly giggled. "It's nearer the bathroom, you know."

"Tough."

"Don't be so hardhearted, darling. She's going to take Proffy off our hands, unless I miss my guess. Have you seen Noah?" Holly's voice was determinedly cool, but Anne wasn't fooled for a minute.

"I just saw him. And offended him deeply, apparently."

"Did you? How did you manage that?" Holly was genuinely curious.

"I asked him for twenty thousand dollars. I wasn't serious, of course. Speaking of which, Holly, I—"

"Don't start on me now, Annie," she protested. "I barely have time to shower and change before we're due at the gallery. We can talk later."

"Proffy's told you about our problem?"

"Proffy told me about the house," she said evasively. "Now I really must run. I'll see you at the gallery. Tell me, is Wilson coming?"

Her studied indifference didn't fool Anne for a moment. "He'll be at dinner. I forgot to ask him whether he was bringing your car."

"Oh, that's all right. I already picked it up," Holly assured her blithely.

"When?" Surprise made the question sound abrupt, and Holly blushed with unaccustomed guilt.

"Don't be paranoid, darling. I came down on a flying trip last week—I didn't have a moment to even call you. Don't worry, you can trust Wilson."

"Pity," Anne said silkily, and Holly shot her a disbelieving glance.

"Don't tease, darling. I'll see you at the gallery." And with that she raced down the hall before her older sister could make any more uncomfortable remarks. Anne watched her go, a smile hovering around her mouth, not even noticing that her sister was heading in the same direction Noah had recently traveled. Lost in a maze of contradictory thoughts, she headed back toward her room prepared to beard the Merry Widow in her den and fight for the right to the bed, if need be.

Chapter Eleven

"Oh, my God!"

"Anne, dear," the Merry Widow protested faintly, "I wish you wouldn't swear. I can't abide it. Please humor me in this matter, dear. I know it's hopelessly antique of me, but I can't help it."

Anne ignored her protests, staring into the closet with grim shock. "Were you with Holly when she took her dress?"

"Of course I was. How else do you suppose she got in here? I trust the hotel management isn't in the habit of handing out keys to every Tom, Dick and Harry who happens to ask for one. I won't rest easy if that's the case."

Anne ignored the faintly querulous tone. "Did she look at both dresses?"

"Of course she did. She took the green one first, then changed her mind and took the purple one instead. I can't imagine why it should matter—the dresses look very much alike to me."

"The purple one was mine," Anne wailed, panic breaking through her grim resolve. "I can't possibly wear the green one."

"And why not? It will look quite stunning with your eyes."

"I haven't got the figure to carry it off, for one thing. Or the guts. Holly likes her clothes a bit more risqué than I do. This dress is bordering on indecent; the purple was demure and modest."

"I'm sure Holly looked at them both carefully before choosing," Mrs. Morgan observed shrewdly. "Maybe she's decided to change her image."

A sudden vision of Wilson flashed through Anne's mind, Wilson with his disapproval and his attraction to Holly. "I'm sure that's what she decided to do," Anne wailed. "But she picked a hell of a time to do it. I haven't got anything else to wear!"

"Your language, Anne," Mrs. Morgan reproved. "And you don't need anything else. You'll look quite charming in the green dress—I expect you'll even surprise yourself. Holly is not the only one in need of a change, my dear. When I was your age I had already been married twice."

Humor born of despair bubbled forth. "But that dress is hardly suitable for an old maid."

"Fortunately such things as old maids are passé," the Merry Widow observed serenely from her perch on the coveted bed. "If you have the right attitude you'll look glorious in that dress. And I wouldn't be surprised if Wilson decides he can't wait till this fall."

Anne ignored the reference to Wilson. By that time he and Holly should be happily in love. But where would she be? "I don't suppose I have any choice," she said doubtfully, eying the silky creation. She had always loved the color, after all. Perhaps it was fate. And what would Wilson say when he saw her in it? Even better, how would Noah react?

WILSON CHOKED on his martini, staring at her, red-faced, when his coughing fit had passed. Holly, firmly attached to his arm and looking radiantly innocent in the purple dress, peered at him through worried eyes, and Anne knew she was having second thoughts about having filched the wrong dress.

Indeed, she realized with a trace of smugness, catching a glimpse of her reflection above the bar, the dress couldn't have suited her better. The deep green darkened her eyes to a clear emerald, artfully enhanced by the Merry Widow's eye shadow. The front clung gently to her unbound breasts, the back dipped enticingly low, and her black hair was a cloud around her animated face. She would never have dared wear such a thing, but she could only be grateful that fate and her acquisitive sister had forced it on her.

Music was throbbing through the room, an artful accompaniment to Ashley's bold canvases. It was a strange mélange—the Pointer sisters fading into Vivaldi and then on to Bruce Springsteen. Anne peered over the edge of her champagne glass, content to eye the wandering crowds, ever alert for Noah's entrance. In the end it was he who found her, coming up behind her when she least expected it. She had just stepped out into the back hallway to catch her breath, away from the suffocating clouds of cigarette smoke and the chattering clatter of high-pitched voices. The hallway was dark, empty and depressing, and she was just about to rejoin the crowds.

"What are you trying to prove in a dress like that, Annie?" His voice was low and seductive just beside her ear, and she could only be glad she was in enough control not to jump.

She turned slowly, looking up into his faintly scowling face and smiling—a slow, sure smile. "That you can't resist me?" she suggested lightly, taking another sip of the champagne she'd brought with her. His own glass was half full.

There was a blessed trace of a smile lighting his dark Gypsy face, and his hand reached up lightly to brush her cheek, the touch sending a tiny shiver down her exposed backbone. "You're probably right. I'm glad to see your bruise faded."

"There are still some lovely yellow traces beneath the makeup," she murmured, trying to still the sudden uprush of hope at his casual words.

"What have you been doing the last two weeks? Falling off roofs or racing into power lines?" He kept his voice light.

"Missing you."

The champagne in his glass spilled slightly, and his eyes darkened. "Did you?" he replied noncommittally.

He wasn't about to give in, she realized in sudden despair. No matter how much he wanted her, he wasn't about to admit it. And there was no way she could be sure he even wanted her. "Yes," she said, turning away.

She had forgotten the effect of her back, or the lack thereof. Before she could move away there was a sudden intake of breath and his hand caught her almost bare shoulder.

"Good God, Annie," he groaned. The silent, empty hallway surrounded them with a velvet solitude. At any moment the door to the crowded exhibit could open and part of that spectacularly plumaged crowd could spill out after them. But for the moment they were alone. His strong hand burned into her shoulder, holding her turned away from him, that long, narrow back exposed to his heated gaze.

Before she could divine his intention she felt the cool, silvery drops of champagne slide down the curve of her back. A moment later his mouth followed, his tongue snaking out to catch the drops he'd showered on her back, slithering down the warm, sensitized skin, its rough texture a soul-destroying caress.

Anne swayed, and it was only the strength of his hand that kept her standing. A helpless little moan of desire had escaped her, but there was no one around to notice.

"Damn you, Annie." His voice was low and almost anguished. "What do you want from me?"

"A two-night stand?" she suggested, not daring to turn around.

The hand released her, reluctantly, the fingers clinging to the silky material for a long moment. When he said nothing she turned around, only to see him disappearing back through the doorway.

It took her a moment to follow him. "How do you like it, Anne, darling?" Ashley weaved his way up to her, and for a moment all thought of Noah Grant fled. Her brother looked absolutely horrible. That he was already very drunk was without question—his eyes were bloodshot from days or weeks or months of constant drinking. His tan had faded to a dissipated yellow, his hair was limp and in need of a cut, and his face was puffy.

"Very impressive," she said vaguely, taking one slender hand in hers. "Are you all right, Ashley?"

"Of course I am, dearest." He withdrew his hand quickly, but not before she recognized the deathly chill in his skin. "Why shouldn't I be? Another smash success, with all my dear, dear friends to celebrate my triumph. Not to mention my glorious family. You're looking quite ravishing, my dear. How did you get Holly to part with that magnificent dress?"

"It was her choice."

"I must say I'm surprised. Maybe she's trying to prove to Wilson how subdued she can be."

"That was my theory," Anne agreed with a forced smile.

"So you finally know about that, do you?" Ashley shoved a nervous hand through his lank blond hair. "I wondered how long it would take you."

"Too long, I suppose. I still don't know whether Wilson realizes it." The two of them eyed the couple in question. Wilson was leaning over Holly, lecturing her very intently, and Holly was listening meekly enough, her slender hand still on his arm.

"I think he might be catching on," Ashley said dryly. "I wonder where that leaves you."

"Splendidly celibate."

"Best way to be," Ashley said sadly. "Listen, darling, Proffy has told me you're desperate for money. I can't help."

"But Ashley, the house is going to fall into rubble if we don't do something!"

"Let it," he said. "Best thing for it, and for you. Really, Anne, I'd like to help, but I simply can't. I'm already up to my ears in debt."

"But how could you be? I know you live rather well, but you also make quite fabulous sums of money. I just need a loan, or if you could cosign a loan with a bank—"

"I'm afraid my credit is worthless, darling, and I haven't even got the money to pay for the reception tonight." He grimaced, draining his glass. "You see, not only do I have expensive...friends, but I've also discovered the myriad pleasures of gambling. Atlantic City is just a little too close for me, I'm afraid."

"Ashley!"

"Sorry, darling. I'm afraid you'll have to count on Holly for help." He turned and walked away.

Elvis Costello had faded into Mozart during the last

few minutes, but anything less like Mozart's delicate fantasies would be hard to imagine in her current state of mind. The world seemed to be closing in on her, and wherever she turned, doors slammed in her face.

Plastering a social smile on her face, Anne wandered through the exhibition, barely touching her champagne, longing to escape back to the hotel, and hoping against hope that the Merry Widow might be indiscreet enough to share her father's single room. If there ever was a night when Anne needed her privacy, tonight was it.

She would have made it through with flying colors if it hadn't been for Marvin Gaye, she realized later. Keeping away from the champagne helped lessen her self-indulgent state of mind. Ignoring Noah's presence also aided her in her resolve. If she could still feel his tongue dancing along her backbone, she sternly ignored it. She was on her way out of the door, heading back to the hotel and a blessed few moments of peace in her room, when the silky, sensual strains of "Sexual Healing" replaced Chick Corea on the sound system. Anne felt her knees melt as the music wove its familiar, seductive spell around her, felt her breasts tingle and a fire begin a slow, escalating conflagration in her loins.

She couldn't go back through that room, the music throbbing at her from strategically placed speakers. Someone would find her cape and fetch it later—at the moment all she needed was escape.

She made her way blindly to the door, but Noah was there ahead of her, her cape over his arm. Startled, she looked up into his face, her eyes meeting his for a long, fiery moment.

"I give up," he said. His hands lingered for breathless moments as they draped the cape around her. "Come on."

She followed him blindly out into the spring night, oblivious of the curious, troubled glances they left behind. When they reached the sidewalk Noah pulled her hand into his, tucking it close to his body as he took off down the street. Without a word she followed him, her feet rushing to keep up with his long stride as they crossed the blocks that led back to the Elgin Hotel. He didn't say a word until they were behind his bedroom door, the lock securely turned.

And then he reached for her, pulling her against his lean, muscled body, his hands firm but gentle as he held her there. "I warned you, Annie, love," he whispered against her midnight-black hair. "I did warn you." He pushed the cape off her shoulders, and it fell in a shimmering pool at their feet as his hands molded her pliant back to his tense frame. And with a sigh she gave herself up to the magic of his embrace, closing her eyes to doubt and the prospect of tomorrow. Her hands were on the buttons of his shirt, fumbling with desperate haste to break through that rough cloth barrier and feel the warmth of his flesh against her. Eagerly she pulled his shirt free from his pants, sliding her hands up inside, her fingertips trailing along the smooth, warm hide of him. And suddenly she couldn't get enough—reaching up, she sought his mouth, desperate in her need for him.

His hands were deft at the back of her gown, and a moment later it followed the cape onto the floor, leaving her standing in the circle of his arms, wearing nothing but a thin wisp of silk panties.

He groaned, deep in his throat, his tongue exploring her mouth with an almost savage thoroughness as his hands traced her curves, cupping her full breasts as they pressed against the frustrating shirtfront. And then his hands joined hers, ripping off his jacket, his shirt, as they tumbled toward the bed.

Anne fell backward across it, Noah's body sprawling across hers, and she looked up at him, breathless with laughter and excitement. "In a hurry?" she murmured, brushing her lips against his, her tongue darting out to trace the contours of his mouth.

"God, yes!" he groaned as her hands slid across his chest. He caught one of those hands, pressing it against his raging desire, and she gasped.

"You're a witch, do you know that?" he whispered hoarsely as she quickly divested him of the rest of his clothing, until he was completely, gloriously naked. "All my good intentions were completely worthless." He quickly stripped away the last barrier, her peach silk panties, and before she realized what was happening he had rolled over onto his back, pulling her with him.

She lay stretched out across his body, her hair a curtain of black silk around them, and a sudden wave of shyness swept over her. But the fever pitch of their emotions was too high. And after only a token resistance she let him arrange her pliant body over his poised, waiting one.

His fingers reached down to find the hot, needing core of her, but she was ready for him. Firm hands caught her hips, levering her forward so that his massive strength rested just outside its haven. And with a desperation born of need, he pulled her down onto him, his glorious hardness filling her to the depths of her very soul.

A helpless little wail of agonized pleasure escaped her lips, and she looked down at him with complete amazement and wonder, her pale face transfixed.

His hands still firm on her hips, he began to move,

arching up into her, then slowly pulling back, and then again, each time filling her more completely. She could feel her body shivering atop his, feel the rigid control in his arms and legs as he tried to slow the pace, to bring her along with him. But she was far ahead, her body shuddering with spasms of need that were rapidly taking over.

And then abruptly his tenuous control abandoned him, and he arched into her as her body went rigid in his arms. And he followed her, locked together through a mindless eternity, his breath hoarse and rasping in her ear as she sobbed against his damp, heaving chest.

His arms went around her, holding her shivering, sweat-damp body against his, both of them still shaking from the hasty, animalistic coupling that had left them both barely sated. His hands were gentle and trembling against her back, and she placed a shy, longing kiss against the warm, tense cord of his neck before trying to slide away.

"Don't you dare," he whispered on a sudden breath of laughter. "You're not going anywhere."

"But I'm too heavy," she protested weakly, leaning her head back on his shoulder, the soft wisps of hair tickling her nose.

"I think I'm strong enough to bear it, Annie, love," he replied, one hand slowly massaging its way up the length of her backbone, the fingers deft and almost as arousing as his tongue had been earlier that night. She stretched into that hand like a luxuriating kitten. "That was only a preliminary. I don't know what sort of witchcraft you used, but I haven't been so inept since I was seventeen years old. I have to retrieve my reputation."

"I wouldn't have called that inept." She groaned beneath the practiced kneading of his fingers.

"Perhaps not." He allowed himself a small, satisfied grin. "But far too brief."

Anne could feel her body melting into his, feel the slow stirring of the coals of passion that had never been completely banked in her still-trembling loins. "But shouldn't we get back to the others? Everyone will be at dinner by now—they'll miss us." Her fingers trailed lightly up to his muscled arms, and she gave in to the temptation and allowed her tongue to gently taste the salty tang of his skin.

"Let them," he murmured, one hand cradling her head against his chest, encouraging her shy explorations.

It was her first chance to enjoy a man's body in full light, and with a sudden shedding of inhibitions she threw herself into her discoveries with zest, her mouth trailing sweet, nibbling kisses down his lean torso, her fingertips tracing delicate, random patterns on the flesh her mouth couldn't quite reach. She would have preferred greater access to the unquestionably beautiful male body beneath her, but his hands still held her captive, still filled her with the renewed proof of his desire.

She had just reached his flat male nipples, her tongue gently teasing them, when she felt her body lifted. A moment later she was flat on her back in the soft bed as Noah leaned over her, his hips pinning her to the bed. His mouth caught the rosy tip of her breast in a glorious retaliation of her sensual explorations, and with an inarticulate cry she arched up against him, against his mouth and his hips, as once more he began to move within her.

This time his control was absolute, now that the white-hot urgency of their desire had been partially slaked. Slowly he moved, pulling away from her, then returning to fill her completely, so that she cried out with the glory of it.

Slowly, inexorably, the tension began to build as a slow, burning fire that quickly flamed out of control began to engulf her. That passion was swiftly climbing to a fever pitch once more, and desperately she tried to increase the pace, to quicken those slow, driving thrusts that were leading her to the edge of madness. Oblivion was just beyond her reach, shimmering beyond her grasp, and desperately she reached for it. But it eluded her and she fell back, sobbing beneath his measured control.

"I can't," she wept against him, hiding her face against his shoulder. "I can't, Noah."

The hands that were bracing his body shifted to gently cup her face, forcing her tear-drenched eyes to meet his. Softly his mouth brushed hers. "Of course you can," he whispered against her trembling lips. "I'll help you."

Slowly he pulled away, separating their bodies, and she clutched for him, emitting a low wail of anguish at his sudden desertion.

Quickly, deftly he turned her over, one arm under her waist, holding her up as he returned to her with a sure, deep thrust that seemed to reach even deeper to the center of her being. She tried to lurch away in sudden shyness and panic, but he held her firmly.

"Don't be frightened, Annie love," he murmured in her ear, his body covering hers, warm and protecting. "I won't hurt you. I promise." He began raining gentle, reassuring kisses across her shoulders as he once more began to move in that slow, sweet rhythm of love. "I don't get to kiss you this way," he continued, his warm, deep voice soothing her initial fright much as his body was once more exercising its mesmerizing effect on her. "I don't get to watch your beautiful eyes when I fill you." Action suited words, and Anne felt that overwhelming tension begin to build once more. "But it still has definite advantages."

The hand that had been supporting her around her waist slid downward, his clever fingers seeking and swiftly discovering their partially hidden goal.

And with the force of a cannon she was catapulted over that edge of oblivion, flung out into the velvet darkness of love. Somewhere in the darkness she felt his arm support her sagging body, heard her voice sobbing her release into the rumpled sheets. And then he followed her in a blaze of glory, and she heard his voice calling her, calling her name, and it was filled with love and wonder.

He collapsed on top of her, and they fell flat against the mattress, his arms tight around her, the fingers almost cruelly possessive for a too brief moment. And then he released her, rolling to one side, an arm flung up to shield his eyes against the brightness of the hotel-room light, his warm, smooth chest rising and falling rapidly.

Reality was returning with distressing rapidity. Anne opened her weary eyes to watch him, eyes filled with an inescapable love and sorrow. Slowly she tried to edge away, but his arm shot out and caught her, dragging her willing body against his.

There was nothing either of them could say. Anne was too profoundly shaken by the last few minutes, by something she'd only dreamed existed. She couldn't guess for one moment that Noah was suffering the same wonder and amazement.

And then his breathing slowed, his heartbeat lessened, and she realized with a combination of tenderness and annoyance that he had fallen soundly, blissfully asleep. It was far too easy to pull out of his arms then—his hands clutched at her instinctively before falling back to sleep once more. Slowly, carefully, so as not to disturb him, she slipped from the bed. Scooping up her scattered clothes from the floor, she made a silent exit into the bathroom. Much as she wanted to stay in that bed with him, curled up against the warm strength of his beautiful body, she knew if she stayed it would take nothing short of physical violence to dislodge her. She had to keep reality firmly in mind.

Quietly she closed the bathroom door behind her, then turned to the mirror to survey the ravages the last hour had wrought on her body. She looked well and truly loved, she noted with a sigh. The kiss-swollen lips, the faint redness from his closely shaven beard, even the tiny mark of his teeth on her shoulder. Her green eyes were smiling and sultry, and she might as well wear a scarlet "A" on her chest if she thought she had a chance in hell of fooling her inquisitive family.

Still smiling, she reached for a towel. And for the first time saw the reflection of the lavender silk robe in the mirror. The robe she'd given Holly for Christmas two years ago.

Looking down, she noticed her sister's jumbled cosmetics littering the top of the sink. She stared at them numbly, as her clumsy fingers pulled the emerald dress around her shivering body. Her evening sandals were on the bathroom floor, inches away from Holly's slippers.

With a low moan of pain Anne slammed barefoot out of the bathroom, her dress held clumsily about her shivering body. She didn't even look at the figure of the man sitting bolt upright in the bed, watching her out of darkly troubled eyes as she scooped up her cape with shaking hands. A moment later she was gone, the door slammed behind her, racing down the deserted hallway as if the hounds of hell were after her.

Noah stared after her. The scent of her perfume was still in the air, the feel of her was still imprinted on his flesh. Never had Nialla seemed farther away.

Punching up some pillows behind him, he leaned back against the headboard and longed for the cigarettes he had given up five years ago. His mind was still clouded with sleep and Anne's precipitous exit, and it took him a moment to realize how alone he was. Even Nialla was gone, his constant companion of the last few years. The anger and rage had left him, finally, after all his efforts to banish them. Left him with a fond and sad memory of a love that had died, leaving him behind to go onward.

Leaving him behind to make an even bigger mess of things than he would have imagined. And at this point there was nothing he could do about it—he was going to betray Anne on her most fundamental level.

He stared at the door, more alone than he had ever been. "Annie," he whispered, uselessly, belatedly. The room only echoed its silence.

Chapter Twelve

It was very late when Anne finally joined the third stage of Ashley's celebrations. Her face was pale but perfectly composed as she glided into the elegantly seedy ballroom, and even the sight of Noah Grant, impeccably dressed and seemingly completely at ease, failed to put a dent in her composure. Besides, he was easy enough to ignore, absorbed as he was in conversation with a short, dapper man whom Anne failed to recognize. The noise of the celebrations had risen proportionally to the amount of spirits consumed, and Anne could only thank heaven that she'd availed herself of both aspirin and a tranquilizer before returning to the bosom of her family.

"Where the hell have you been?" Holly demanded in a loud whisper from directly behind her. "You've been gone for hours. I wondered for a while when I saw Noah was missing, too, but he's been back for ages now. Were you off with him?"

"No."

"Then have you seen Ashley?"

"Ashley? Isn't he here?" Anne scanned the crowd with worried eyes, her gaze slipping over Noah's lean shoulders with indecent haste.

"Didn't even make it through dinner. He was very

drunk, Anne, and acting sort of crazy, even for him. Wilson went looking for him, but he couldn't find any trace of him."

"Did you tell Proffy?"

Holly snorted inelegantly. "He's too busy flirting with the Merry Widow. I'm afraid we're about to have a wicked stepmother."

"She's welcome to him."

"Has she seen him?" Wilson joined them, his handsome face creased with worry, and without thinking he slid his arm protectively around Holly.

A small, resigned grin lit Anne's face at the naturalness of the gesture. "Not a trace," she said. "Did anyone see him go? Was he alone?"

"He must have been—no one else seems to be missing except you. I'm sure he's all right," Wilson insisted, giving Holly's narrow shoulders a reassuring squeeze. She looked up at him, love and gratitude shining out of her china-blue eyes, and Anne felt a sudden, unworthy pain near her heart. *Damn it, Holly shouldn't have everyone,* she thought morosely.

"Of course he is," she agreed, squashing down that nagging jealousy. "In any case, I might go check the lobby."

"That's the first place I looked," Wilson said.

"Well, I can look again," she replied mildly, heading off toward the door. She could feel a tall figure following her, and even though her senses told her no, she hoped and dreaded it might be Noah.

But it was Wilson's hand that stopped her just outside the ballroom, Wilson's handsome face peering earnestly down at her. "Anne, I have to talk to you," he began, tension giving him a faint wheeze. "You've been incredibly elusive these past few weeks, and I've let this go on far too long. Anne—"

She put one slim hand to his lips, a rueful smile playing about her mouth. "There's no need, Wilson," she said lightly. "I just hope she doesn't lead you a merry dance." And slipping off the pearl-and-diamond ring, she placed it in one limp hand, leaning forward to kiss him gently on the lips in a sweet, grateful farewell. As she looked up, her senses once more betrayed her, and from across the room she could see Noah staring at her out of fathomless, wintry eyes.

Let him think what he wanted about that kiss, she told herself grimly as she escaped from the bemused Wilson, who stood there looking after her, the ring still clutched in one hand. Noah was about to lose both Kirkland women. Not that that should bother him— doubtless he already had replacements lined up around the block in New York. And there was always Nialla's sacred memory, she added bitterly, ashamed of herself for her jealousy.

It was well after midnight, and the lobby of the Elgin Hotel was dimly lit, the darkness covering some of its seamier qualities and giving it a mysteriously elegant air. The place was deserted; no sign of her brother or even a desk clerk to be seen. Anne hesitated, common sense telling her she should rejoin the party, even if it was the last thing she felt like doing, an eerie sixth sense warning her to wait.

She listened to that sixth sense for a brief moment. Just long enough to hear the faint voice that floated toward her from a darkened corner of the lobby. Even in that thin thread of sound she recognized Ashley's mocking drawl, and she rushed across the deserted lobby.

He was huddled in a chair in the surrounding darkness, the back shielding him from prying eyes. The light was dim in the corner, but not dim enough to hide his condition from his sister's worried eyes.

"Oh, my God, Ashley, what happened?" she breathed, almost afraid to touch him.

There didn't seem to be a part of his body that was undamaged. The black silk suit was in tatters around his scrawny frame, his hands were cut and bloody, his entire body seemed to vibrate with pain. His face was the most horrifying of all—one eye was completely closed by the purplish swelling, and the entire expanse was covered with cuts and bruises. His noble beak of a nose was broken, his lips were split and swollen, and the one eye that was still capable of looking up at her was curiously resigned.

"I ran into a door," he said lightly, his voice muffled through the damaged lips.

"Who did this to you, Ashley?" she demanded, squatting down beside him, ignoring her dress trailing on the none-too-clean carpet as she took one hand in hers. He winced, and a deeper panic filled her heart.

"Did they hurt your hands, Ashley?" she demanded hoarsely. If Ashley could no longer paint they might just as well have killed him.

Slowly, painfully he flexed them. "Nothing permanent," he reassured her, his wry smile macabre in his battered face. "Don't look so stricken, sister dear. These things happen."

"Well, they shouldn't," she said fiercely. "Especially not to my brother."

He appeared to consider it for a moment, then sighed, a long, sad sound. "You're right, of course. I think I'd better learn to be more careful." She opened her mouth to speak, but he raised one wounded hand in protest, the fingers trembling slightly. "Don't preach at me, I beg of you, Anne. I think I've reached about the limit of my endurance tonight."

"I won't preach, Ashley. I never have," she said. "I'm not about to ask you to change your life for me."

"I don't think I could if I wanted to," he said harshly.

"But I can ask you to take better care of yourself. I love you, Ashley, and I don't want to wake up one morning and find you dead in some alleyway."

"You won't, Annie. It's not in my karma. But you have a point." He sighed, and even that made his body shiver with pain. "Perhaps a bout of celibacy might do wonders for me. Abstinence of all sorts—I could go on a retreat to some secluded place. Perhaps a monastery in New Mexico."

"Oh, no, the poor monks," Anne shot back on a breath of laughter, and Ashley did his best to glare at her through his ravaged face.

"You lack respect, darling. Help me to my feet."

"You're not going back to the party?"

Ashley smirked, the smile off center on the swollen lips. "It would make a gloriously dramatic touch, don't you think? But no. I would be more than grateful if you would help me back to my room. It's just down the corridor from the one Holly and Noah are sharing."

There were times when Anne and her brother understood each other very well. "Yes, I know about that," she replied calmly. "I just wonder where she's going to put Wilson." He leaned heavily against her as they made their slow, halting way down the corridor.

"You made the break then? Good girl."

"It was long overdue."

Ashley sighed. "Maybe now she'll stop throwing Grant in your face all the time."

"I think Noah's doing his part," she said.

"Poor Anne. You're worth more than the lot of us put together, do you know that?" He shook his head sadly. "You should never trust us—we'll just use you and betray you when your back is turned."

Anne smiled up at him, worry still clouding her eyes. "I trust you."

"You shouldn't," he said abruptly, halting outside his door.

"Do you want me to come in with you? Help clean up some of your cuts?"

He shook his head. "I can take care of it. What I need now is about forty-eight hours of sleep. Not that I'm going to get it. I'll be out for lunch tomorrow."

"Good," she said firmly. "Why don't you come alone and stay for a while? I can even get rid of Proffy and Holly if you want real peace and quiet. You know how peaceful the old house is."

"I know." He waited in his open doorway, his one undamaged eye sad and knowing.

"You're sure I can't do anything more?"

"Positive."

"Then I'll see you tomorrow." She was loath to leave him like that, but she had little choice. "And Ashley—"

"Yes?"

"I think New Mexico is a very good idea. As long as you keep your hands off the monks."

He gave her a travesty of a grin in reply to her sally, stepped inside his room, and shut the door behind him.

"Is he all right?"

She should have known he'd be there. Indeed, part of her had been uncannily aware of his presence at the end of the hall, and Ashley of course had a full view of him just beyond her shoulder.

She turned to face him, her expression impassive. "I don't really know," she replied. "I hope so."

"What happened to him?"

"He wouldn't tell me. It sounds like it wasn't the first time something like that happened."

"It probably wasn't," Noah said coolly. "What are you going to tell the others?"

That was a new problem. "I don't know," she said, turning over the problem in her head. "Maybe I won't have to say a thing. After all, Ashley delights in being eccentric—it's just like him to abandon his first opening in almost two years."

He was curiously subdued, the man beside her, surprisingly uncertain of both himself and her. Gone was that bone-melting smile, that damnable self-assurance that held him back from her. In its place was a pain and vulnerability that matched her own. "Why did you leave like that?" he said suddenly, and Anne could feel what little color she had left drain from her face.

"I didn't fancy running into your roommate," she snapped.

He flinched as if struck. "Anne," he said, and his voice was low and troubled and deeply moving. "I have to—"

"There you are!" Holly swept down the hall, Wilson in tow, a fatuous expression on his face. "You missed all the excitement, both of you, and for the second time tonight."

"Oh, I wouldn't say so," Noah murmured, a trace of his old wicked smile lighting his face for a moment.

"Well, you missed a fabulous dinner!" Holly said. "It would have quite put you in the shade, Anne."

"I sincerely doubt that," Noah drawled again, his hand reaching out for Anne's. Deftly she avoided it— the last thing she wanted was the demoralizing touch of his hand on her flesh. Noah ignored her skittishness, moving closer with a casual grace, the closeness of his lean body lending a subtle support that she sorely needed. "Anything else earth-shattering besides the dinner?"

Holly giggled. "Of course, silly!" She waved her hand at him. Anne's ring now adorned her slender hand, the sparkle of the diamonds matching the brightness of her eyes. "We're going to have a double wedding."

"A double wedding?" Anne echoed faintly.

"Proffy just made his announcement. Not that it came as a surprise to any of us. The Merry Widow is positively preening, and I think it'll be an absolute stitch to get married together. We'll have to hurry, though, if we're going to do it before..." The words trailed off as an astonishing guilt darkened Holly's eager face. "Before I have to go back on tour," she continued firmly.

"That wasn't what you were about to say," Anne said very quietly.

"You're not psychic, Anne," Holly shot back with a little too much sharpness. "You'll help me with my wedding dress, won't you, darling? We can start planning tomorrow."

"Are you coming out to the house, too?"

"For lunch," she said, and the tension surrounding them was thick with hidden meanings.

Anne stared at her sister for a long moment. The source of the tension was logical—Wilson had made an obscenely fast switch of his affections, and heaven only knew what Noah was thinking. But there was something else going on, something she couldn't quite fathom. And she had little doubt that none of the three was about to enlighten her.

"Well," she said finally, "congratulations. I guess I'd better go find Proffy and Letitia and wish them well."

"I'll come with you," Noah said with alacrity. "We still have something to talk about."

"No." It came out a little louder than she expected, and the three of them stared at her. There was no surprise on Noah's face, only a determination that didn't augur well for her success in avoiding him.

"Yes," he said just as firmly, catching her arm in an iron grip and half dragging her down the hallway as Wilson and Holly looked on, bemused.

They were at the end of the hall when she made her move. His skin seemed to burn through the light silk of her dress, his nearness an intoxication that threatened to overwhelm her. If she didn't break free soon she'd be lost, and she didn't think she could bear the sweet, soul-destroying agony of it again.

"No," she said.

It took only a moment. Bringing her heel down sharply on his instep, she yanked her arm free, lifting her skirts and racing down the hallway. Proffy and the Merry Widow could wait—no doubt they'd be there for lunch along with the rest of her motley clan. In the meantime she needed most of all to keep out of Noah Grant's seductive reach. Her hotel room was back in the other direction, past Noah's long reach, and nothing on God's green earth would make her head back that way. Besides, she was in no mood to put up with the Merry Widow's girlish glee as she contemplated husband number three. Or would Proffy make number four? It scarcely mattered. What mattered was getting back to the comfort and safety of the house. If she left right now she could make it there in under an hour and be blissfully alone, with no intrusive family to interrupt the healing flow of the house's energy around her.

She had nothing in her evening purse but her keys and a five-dollar bill. She could only hope she'd left enough gas in the Volvo to see her home. It would be a close call.

The night air was cool against her skin, but she didn't even dare go back for her evening cape. At least her car heater was strong—she'd be warm enough before she even crossed the Delaware River.

It took all her concentration to keep from speeding down the deserted roads. Each time the needle slipped past sixty she eased up the pressure of her sandaled foot. For one thing, she could hardly afford to be stopped by the police when she didn't have her license with her; for another, the gas supply would be a near thing. She wasn't about to stop at one of the few all-night gas stations wearing that indecent silk dress—she could only nurse her gasoline supply and pray to the unseeing god of Volvos that she make it home all right.

Fate was disposed to smile on her at last. She fell into the house with a gasp of relief, leaning against the inside of the kitchen door to drink in the welcoming ambience of the ancient house.

But it failed to come. Her eyes shot open again in sudden dismay, looking about her in bewilderment. Always before the house had seemed to stretch out welcoming arms, protecting her from the cruelties of the outside world. But that protection was gone, ripped away by Noah Grant and the events of the last few weeks, and particularly the last few hours. The house was no longer her haven, her protection, her safety. It was simply a house.

It was more than she could comprehend or accept at two o'clock in the morning. Shaking her head in silent denial, she made her way up the winding stairs, down the halls that suddenly seemed so empty. It would come back, she promised herself grimly as she collapsed fully clothed on her bed and pulled a quilt around her shivering body. It had to come back, that feeling of peace and belonging. But as she shut her eyes against the sudden stinging of tears, she knew through her exhaustion that it was gone for good.

WHEN ANNE FINALLY dragged herself out of her bed late the next morning the house was still silent and deserted. Never had its beloved halls felt so empty. A long hot shower did little to restore her equilibrium, and this time when the hot water ran out prematurely her reaction was a shaky annoyance instead of her usual tolerance. The stone floors were cold beneath her feet, but nothing could destroy her pleasure in the graceful lines of the old rooms as she made her way down to the kitchen. It was still a very beautiful house, she recognized sadly as she went through the ritual of brewing a decent cup of coffee. It simply wasn't enough anymore.

By one o'clock there was still no sign of her errant family. A good thing she knew them well enough to have made quiche instead of a soufflé, she thought with a distant trace of humor, staring out into the slowly greening woodland that surrounded the old house. At times it seemed as if she had spent all her life waiting to feed her family.

She was curled up in front of the empty fireplace in the living room, having assiduously avoided the memory-ridden library for the past few weeks, when she heard several cars make their slow, tortuous way up the potholed driveway to the house. The downed oaks hadn't helped the road, either, Anne noted with distant satisfaction as she sipped her sherry. It was Harvey's, the best she could buy, and she left it out for her doubtless hung-over relatives. If there was any chance of her regaining some feeling of contentment, she was close to it now. The warmth of the sherry, the soft comfort of her oldest Levi's and the often-washed flannel shirt all contributed to a transient sense of well-being. Just how transient it was was made abundantly clear to her when Noah Grant followed her family into the room.

Ashley was definitely looking the worse for wear. His other eye had almost equaled the first in swelling and color, so that he had to make do with only a tiny amount of vision out of the narrow slit. He leaned heavily on a cane, his face so distorted from the beating that Anne wouldn't have recognized him. Proffy looked both uneasy and disapproving as his eyes met those of his elder daughter, and Holly looked downright nervous.

"No fiancés for lunch?" Anne queried brightly. "I expected both Wilson and Mrs. Morgan—there's more than enough. Although I didn't expect you." Her eyes were turned with wintry effect on the unmoved Noah.

Ashley lowered himself gingerly into a chair, stretching one leg stiffly out in front of him. "Proffy's sulking about my current condition, Annie," he drawled. "Be patient with him." He smiled faintly. "He's also scared to death of you."

Slowly Anne uncurled her bare feet. "Scared of me?" she echoed. "Why?"

"Guilty conscience, I suppose. It's a good thing I don't have a conscience myself, or I'd be feeling equally miserable. Put that sherry away, darling. It's far too tempting, and I've sworn off it."

"Why should Proffy have a guilty conscience, Ashley?" Anne inquired with a deathly calm.

"Didn't you tell her?" Noah demanded, his voice rich with horror. "You told me she knew."

"I haven't had the chance." Proffy's defense bordered on a whine.

"I'm going to call Wilson," Holly said hastily, dashing from the room. "See you at lunch."

"All right. What's going on?" Anne was surprised how level her voice could be. She could feel her world slipping away from her, and she knew it would do no good to try to catch it. She could only let it go.

Proffy continued to look guilty, refusing to say a word, and Ashley contented himself with a barely recognizable smirk. It was up to a furious Noah to tell her. Serves him right, she thought dazedly.

"We signed the papers for the house today, Annie," he said gently.

"What papers?" Still that deadly calm. She could be quite proud of herself.

Proffy finally decided to bestir himself. "We had the closing on the house this morning before we came back. That's why we're late."

"You've sold the house." She could have been discussing the luncheon menu, she thought dazedly. "To whom?"

"The Allibet Foundation. They've been looking for a suitable artists' center, centrally located between New York and Philadelphia. They'll do a marvelous job with the house, Anne, pour all the money we could never afford into it."

"I don't think that's what Anne wants to hear, Proffy," Ashley drawled, eying her out of that swollen slit. "Do you, darling?"

"No. I want to know what Noah had to do with it."

If anything, Proffy looked even more guilty, and he stared down at the carpet, once more abdicating responsibility. It was up to Noah.

"I've been negotiating with your family on behalf of the foundation. Wendell James is the chairman of the board and my wife's father. He asked me to handle this as a favor to him and I agreed." His words were clipped, expressionless.

The pain that had been strangely absent suddenly ripped through her with lightning speed. Noah saw her flinch, her mouth tremble with pain before tightening once more into a grim smile. "Well," she said in that same calm, dead voice. "I suppose that's that. I'll serve lunch." Slowly, gracefully she rose from the sofa, moving across the room without a trace of hurry, her emotions under iron control. As she passed Noah he reached out a hand toward her, then withdrew it as she turned that chill, cold face on him before continuing on her way to the kitchen.

She moved through the next hour with the liveliness of a robot, and her entire family eyed her with wary relief. She didn't take a bite of the quiche, merely pushed it around on her plate, and no one else seemed particularly hungry, either. Proffy did his best to lighten the situation with what he fondly supposed to be cheerful conversation.

"We're going to be here for another two months, Anne. That'll give us plenty of time to organize the packing, decide what we're going to take with us and what we're going to sell. Noah tells me that the foundation would be more than happy to buy whatever of the furniture we don't want to take with us. And we'll be able to have the weddings in the rose garden in mid-May. It will be beautiful by then and a fitting farewell to the house, don't you think?"

"It sounds charming," she murmured quietly.

"I'm glad you're being so reasonable about this, Anne," he said, obviously much relieved. "I told the others they were making a mountain out of a molehill. I'm only sorry it didn't work out with you and Wilson."

"Yes, it would have made things tidier," she agreed calmly.

"Listen, Anne, anything you want in this house you can have," he said earnestly, her lifelessness slowly penetrating. "The Stuart painting, the Chinese Chippendale, the Duncan Phyfe chairs. I'm sure your sister and brother will agree with me that you have more claim on these things than they do."

"Of course, Annie," Holly said in a rush. "You've always loved the Constable landscape in my bedroom. It's yours."

Anne said nothing, smiling a faint, agreeable smile.

"I'll tell you what, Anne. Why don't you rest this afternoon, and make a list of things you want to take with you? Letitia and I want you to stay with us if you like, but of course there'll be more than enough money for you to buy yourself a little condominium. Think how nice that will be—no repairs, no slogging in the mud, abundant hot water. You'll love it."

"Sure she will," Ashley drawled.

"If you can't say anything pleasant don't say it!" Proffy snapped. "Anne is taking this all very well—don't be upsetting her further."

"He's not upsetting me," Anne said gently. "And I think I will take a nap. I'm really very tired. Will you excuse me?" Without waiting for a reply she rose. Noah hadn't said more than a dozen words since the meal began, and whenever she had been forced to raise her head from her solemn perusal of her plate she would find his blue eyes on her, clouded with concern and caring. A concern and caring she knew to be completely false. She passed very close to his body, wishing she could summon the energy to tell him what she thought of him, the hatred to start throwing things at his beautiful head. But she was drained of everything, even hatred. With a faint smile in his direction, she left the room, heading down to the cellar of the old house.

She paused a moment to notice the cracked foundation walls, the moisture seeping in, the aging wiring she had just begun to replace, before heading toward the laundry area. It was fortunate she had just done several loads of laundry before leaving for Philadelphia—she would have enough to last her without making an incriminating trip up to her bedroom.

With calm, measured movements she stuffed the clothes into a clean trash bag and carried them back upstairs. The Volvo was parked just outside the kitchen door, and it took no more than three trips to fill the back seat with her clothes, her paints, an armful of books and her music. There was two thousand dollars in her savings account. She owed it to the carpenters who were still struggling with the slate roof, but this time it would be up to Proffy. He could take her share of the blood profits from the house to pay for it.

No one heard her as she stepped out into the late-spring sunshine, her sneakered feet silent on the damp spring earth, the electric coffee grinder under one arm. She could see the bright yellow heads of the daffodils lining the edge of the woods, smell the faint, heavenly scent of the hyacinths she'd planted two years ago by the kitchen window. To leave in spring was the cruelest cut of all, she thought wearily. Climbing into the Volvo, she rolled down the window to get a final whiff of spring before grinding the noisy old motor into life. And then she was off down the road, driving as fast as her car would carry her over the rutted driveway, the potholes tossing the car this way and that. When she reached the end of her mad dash down the drive her muffler fell off.

With a hysterical laugh at the absurdity of it all, she took off down the road with an unmuffled roar, unshed tears bright in her eyes.

Chapter Thirteen

Aunt Lillian was, at best, a mixed blessing. On the plus side, there was the seclusion of her small farm in southern Vermont, the security of knowing that although her family knew exactly where she was, they were far too intimidated by Aunt Lillian's legendary temper to try to interfere more than once. Anne had the space and freedom to paint, to play the piano, even to cook. Unfortunately she only painted very pretty, lavender-hued, rain-drenched landscapes, she only played and sang lilting, mournful dirges, and everything she cooked she ate, swiftly adding ten pounds to her slender frame.

The drawbacks to Aunt Lillian's hospitality were equally manifold. Lillian Westerby was, in actuality, Anne's great-aunt, her mother's father's sister. She had been a suffragette as a teenager, a flapper in the twenties, a factory worker in the forties, a civil rights worker in the fifties and sixties. In the seventies, crippled from arthritis and filled with a profound disgust at the modern hedonism, she retired to her farm to raise chickens. What she'd done instead was raise hell. She was now on the board of selectmen of the small town, and she struck terror into the heart of every bureaucrat from Brattleboro to Burlington. She enjoyed herself tremendously in her troublemaking and relished having her favorite niece join her, even if it was to nurse a broken heart. Most of all she enjoyed prying into Anne's past, exhorting her to seek a new life or, failing that, revenge. Her version of the facts was extremely garbled, since Anne steadfastly refused to discuss it, and she had to glean her information from the various disgruntled Kirklands.

"Heard the weddings went well," Aunt Lillian cackled as she wheeled herself into the kitchen one morning. By afternoon she could get around quite well with a walker, but first thing in the morning her joints were too stiff and swollen to allow her much mobility. "Got a cup of that fancy coffee of yours?"

"Sure thing." Anne slid off the stool and poured her aunt a cup.

Lillian took a deep, soulful sip. "Yes, it was a great success apparently." She eyed her niece with a sly expression. "Even if it rained on them in the rose garden."

At that Anne smiled with faint, unaccustomed malice. "Good," she murmured, biting daintily into a freshly baked croissant. "They deserved it."

"I still say we should have gone down there. After all, how often do your father and sister get married in one afternoon?"

"No, thank you." She finished the croissant in two bites, reaching for another without hesitation.

"Still angry about the house?" Lillian queried shrewdly. "I would have thought you'd realized that was no life you were living. You always struck me as the sensible one in your family."

"That's me," she said bitterly. "Sensible Anne, adrift in a family of peacocks."

Lillian watched her out of troubled eyes. "They

don't realize how much they've hurt you," she said. "You've always been a tower of strength for the bunch of them. I can't imagine they're doing very well without you."

"A tower of strength!" Anne mocked. "You must be kidding."

"Hell, no. You've been so strong all your life that the others have been happy enough to let you do everything. They're learning that they have to take some responsibility now, and it's good for them. Good for you, too."

"Sure it is."

"You never used to feel sorry for yourself, my girl," Lillian snapped. "I may have to revise my opinion of you being the strong one in your family."

"I don't feel like the strong one," Anne said quietly.

"And you never used to eat so much," Lillian continued, ignoring the little pang of pity that filled her at Anne's woebegone face. "Put that croissant down— you'll burst your jeans at this rate."

The goad had its intended effect, banishing her self-pity and replacing it with a healthy anger. Defiantly Anne shoved the entire croissant into her mouth. Lillian watched her with mixed exasperation and affection. "Though I did wonder if it's the house you're sulking about," she added sagely.

"I'm not sulking." Anne washed down the croissant with the last of her coffee. "I'm leading a very productive life."

"And what does that productive life consist of? Driving a crippled old woman around, making up depressing songs, watching sad movies on television, and crying. Heavens, I even saw you cry over a baseball game!"

"It was a very touching game," she defended herself weakly.

"And did I mention eating? I believe I did. First you won't touch a speck of food for almost a week, and then I never see you without something in your mouth or well on its way there. If I didn't know you better I'd say you were in love or pregnant."

"Not pregnant," Anne said morosely, having ascertained that fact the morning of the lachrymose baseball game.

"Thank heavens for small favors. Not that I wouldn't welcome a great-great-niece or nephew, but I don't think it's the best possible thing for you right now. So you're in love."

"What? Strong, sensible Anne in love? Don't be ridiculous."

"Tsk, tsk. That self-pity is cropping up again. Ugly emotion." Aunt Lillian shook her grizzled white head. "Not that we're not all prey to it every now and then, but it should be resisted most strenuously, Anne, dear."

Anne reached for another croissant, caught her aunt's glare, and withdrew her hand, settling for another cup of rich black coffee. Her jeans were getting a little snug, and she wasn't in the mood for clothes shopping.

"So are you still in love with that dull stick your sister married? What was his name? Winston?"

"Wilson." Anne allowed herself a small sigh at the absurdity of the thought. "No, I'm not still in love with Wilson. I doubt I ever was. I hope he and Holly will be very happy."

"That's good. You deserve someone with a little more fire than that stuffy old banker."

"Lawyer," Anne corrected, and the word sent an unexpected shaft of pain through her.

"Almost as bad as a banker. I hold no brief for lawyers," Lillian announced, chuckling to herself. The terrible joke brought a fresh searing through Anne's heart, as unwillingly she imagined Noah's diabolical appreciation. "You know, I'd hate to think of you settling for anything less than you deserve," Lillian continued, oblivious to Anne's flinch.

"It doesn't appear that I will."

"Not if you keep on this way. You've got to do more with your life than sit around baby-sitting an old woman and eating yourself into a stupor. You either have to go after your lawyer and tell him you want him, or forget him and find someone new. You can't spend the rest of your life moping."

"I told you I couldn't care less about Wilson!" Anne shot back, reaching for a croissant.

Lillian smacked her hand, and the croissant crumbled into a flaky pile onto the plate. "I'm talking about the other one, you ninny! Noah, isn't that his name?"

Anne stared at her, openmouthed. "Who told you?"

"Who do you think? You're a big-mouthed family. Proffy, Holly, even Ashley made sure I knew all about it. I just wish you'd tell me your version of the story. Their three versions were confusing, to say the least."

"What's the use? It's all ancient history by now." Very daintily she licked her fingertips and picked up a few stray crumbs from the plate.

"It doesn't have to be."

"Darling Aunt Lillian, I'd really rather not discuss it." With her usual lithe grace Anne slipped off the kitchen stool, carrying her refilled coffee mug with her. "I'm going to finish this out on the porch."

"Put on some shoes!" Lillian shouted after her. "It's

still cool out there. I don't want to have to nurse you through pneumonia along with your broken heart."

"I do not have a broken heart!" Anne yelled as the screen door slammed shut behind her.

Lillian, never content to let a young upstart have the last word, wheeled herself over to the door. "And what do you have planned today, missy?"

"I'm going to repair the east wall of the stables. The bottom boards have been resting in the mud and they're rotted through."

"You're the best carpenter this place has seen in many a year," Lillian admitted grudgingly. "Not to mention plumber and electrician. You ought to do something with all that experience."

"Like what? I can't really see me building condominiums in Bennington," Anne said, digging her toes into the cool spring earth beneath her.

Lillian's eyes softened for a moment as they surveyed her niece's bowed head. "We'll see. I wouldn't be surprised if something could be found for you to do."

"I have plenty to do. When I'm finished with the wall, I'm going to fix the overhead light in the pantry, and then I'll probably work on my music for a while."

"Saints preserve us!" Lillian moaned. "That song is enough to make a Pollyanna slash her wrists."

Anne grinned over her shoulder. "Okay, I'll spend the rest of the afternoon eating."

"Strong is one thing, Anne Kirkland, stubborn is another," Lillian grumbled as she wheeled herself away.

Anne leaned back, sipping her rapidly cooling coffee, contemplating Lillian's words with a distant interest. The strong one in the family, was she? She had never felt less strong in her entire life. She felt weak and miserable and unhappy, and totally incapable of doing anything to stir herself from the miasma that had settled over her when she left New Jersey.

Even the glories of the late Vermont spring couldn't shake the massive depression that had engulfed her. The smell of the damp earth, the daffodils poking their heads through the fresh green grass, the warmth of the sun on her shoulders, all should have contributed to the easing of the hard knot that lodged between her breasts. But they brought no more than a faint, fleeting smile. Lillian was right, of course. She could only spend so much time hidden away in Vermont, keeping herself busy with a dozen useless projects. But she still couldn't decide where she could go, what she could do.

Edmund Jolles had begged her to return to the small publishing house in Bucks County whenever she felt like it, had also promised her glowing recommendations if she wanted to find an editing job elsewhere. But still she sat, eating too much, singing dirges—much to Lillian's disgust.

Because, of course, Lillian was absolutely right. Despite Anne's years of possessive love for her pre-Revolutionary War farmhouse, what really tore her apart was Noah Grant's betrayal. The loss of her home and her family's deviousness were nothing compared to the loss of Noah Grant.

Not that she'd ever had him, she mused. Nialla had him firmly chained to her memory, chained by guilt and love, and Anne couldn't begin to guess which was stronger. From the very first Noah had warned her, as obliquely as possible, that he was nothing but trouble. Why hadn't she believed him? Why had she made the incredibly stupid mistake of falling in love with him anyway? And why couldn't she find even a scrap of comfort in the peace surrounding her?

Sighing, she drained her coffee, rose and went in search of more croissants.

NOAH GRANT SHOULD HAVE been enjoying his freedom. He was walking away from the law firm that had employed him for the last six years, the firm that had just offered him a partnership if he'd stay, that had treated him as well as anyone could expect to be treated. He was walking away without a backward glance or a single regret, heading toward a future that was, at best, nebulous.

He still couldn't quite figure why he thought being a public defender in a thriving Connecticut city would be any more rewarding than finding tax dodges for obscenely wealthy corporations. Maybe he was just nostalgic for the past, for the year he'd spent doing the same work for the City of New York. He'd had a sense of purpose then, a feeling of involvement that had been lacking for too long. He wanted that feeling back; he wanted life back. He'd been only half alive for too long, half of him in the grave with Nialla.

Nialla was gone now, had been since that night at the Elgin Hotel less than a month ago. No longer did she hover at his shoulder, dark eyes reproaching his anger. He remembered her with love and sorrow, the rage absent now, but she was fading fast, not much more than a sweet memory.

He had a new ghost now, one that was going to prove much harder to exorcise. He had steeled himself for the Kirkland weddings, determined to back Anne into a corner and force her to listen to him. He had been in a white-knuckled panic during the drive down to Lambertville, and all for nothing. Anne was still gone, and it had taken nothing short of threats to get her address from the disapproving Wilson.

Not that it had done him any good. The old dragon who had taken her in steadfastly refused to put her on the phone, to relay his messages, to give him any help at all. It wasn't the slightest bit encouraging to realize that Lillian was sympathetic and longing to be helpful. Her opinions were strong on the subject—Anne needed time and distance, and she didn't need to be bothered before she could make up her mind what she wanted.

It took him a while before he realized that Lillian was willing, even eager to be an ally. But only on her terms. In the meantime the summer stretched in front of him, bleak and hot and empty without her. His time would be filled with starting the new job, dealing with the vagaries of apartment life while his house was being built. And when the weekends proved too long he would go out to the ocean and work on the rambling cottage his architect brother had designed for him. His hours would be filled with activity, and his life would be empty.

He could always ignore Lillian's warnings and drive up to Vermont. There were times when he thought that if he didn't see Anne soon he'd go crazy. But his regret always stopped him.

When it came right down to it, he had a hell of a lot of nerve, he told himself with weary self-disgust. He'd spent the three years since Nialla's death dodging commitments, dodging love. He'd tricked Anne, in effect lied to her, and offered her nothing. And now that he'd changed his mind, decided maybe he could offer her more than just a short, sweet affair, he had the colossal gall to hope she'd welcome him with open arms.

He didn't deserve her. And the least he could give her was the time she needed. If in the end she decided to listen to him, it would still take her a long time to forgive him his betrayal in taking the house from her. If she ever would. And if he had to suffer while she came to terms with it, then that was his deserved penance. But it seemed to be taking forever.

"YOU'RE GOING TO HAVE to leave," Lillian announced abruptly several nights later. Anne looked up from the lugubrious Russian novel she was wading through with a question in her shadowed eyes.

"Driven you nuts, have I?" she questioned calmly, trying to still the little spurt of panic that clutched at her stomach. She wasn't ready to make decisions, to face the real world as yet. She knew she had to, sooner or later. But later would have been much more appealing.

"I've survived worse," her aunt replied dryly. "No, it's you I'm thinking of. Your family is descending, almost en masse, to try to drag you back to New Jersey. Apparently the task of packing up a century's worth of accumulations is more than Proffy and Holly can manage."

"And they want me to come back and help?"

"Knowing your family, I expect they want you to come back and do it all," Lillian replied. "Holly said they were going to throw themselves on your mercy."

Anne snorted, closing the turgid novel with a snap. "That's like asking someone to assist at his own execution."

"Well, you can't really blame them, can you? After all, you've never told them no before. They think you're Superwoman, with nerves and heart of steel. It's only natural they think they can talk you into anything without you doing more than blinking."

"Not this time."

"So I told them. But they're coming anyway, and I think you should be gone when they get here."

"Is that who's been calling all the time?" she asked, not really curious.

Lillian smiled faintly, refusing to answer. "When can you be ready to leave?"

"Whenever," Anne replied with a shrug. "I'll have to decide where to go, though."

"That's the best part." Lillian looked quite pleased with herself. "I've been busy the past few days. I've found you a job."

"I don't need a job."

"You do, and you're going to take it. I went to a lot of trouble arranging this for you, and I'm not going to have you turn up your nose at this and make me look like a fool," Lillian snapped. "Besides, it's right up your alley."

"I'm not interested in editing at the moment."

"The hell with editing. I've gotten you a construction job."

"What?"

"A friend of mine is building a house on a stretch of oceanfront property in Connecticut. It's a simple, almost experimental affair. Lots of passive solar heating and other such newfangled ideas. He wanted to build it himself but things have gotten a little out of hand with his work. He's got a new job, so he's had to hire helpers. You'd be working with Sam Oliver during the week, and the owner would come out and putter on the weekends."

"You must be kidding."

"Absolutely not. I had the devil's own time convincing Sam to hire you. He usually makes do with a couple of teenagers during the summer, but his usual boy has gone into the army and he's been having trouble finding someone else. He said he was willing to give you a chance."

"What about the owner? How does he feel about women's work?" Despite her initial dismay the idea was beginning to appeal to her.

"Oh, he doesn't care—he leaves it up to Sam. I don't think you'd even run into him."

A sudden absurd suspicion flared into Anne's admittedly paranoid brain. "Who's the owner?"

"Fellow by the name of Matthews," Lillian lied without batting an eye. "You'll like it down in Wilbury, Anne. I've visited when I was younger—a perfect little New England village, looks more like Maine than Connecticut. And Matthews is building right by the sea—you can take a swim on your lunch break."

"You think I won't do it," Anne challenged the older woman.

Lillian smiled serenely. "I don't know anymore what you'll do. You'd be crazy not to jump at the chance. You could room at the local boardinghouse and have a peaceful summer doing good hard physical labor that will leave you too tired to brood. Get a good tan and a feeling of accomplishment, and then come fall you can look at life from a different perspective."

"You take a lot for granted, Aunt Lil."

"I was counting on your still having a lick of gumption beneath that mournful exterior. Was I right?"

Anne hesitated for only a moment longer. There had been no word from Noah, no message. Not that she'd expected anything, she maintained stoutly. But an apology, no matter how feeble, would have been something. Lillian's badgering was well founded—she had spent far too much time mourning a lost cause.

"You were right, Aunt Lil." Getting up from her perch on the comfortable old sofa, Anne crossed the room and pressed a kiss against her aunt's papery cheek. "Thank you, Lillian. I'll miss you."

The old lady's eyes misted. "I'll miss you too, darling. You write me from that place. And don't let Sam Oliver push you around. He knows his stuff—you couldn't work for a better man. But he has a tendency to be a mite autocratic. Not to mention sexist."

"Sexist? Then why in the world is he hiring a woman construction worker?"

Lillian grinned. "Because the fool man never could say no to me," she said with deep satisfaction.

Anne stretched to her full height. "Well, whatever his misgivings, I'll make sure he doesn't regret this. I think you may have saved my life, Aunt Lil. I'm going to love this."

Chapter Fourteen

Love was not the operative word, Anne thought later of her first few weeks as a laborer. Exhaustion, frustration, annoyance, discomfort and a rough satisfaction were more accurate. Sam Oliver had proven to be cut from the same cloth as Aunt Lillian—opinionated, irascible, with a warm heart beneath that grumpy exterior. He was also an incredible craftsman, and his demands on Anne, even from the first, were phenomenal. Every nail had to be nailed at the exact angle called for, every measurement had to be done three times at least to be sure of its exactness. Even with something as fast-moving and rudimentary as framing the rambling modern house was accomplished with a care for details. Anne both dreaded and anticipated the more exacting finishing work when it came along. If Sam would put up with her. And despite his vociferous complaints, she could tell that on occasion he was not displeased with her work.

The first week was a disaster. Her stamina for the rough physical labor of hauling two-by-fours around was limited to four hours a day. By the second week she found she could push herself to eight hours, and by the end of the month her pace for the twelve-hour working days Sam favored almost equaled his.

Her soft, lean arms grew lovely muscles, her pale skin first burned in the bright early summer sunshine, then turned a deep golden tan. The worst part of the whole experience, Anne mused, was early June, when the mosquitoes were at their worst. She was roofing then, the hot sun beating down on her, and all the odoriferous Woodsman's Fly Dope couldn't keep the little monsters from feeding on her succulent flesh. They left Sam's leathery hide completely alone—"too tough for 'em," he said smugly. That night when she looked into the mirror, her face blistered from the sunburn, swollen from a thousand and one mosquito bites, she burst into tears. But a good long soak in a baking-soda-filled bath and a sound night's sleep, and she went back to the roof with the resignation of an early Christian martyr, determined to do her duty no matter what the cost.

June slipped into July, and the house began to assume some shape. Sam and Anne would work all week long—framing, sheathing, roofing—and then have the weekend off. Anne grew to hate those weekends. For the first part of them she was content to walk along the tourist-crowded streets of the little town, to hike along the ocean, to lie in the sun and read something a bit more cheerful than Russian novels. But as Sunday lengthened and her body rested, the events of the spring would return and she recalled with a pang of regret Noah Grant's laughing blue eyes in his dark Gypsy face. She never slept well on Sunday nights, and when she did her dreams were of Noah and she would wake, bereft once more.

Her least favorite job on the whole house was the wall of windows facing out toward the sea. Each sliding window had weighed in at several hundred pounds, and despite her newly formed muscles she was exhausted by the third one. "I sure the hell hope Matthews is going to appreciate this house," she said, panting, one Friday afternoon late in July as they settled the window into place. "It's going to be hard enough giving this up after we've worked so hard on it. I just hope he has the sense to love it, too."

"Pretty possessive, aren't you?" Sam drawled, tapping the corner of the window against the frame with just the right amount of force. "You forget that he comes and works on it every weekend."

"I haven't forgotten. His work isn't as good as yours is—I can always recognize anything he's done."

"Nobody's as good as me," he replied, a calm statement of fact. "Not even you, young lady. But he does a good enough job, for all that." Which was high praise indeed, given Sam's high standards. Praise that even a jealous Anne had to admit was deserved. "If you're going to keep building houses, you're going to have to let go, Annie."

"Even if I don't build houses I'm going to have to learn to let go," she said darkly.

"We all have to, sooner or later," Sam agreed, setting the window in place with a few short perfect taps of his hammer. "You want to help me with the last one, or could you use a trip into town about now?"

"A trip into town would be wonderful. I'm out of Coke."

"You and that bellywash. Why can't you make do with coffee like me?" he demanded.

"Because mediocre coffee isn't worth drinking, and the stuff in your thermos would be deeply flattered to even be called bad. What do you need in town?"

"We're about ready for kitchen cabinets. And unless

you want to try your hand at building them you'll have to go pick out some ready-mades at the home-building center."

"Could I build them?" she asked curiously.

"You could. But they're a pain in the butt. I won't do 'em anymore, and if I were you I'd settle for store-bought. They've got some nice ones down there—take your pick."

"But doesn't the owner want to choose? Or his wife?"

"Ain't got a wife. At least, not yet. That's why he's building this house, to try and win her. And I guess he figures that one woman's opinion is as good as another's in these matters."

"That kind of attitude is hardly going to endear him to the lady in question," Anne observed wryly. "You sure you don't need any more help?"

"Nope. I'm just going to finish hanging the bedroom door and then head on home. You do the same—don't bother coming back after you place the order. You've had a long week."

Anne stretched her weary muscles, a slow, luxurious stretch like a cat's. "True enough. I enjoyed it, though."

Sam snorted inelegantly. "Glutton for punishment, I'd say. Get on with you." Anne was halfway out the door when his rough voice called her back.

"By the way, young lady," he said, and she waited for the ax to fall. He only used that tone of voice when he was about to point out some incredibly stupid mistake. "You did a damned fine job on the windows."

A slow grin lit her face at his unaccustomed praise, and she surveyed the wall of windows with unrestrained pride. "I did, didn't I?" she replied, in a perfect mimic of Sam's laconic tones.

He gave a bark of laughter. "See you Monday, squirt. Seven o'clock and no later."

"Yes, sir!"

As she pulled into the home-building center she gave her yellow Volvo an affectionate pat on its peeling dashboard. It had served her well the last few months, once she'd replaced the muffler. Even now it was still a little noisier than she would have liked, but she accepted the fact that its engine would herald her appearance. She was already somewhat of a conversation piece in the small seaside town, she realized, casting a quick, untroubled glance at her reflection in the rearview mirror. Her long black hair was caught in a single braid down her back, though the heat and humidity had combined with the day's exertions to leave a halo of wisps around her face. With her deep tan, slightly hollow cheeks and straight, strong nose she looked like an exotic Indian. Until one took in the deep-green eyes, the baggy carpenter jeans that rode low on her hips, and the sleeveless jersey that exhibited an expanse of long, muscled arms. She did love her muscles, she realized with a sigh. If she ever went back to a desk job she would miss the exercise.

She didn't take long in her choice of cabinets. Matthews had more than enough money, and while the rustic oceanside house was in no way elegant, no corners had been cut, either. She chose solid oak cabinets with a raised panel door, consulting the little plan she'd drawn up earlier several times as she chose the pieces that appealed to her. Too bad if the future Mrs. Matthews didn't like to cook—she was getting a food preparation center that would hold a mixer, food processor and blender within a modicum of space. Too bad if she preferred a single sink—Anne picked out the champagne of double sinks, with every accoutrement a dedicated cook could ask for. The only thing that stumped her was the countertops—she couldn't decide whether she wanted Formica in a nice primary color with a matte finish or solid wood butcher block.

"Why don't you go ahead and send this out on Monday and I'll let you know about the countertops," she said finally, signing her name to the order with a scrawl.

"That's the old Matthews place, right?" The teen-aged clerk staggered back under the weight of the first cabinet, and it was all Anne could do not to come to his aid. Sternly she repressed the urge, waiting until he dropped it with an ominous thud. She knew how fragile male pride could be at that age, and she'd always had a fondness for that particular clerk.

"That's right," she said pleasantly. "We'll be there to give you a hand unloading."

"Oh, I won't need any help," he said righteously, mopping his sweating brow. "How's the house coming?"

He almost, but not quite, could have been her son, Anne mused, but the look in his eye was faintly swaggering. Maybe she should have helped him with the cabinet—it would have cooled his ardor a bit. She gave him her easiest smile. "It's beautiful," she said. "Another few weeks and we should be just about done." She didn't like to think about it, didn't want to think about leaving her house by the ocean and the small town of Wilbury that she had come to love.

"Hey, that's great. I can't wait to see it. Is it a real palace?"

"Actually, it's quite simple. Very pleasing aesthetically." *Almost too pleasing,* she thought mournfully. "But nothing fancy."

The boy shook his head. "Sure am glad old Matthews decided to sell. It's been great for business and it's brought some welcome strangers into town." His puppy-dog glance left no doubt as to who the welcome stranger was.

Anne smiled uneasily. "You're very kind. Now, I think I'd better—" Suddenly the rest of his words penetrated. "Did you say old Matthews decided to sell? When was this?" Perhaps his lady had turned him down after all. Perhaps Anne wouldn't have to lose the second house she'd poured her life and blood and soul into. So far she had steadfastly refused to accept any part of the money from the sale of the old farmhouse. Her share came to over a hundred thousand dollars—she had no idea what Matthews would charge, but that would surely be enough to cover a goodly share of it. She could...

The boy shattered her dreams a second later. "He sold his place three years ago. It's taken this long to get the old ruins torn down and the new house started. It's a lucky thing Mr. Grant finally got around to it—that place was dangerous, sitting around unused, with the floors caving in and all. After all, there aren't any neighbors around, and kids used to go out there all the time. To...you know...neck and all." He smirked lasciviously, but Anne was beyond noticing.

"Grant?" she echoed, her voice a hoarse croak. "Noah Grant?"

"Sure. Didn't you even know whom you were working for?" The boy stared at her in amazement.

"I do now," she said grimly, turning on her heel and stalking toward the door.

"Hey!" the boy called after her. "What time do you want these delivered?"

Anne's reply was succinct, obscene and quite loud before she sailed out the door, slamming it violently.

How could he have done it to me again, she demanded

in white-hot rage as her battered Volvo tore down the road. Did he get some sort of perverse pleasure in using her, making a fool of her? Or maybe, worst of all, he felt sorry for her. He carried such a burden of guilt already, maybe he simply added her to it, drumming up this job as therapy and to absolve himself of his responsibility in ripping her house from her.

Well, this time he wasn't going to get away with it. Hadn't Aunt Lillian suggested revenge? Though Aunt Lillian's part in this was none too pure, she realized belatedly. She'd been in on the setup all along, sending her straight into the lion's den without a second's hesitation. The traitor.

Well, revenge might not be sweet, but it would be infinitely satisfying. Noah Grant was not going to live in the house she had sweated over, wasn't going to bring one of his New York sweeties to live in her house.

The Volvo raced at forty miles an hour down the rutted road that led to the house. In her red-hot fury Anne heard several pieces of metal fall off with a crash, and her foot pressed even harder on the accelerator. She wasn't going to let second thoughts stop her this time. She'd leave Noah Grant a clear message as to what she thought of him.

Sam had left long ago by the time she pulled up with a screech. She slammed the car into first and wrenched out the key, stalking from the car like a hunter stalking its prey. And even through her haze of anger she recognized the beauty of the house as it stood there in the late afternoon sunlight. The cedar shingles were stained a light gray; the row of windows reflected the setting sunlight with a rosy glow. For a moment Anne hesitated, tears of rage and pain bright in her eyes.

Give it a minute or two, she ordered herself, trying for a semblance of calm. *Make sure you want to do it.*

She started off down the beach, half walking, half running, trying to drive the demons of anger and hurt from her heart. She ran until she dropped, sinking into the sand, her breath coming in short, deep gasps, her heart pounding. She lay there for a long, long time, listening to the sound of the ocean lapping on the beach and the slow, steady pounding of her heart, her eyes following the trail of the sun as it dipped slowly in the west.

It took her a lot longer to walk back to the house than it had taken her to run from it, and as she walked her determination crystallized. She was going to take a rock and smash every one of those windows she'd worked so hard on. It didn't matter that it was her own handiwork she was destroying; indeed, she couldn't have brought herself to hurt either Sam's careful work or even Noah's weekend projects. She only had the right to destroy her own efforts, and destroy them she would, with a fine crashing of glass.

There were stones piled in the living room, waiting for the mason to build the massive fireplace that was the heart of the house. Her sneakered feet were silent as they bounded up the steps to the balcony that surrounded the house on three sides. The house was dark and silent in the twilight, all of Sam's tools put away with his customary care and neatness. Forcing herself to move forward with careful deliberation, she picked up a good-sized rock and moved to face the wall of windows.

The house sat facing southwest on a spit of land jutting into the ocean, and the setting sun reflected on the sea in front of her, gilding the water with a fiery glow. It would be a beautiful room for Noah and his memories, she thought bitterly. He could lie there in front of the fire with whatever short-term fling accompanied him,

watching the ever-changing ocean through the expanse
of windows. She hefted the rock in one hand, staring
mesmerized out at the ocean. And then she let it fall
out of numb fingers. She sank down on the plywood
subfloor and dropped her head in her hands.

"I knew you couldn't do it." Noah's voice came
from directly behind her.

Anne's back stiffened and slowly she raised her
head. "How did you know?" she asked in a conversa-
tional, if somewhat hoarse, voice. "I didn't know it
myself."

"In some ways I know you better than you know
yourself." She felt him kneel down beside her, and she
kept her face staring out at the ocean, frightened to
look at him, frightened of the overwhelming emotions
that swept over her—anger, betrayal, regret and love,
all tied up in a jumble that left her hopelessly confused.

She could see his long legs stretched out beside her,
clad in a pair of faded corduroys. He was wearing an old
pair of running shoes that had definitely seen better
days. What would his face look like if she turned to see
him, she wondered. Better wait until it was darker. It
wasn't so much the problem of her seeing him, great as
it was. She already knew every inch of his body, had it
emblazoned into her memory. No, even more dangerous would be his knowing blue eyes looking into hers,
all vulnerable with love and longing. She would just as
soon keep that from him for as long as possible. He was
right—at times he did know her better than she knew
herself.

"I've missed you, Annie," he said, and she gritted
her teeth.

"I'm sure you did," she replied evenly, tonelessly.
"And of course there's no need to ask where I've been.
Aunt Lillian must have been more than helpful."

"Don't blame her—it's not her fault I talked her into helping me."

She couldn't stop herself; she had to turn at that. Immediately she regretted it. His face was lean and strong in the waning sunlight, his eyes glowing with a blue intensity that took her breath away. And his mouth, that beautiful mouth that knew so well how to give her pleasure, was parted slightly, waiting for her.

Quickly she scrambled to her feet, moving out of his reach. "I'm sure you were very persuasive," she said bitterly. "I know just how persuasive you can be."

"That's not fair," he shot back, jumping to his feet in one fluid move. She backed farther away, and he ran an exasperated hand through his curly mop of hair. She could see strands of gray in the black curls, gray that hadn't been there last time she'd seen him. "Don't be afraid of me, Annie," he added in a gentler tone. "I'm not going to hurt you."

"That's right, you're not. Not ever again." She headed for the door, but he was there ahead of her, his tall figure blocking the exit.

"Are you going to listen to me?" he demanded hoarsely.

"No."

"Don't be ridiculous, Annie. You're acting like a child!" he shot back angrily, all his well-planned explanations vanishing in a burst of frustrated temper.

"That's my prerogative," she said sweetly. "And you can't keep me here. There are five different doors to outside, and I can reach one of them before you can stop me. Not that you should want to. You've accomplished what you set out to do."

"And what did I set out to do, Annie? What have I accomplished?"

"Why, you appeased your conscience and got your house built at the same time. Very efficient, if I do say so. And I can assure you, I'm a lot better off than I was three months ago. I've resigned myself to the loss of the house, resigned myself to—"

"To the loss of me?" he questioned softly.

"I never had you to lose," she replied flatly, ignoring the searing pain that swept through her when he looked at her like that. "Why did you do this, Noah? Why did you trick me?"

"I owed you a house," he said stiffly. "I helped take one from you. I thought I could give you one in return."

"I don't need your help, Noah, or your condescension. You can finish your house by yourself and live in it with your guilt and your memories." She started for the door, but his voice, rich and vibrant and unbearably seductive, stopped her.

"I only want to live in it with you," he said.

She turned very slowly, halfway across the room from him, determined not to move closer. "This is a small house, Noah. I don't think there's room for the three of us."

"Nialla's gone, Annie. Laid to rest, as she deserved to be long ago. There's only me here, waiting for you."

She stood very still. She wasn't going to settle for crumbs, for half measures after all this time. Her family thought she was strong, and she was about to prove them right. She was strong enough to make it without him. It would hurt, it would hurt like hell, but she could do it if she had to. No, she couldn't, she thought suddenly. To hell with pride. She took a small, symbolic step toward his waiting figure. "What do you want from me, Noah?"

Slowly he moved toward her in long, measured

strides, and firmly she held her ground. "I have no right to ask you, Annie love," he said. "I want you to marry me and live with me in this house. But you're right, it's too small for three. I have to be honest with you. I don't want children. It's wrong of me to ask you to be with me anyway, but I can't help myself."

"Why don't you want children?" She kept her voice level with an effort.

"Because I'd be too afraid of losing you." He was standing directly in front of her, and the heat from his body radiated outward, penetrating her bones, which had been so cold for so long. "I love you, Annie, and I can't live without you. I should have left you alone, let you marry Wilson and have lots of babies, but I couldn't. Please, Annie, stay with me." There was just the faint hint of a break in his voice, and she melted.

He could have told her anything, put any restrictions on their relationship, and she would have given in. Without hesitation she consigned all her babies to the four winds, moving another step toward his lean, waiting figure, the tension in his body pulsing like a highly strung wire.

"You want to marry me?" she said doubtfully, not quite believing him.

He made no further move toward her, content to let her come to him. "As soon as possible. I'm tired of being celibate," he said lightly, a small hint of a smile flashing across his face.

"Celibate? The great lover celibate?" she scoffed.

"If you don't believe me ask your sister. I haven't slept with anyone since that night in Philadelphia."

"Goodness, you must love me," she breathed, a hint of laughter in her voice.

His hands reached out then to catch her shoulders, drawing her slowly against his lean body, and there was an answering glint in his eyes. "I do," he whispered, his lips brushing hers with a slow, tantalizing pressure she had thought never to feel again. "And you love me, don't you, Annie?"

"Do I?" she murmured beneath his mouth, and in reward his strong white teeth bit into her lower lip.

"Witch," he whispered. "You've already told me so."

"When?" Somehow her arms had slid around his waist, her hands trailing up under the cotton knit shirt to explore the flesh that had been denied her for so long.

"That night in Philadelphia. I realize a gentleman shouldn't pay any attention to words uttered in the throes of passion, but then, I never was a gentleman." He'd managed to pull her top free from the loose jeans, and as his mouth still traced tantalizing little kisses around her lips his hands were deftly pulling the shirt up her torso.

"You said a few things at the time," she protested huskily as she pulled back to allow him to draw the shirt over her head.

"Then why didn't you believe me?" He buried his face against her full, soft breasts, his mouth seeking and finding one aroused bud beneath the wisp of lavender bra.

"A lady doesn't pay attention to words uttered in the throes of passion," she echoed innocently, then gasped as he pulled her closer against him, his heated maleness pressing against her soft hips.

"I think we'd better believe each other," he groaned against her cheek, his hands reaching down to unfasten the loose carpenter's pants.

"If you think we're going to make love on the floor here you've got another think coming," she threatened him sternly, even as she aided him in stepping out of the jeans.

"Why not?" He pulled the knit shirt over his head and tossed it in the corner, exposing his beautiful bronzed torso to her hungry gaze. *It had been so damned long.* Unable to resist herself, she slid her hands through the fine mesh of hair that drifted over his muscles.

"Because plywood subflooring is full of splinters," she replied in a low groan. "Unless you want to be on the bottom."

He looked out into the gathering nightfall. "Sand isn't a lot better." Her hands were already on the zipper of his corduroy pants.

"I agree," she whispered, sliding the pants down his narrow hips. "What are we going to do?"

"Well, we do have to seal the bargain, don't we?" he murmured, leaning down for his mouth to capture the rosy-tipped breast that the removal of her bra had exposed.

"What bargain?" she echoed dazedly.

"You're going to marry me, aren't you?" He caught the other breast, and a low, agonized wail escaped her breathlessly parted lips. His hand reached down between her legs, teasing her unmercifully, and she parted them willingly.

"Yes," she moaned, no longer sure what she was saying yes to.

Gently she found herself pressed up against the wall, his hands still firm and arousing on her heated flesh. "No splinters in Sheetrock, are there?" he whispered in her ear, his hand driving her to distraction.

Wordlessly she shook her head, her arms around his shoulders, her face buried in his neck. "Please, Noah," she whispered breathlessly. "I need you."

"And I need you. I can't wait for a bed, Annie."

And he levered forward, filling her with one deep, strong thrust, the force of his body lifting her in the air as the wall supported her back.

Instinctively she wrapped her long legs around his as his large, strong hands cupped her buttocks. All she could do was cling to him, arms and legs wrapped tight around his straining body, as he moved within her, the rhythm steady, irregular and then overwhelming. There was no room for the passion to build—it was already well beyond fever pitch. As she drew him ever deeper she could feel her body clench around him, feel the spasms ripple through her as she sobbed against the smoothness of his shoulder. And then he joined her in that midnight darkness, thrusting into her as he pressed her up against the wall.

Together they collapsed on the floor, his body cushioning hers, oblivious to the danger of splinters. His hands were infinitely gentle on her fevered flesh, his voice full of words of praise and love and commitment. Closing her eyes, she flowed against him, home at last. For a moment the question of birth control reared its ugly head; then she banished it. He had done nothing about it, she had done nothing about it. It was too late now—they would just have to be more careful in the future. She opened her eyes to meet his soft, almost reverent gaze. "I do love you, you know," she whispered.

And he smiled, that dazzlingly sweet Gypsy smile that he reserved for her alone. "I know," he said, and kissed her again.

"HOW ARE YOU DOING, Annie?" Elena Mendoza Richardson leaned over her friend, concern in her warm dark eyes as she placed a gentle hand on Annie's hugely rounded belly. "Won't be long now."

A fine sheen of sweat covered Anne's face, but she managed to smile up at her old friend. "I don't suppose you could perform a cesarean in the hallway? It's pretty bad."

Sadly Elena shook her head. "Don't worry, one of the operating rooms will be free in a few moments. It's a shame you didn't take Lamaze classes—it would help you through the pains. Your husband might help even more."

"Don't." The word came out on seven syllables as the next pain caught her. "It seemed a waste of time when we knew I had to go in for a planned c-section."

"Not to mention the fact that you had nobody to go with you." Elena frowned. "You should have at least attended a few classes. There was always the chance you'd go into labor before the date we set."

"Well, it happened." She managed a weak grin. "And I'm just fine, I promise you."

"Then where's your damned husband? It's his baby you're having, not just your own."

"There's a lot more involved that you're not aware of," Anne said wearily. "This baby wasn't planned."

"So what? I'm sure half the babies I deliver aren't planned, and the fathers stick by their wives anyway. We allow husbands in the operating room now, Anne, as long as the wife is awake. He could be with you."

"You don't understand, Elena. He's afraid I'm going to die."

"If I weren't so insulted I'd laugh. Does he think I'm a complete charlatan? I'm not about to let my best friend die in childbirth."

"Elena, his first wife died because she was pregnant. He's terrified that I will, too. The fact that I had to have a cesarean was more than he could stand," Anne explained with an attempt at calm, even as another pain twisted her body. "It's not because he doesn't love me enough; he loves me too much to be here."

"Humph," Elena sniffed, unconvinced. "Give me your hand."

Blindly Anne reached out, clutching her friend's strong, capable hand with a grip that could have broken bones with a weaker woman. "It's been a hell of a nine months, Elena," she said, sighing. "Every time he's looked at me he buries me; every time I felt a twinge he'd go into a panic. I've got Wilson and Holly pouring cognac down his throat to try to keep him calm."

"Where is he?" Elena had a light in her brown eyes.

"I don't know. Holly said he took off into the night when they wheeled me away. I only wish I didn't have to worry about him. This—" Another ripple of pain stopped her breath for a moment. "This is distracting enough."

"Operating room seven is ready, Dr. Richardson," a voice announced, and Anne smiled a wan, relieved smile.

"Are you sure you want to be awake for this, Annie?" Elena questioned.

"Of course I do. After nine months I don't want to have to wait a minute longer than I have to to see my baby."

She heard the noise distantly as she was wheeled into the operating room. Elena had insisted on a small amount of Demerol to take the edge off the pain, and the bright lights of the room gave a curious haze to everything. Loud voices were arguing behind her, but the words all blurred together. The spinal anesthetic was beginning to take hold, but not enough to blot out the next swath of pain that stretched across her. The drugs had eased her inhibitions enough for her to let out a loud, uninhibited yell.

"Be quiet!" Elena said crossly, and Anne bit her lip. "Not you, Annie," she reassured her, patting her hand. "That fool man."

They were draping her belly and washing it with bright orange liquid when another pain came, this one milder than the earlier ones. The anesthetic must be taking place. "You won't cut me until I'm numb, will you?" she asked meekly.

"I wish someone here would trust me," Elena announced plaintively to the world in general.

Another jumble of voices. The pains in her stomach were easing, and the endless painting of orange finally stopped. And then one more contraction, this one strong enough to break through the anesthetic. "Elena," she gasped, and felt a strong, calloused hand envelop her own. She didn't even have to turn her head. "Noah," she breathed. "Thank God."

"If you're all quite ready," Elena said sarcastically, "I would like to get this baby born."

"We're ready," Noah said, his voice steady, his hand clutching hers tightly.

Anne smiled up at him. "We're ready," she echoed. He moved down to put his head by hers, never relinquishing his grip on her, as together they turned to watch in the mirror.

A FEW HOURS LATER Holly sent a telegram to Ashley Kirkland, care of the Sangre de Cristos Monastery in New Mexico.

ANNIE GAVE BIRTH TO BABY GIRL LILLIAN THIS A.M. MOTHER AND DAUGHTER DOING FINE, FATHER STILL RECOVERING. MUCH LOVE, HOLLY.

EYE OF THE STORM

MAURA SEGER

A powerful portrayal of the events of World War II in the Pacific, *Eye of the Storm* is a riveting story of how love triumphs over hatred. In this, the first of a three book chronicle, Army nurse Maggie Lawrence meets Marine Sgt. Anthony Gargano. Despite military regulations against fraternization, they resolve to face together whatever lies ahead.... Also known by her fans as Laurel Winslow, Sara Jennings, Anne MacNeil and Jenny Bates, Maura Seger, author of this searing novel, was named by ROMANTIC TIMES as 1984's Most Versatile Romance Author.

At your favorite bookstore in March.

EYE-B-1

Enter a uniquely exciting new world with

Harlequin American Romance ™·

Harlequin American Romances are the first romances to explore today's love relationships. These compelling novels reach into the hearts and minds of women across America... probing the most intimate moments of romance, love and desire.

You'll follow romantic heroines and irresistible men as they boldly face confusing choices. Career first, love later? Love without marriage? Long-distance relationships? All the experiences that make love real are captured in the tender, loving pages of **Harlequin American Romances**.

What makes American women so different when it comes to love? Find out with **Harlequin American Romance!**

Send for your introductory FREE book now!

Get this book FREE!

Mail to:
Harlequin Reader Service

In the U.S.A.
2504 West Southern Avenue
Tempe, AZ 85282

In Canada
P.O. Box 2800, Postal Station A
5170 Yonge Street, Willowdale, Ont. M2N 6J3

YES! I want to be one of the first to discover **Harlequin American Romance.** Send me FREE and without obligation *Twice in a Lifetime.* If you do not hear from me after I have examined my FREE book, please send me the 4 new **Harlequin American Romances** each month as soon as they come off the presses. I understand that I will be billed only $2.25 for each book (total $9.00). There are no shipping or handling charges. There is no minimum number of books that I have to purchase. In fact, I may cancel this arrangement at any time. *Twice in a Lifetime* is mine to keep as a FREE gift, even if I do not buy any additional books.

154-BPA-NAZJ

Name _____ (please print)

Address _____ Apt. no.

City _____ State/Prov. _____ Zip/Postal Code

Signature (If under 18, parent or guardian must sign.)

AMR-SUB-3

Readers rave about Harlequin American Romance!